Publisher's Note

Readers BEWARE

This is a novel built in layers. Snippets of details and the emotions of what seems to be, at first, a confused and lost narrator are put into short "Dispatches" that slowly evolve into a dystopian world where books and the cleaning of old books stacked in endless rows become the center of existence. There is first a bookkeeper and then the bookkeeper is gone as the narrator struggles to learn about his job in an enormous, dusty warehouse. And what about Paige? Who is the young girl in the earliest dispatches?

This is not our everyday world, although we are never sure whether the story is set in our world or in some timeless universe where books are everything. Characters appear and disappear as the trilogy's three books unfurl. Cats and a dog become important as the story rollicks onward. Robots (or are they robots?) take over the writer's, the trilogy's, I and then lead him away from the reality he believes he has lived, the one with the enigmatic woman in his bed. Then there are the story characters running and roaming as they try to avoid fates that seem to hover just beyond where they are. And always, always, there are the books you blow on to clean, bringing them back to life so that their pages become part of who you are.

This is as unusual a book of literature you will ever read even if you love Kurt Vonnegut or Franz Kafka.

The Breathing Pages trilogy

By Philip Todd Pfuehler

The Breathing Pages trilogy

By Philip Todd Pfuehler

Four Windows Press

Sturgeon Bay, WI 54235

Fourwindowspress1@gmail.com

Dedication

For bookworms, wherever they may be unearthed

Acknowledgements

For Tom Davis and Brian Evenson, both of whom provided emotional lifts when it was truly needed; for Mike Longaecker, my sounding board for years; and for reader Ruth Wood and her "English teacher" field of vision.

CONTENTS

Book 1

From the Vault: The Bookkeeper's
Dog-Eared Delirious Dispatches

Dispatch #1

Taking a break from blowing, I browse a few pages and am moved and then distracted by the reading of one simple passage. I look up from the words and stare off into space, not even seeing the motes of dust in the air. Before I resume blowing, I read the passage a second time:

The pleasure, while leafing through a book, of noticing by the way some of the pages stick together that I am the first reader.

Dispatch #2

One of the first things Paige asked – after she stopped being the girl I may have followed on walks and who may also have followed me – was how I caught my strain of reading virus.

Because of writer's block, I explained, shaking my head. I tried writing, again and again, hit a block in my writing, again and again, so I turned to reading, again and again. Through reading I papered over the tortures of my blocked writing.

I absorbed the contents of whatever I read. Often fiction, make believe, for my made-up life...Tens of thousands of pages, countless stories and their characters. I absorbed the words I read as if I had written them myself. In my mind I read, reread, revised, rewrote and relived the lives of countless story characters.

Anyway, I told Paige, that's how I recalled it. I admitted my recalling was unreliable. Often it seemed as if, whether through the reading or the writing, I was hardly more than a story character myself.

Paige asked if I thought my writing block would ever end. I said possibly, but not in a way that could be explained.

Paige did not ask me to explain. She knew better. The unexplainable was best left unexplained.

Much later, before the walls here came crashing down, Paige found what she was looking for – a lost book. The story inside the pages of that book was meant for me alone to read. Reading it would bring an end.

Turns out I was waiting for that ending to find me.

Dispatch #3

Wham!

A solitary man, a reclusive writer, takes what might be described as a walloping – to the back of the head.

This happens too quick to hurt. The assailant, if there was one, is unknown. Maybe it was merely a fall, a backward fall. Either way, having been knocked out by the walloping, the man is unable to decipher what follows.

The knockout wallop sends him somersaulting – in his head – down through an opening like that of a trapdoor.

Whoosh!

It feels like a long way going down but he quickly somersaults the distance. Being knocked out, all that follows seems like a delirium.

On the way down he feels an updraft of stale, dusty air. Someone, some blurry shape, passes him going up as he goes down. Or is he the one going up at the same time as he's going down?

Never mind, too delirious to know what's what.

When he hits bottom, lands on his ass, the man bounces, once, then lands again on his ass but doesn't bounce as high the second time. His eyes shut tight. He grimaces. The bouncy landing gives him a pain in the ass.

Next the man has a coughing fit. He begins counting each cough. Shaking his head as if to loosen mental cobwebs, he spits out a gob of saliva mixed with dust. He rubs his eyes before they reopen on their own.

Even with eyes open wide, it's too dim and dusty to see anything clearly. But wait. He cups both ears: Hear that? Those sounds? How peculiar.

Knees raised, he bends forward on his painful ass, ears still cupped: Can the sounds be ID'd? First, a sort of clacking – from a keyboard, maybe a manual typewriter? Second, is that groaning? Chorus of deep groans? Human? Then, something else, something animal-like: Some kind of meowing maybe...and finally, another sound, small animal, high-pitched and faint: Squeak-squeak...squeak, squeak, squeak...

Dispatch #4

Something from far above sparkles until it gets my attention. I look up, way up, to the vertical windows on the upper level.

I blink at whatever is sparkling up there, at the upper level referred to as the mezzanine.

What I'm seeing up and beyond the mezzanine railing is not possible. I am certain that what I see is impossible. But there it is – small flakes that sparkle in the slanting natural light.

What I believe I see up there – what I can't be seeing – is falling snow.

Seeing snow falling inside here is not a sight I, nor anyone, would expect to see. So seeing that makes me fear for my sanity.

I stop blinking at what I can't be seeing and make myself look down at the floor, mentally ticking off a half minute – exactly 30 seconds by my count – before looking back up to the mezzanine windows.

And yet there it is, still there, inside here – sparkling, falling snow. Down fall the snowflakes, all around, some even fall on me.

It's a dazzling sight, but still, snowfall here – inside here? I try to clear my mind, fearing the vision confirms my insanity.

Dispatch #5

I can't stop blinking at this snowy shower falling all around and even down on me. I shake and brush myself so the snowflakes fall off.

I admit I get confused, more like fooled, but I try to keep my head. I also believe that, overall, I am sane. I cling to that belief.

I believe I have been working here, inside this place, for some time. More than that I believe that snow only falls outside – not inside here, in this place where I work.

Or inside where anyone works – or, for that matter, working or not, anywhere inside, at least inside where there's a roof. Snowfall only happens on the outside.

Yet because of what I'm seeing – or not seeing – I have doubts. If the doubting goes on I fear it could trigger another foolish vision.

These happen to me – visions. They happen as I go about with my work here. My response is to keep my head and go on working.

At the same time, as any sane person would, I must decipher the latest vision before fear blows up my sanity.

Dispatch #6

I act on my fear by reaching up with my arms and hands. I must touch and feel these falling snowflakes. Touching and feeling will give evidence to decipher.

I slide back from my chair and stand, hands up. The powdery flakes reach my fingertips, then my upturned palms.

I wait but feel nothing to the touch – no moisture, no coolness, no tingling.

I ponder why there is nothing to feel from touching the falling snow. Why do I feel nothing on my skin?

And why have the snowflakes not melted? They are still cupped in my palms. They are very small, almost tiny. I brush my hands till the falling flakes have spotted my shoes. There they remain, on my toes and shoelaces, not melting.

I recall being fooled before by visions of this nature – with falling snow inside this very place. History must be repeating.

Does weather inside here function in another dimension? Or have I forgotten the basics of real weather?

Well, I am not so clear-headed after all, but I must keep deciphering.

And I must face the facts. I must. These so-called visions are nothing but figments of a delirious mind.

So call them deliriums. Call them mine. My deliriums, my dispatches.

Dispatch #7

I tell myself OK, OK, whatever you call them does not change facts. You're a delirious fool. The verdict unfurls like a banner before my eyes.

As if looking for a reprieve, I look up again at the windows. I squint at the natural light. I close and rub my watering eyes until the wetness rubs off and goes away.

When I reopen my eyes, now dried, I see that the falling snow, as if by coincidence, has also gone away.

Absent the snowflakes, the sparkling has gone away too, replaced by slanting beams of sheer golden sunlight.

I stop looking up and look down to the floor. What I see there, highlighted in gold, is a maze of overlapping footprints.

Dispatch #8

There are far too many footprints to count on the snowy floor. Yet I am one who cannot resist counting.

Even with my counting impulse, I must admit the overlapping footprints are uncountable. I have better ways to spend my work time. In this case, further counting is pointless.

Since I am here by myself, most often alone, I reason that all these snowy footprints, or nearly all, are mine.

But the reasoning – deciphering – is flawed. Even a fool knows that snow only falls outside, that cold snow is felt on skin and melts when warmed. To my knowledge, this is basic weather.

If not snow, then what? I swear to myself, swear at myself, swear for being fooled again by these deliriums.

Dispatch #9

My swearing fit takes aim at the delirious way my mind drifts, how there's no control to the drifting. When I drift off, I'm like a mote of dust carried whatever way a current of air blows.

Despite all the swearing – there's also no controlling deliriums – my mind drifts again, drifting back to the past and another season of weather.

I drift back to childhood. I see myself on the inside again, in a cozy, two-story red-brick house. Feels warm inside. I am looking outside where it's wintry cold with gusts of snow.

I look through a tall living room window as a slim man, my father, bundled up, bends over to dig and shovel away towering snowdrifts.

I watch him take on the weatherly elements. His coattails lift and drop. Ragged white clouds puff from his mouth.

The snowdrifts are like shape-shifting sculpture. The wind scatters their crowns in swirling funnels. Father barely advances toward clearing a path across the front sidewalk by the road.

The patterns of drifting, swirling snow remind me of my school geography book. The cover art had sand dunes extending across a vast desert.

Now I drift forward in time to here, back inside to this place where I work. Here where I'm delirious and can make no sense of indoor seasonal weather with unmelting snow.

Dispatch #10

What I can report is this: the roof above me should keep out falling snow. And there is also furnace heat. I can feel its waves of warmth, so that if snow somehow falls inside, heat from the vents should melt it.

So what fell on me, from way up, above the mezzanine railing and the shelving, reaching down to where I stood looking up?

I know I've had this delirium before – history repeats – as I walk, work this job and leave overlapping footprints.

Oh, enough with this. I decide to pause deciphering. I'll try clearing and resetting my delirious head by taking a catnap.

I fall back in the chair. In no time I am dozing. Last thing I vaguely recall is my chin falling to my chest.

When I wake later, I recall having a seasonal dream where snow piled up in endless waves, leaving an impression of sand dunes spread across the horizon.

Dispatch #11

Please, bear with me. I cannot say how long it is before, still slouched in the chair, I wake, eyes blinking open. I sit still. Have I come to my senses?

Well, it's darker because sunlight from the mezzanine windows has dimmed. So it must be later in the day, closer to evening.

Unless it is already later the next day and closer to the next evening? But how likely is it that I slept an entire day while slouched in my chair for a catnap?

Actually the question is not all that crazy. It is so easy to lose track of time here.

After waking, my chin popped up off my chest. Yes, my mind had cleared and was as sparkly as a constellation across the night sky.

Suddenly – call it a revelation – my earlier vision was brushed aside. What I knew to be true now came from the dream about snow, which resembles sand, which also resembles...dust.

Of course – dust.

DUST! The reason I'm here, on the inside, working, blowing – because of the never-ending dust.

In my mind, a passage from a short story I once read unfurls into another banner before my eyes:

The apartment was like a snow globe but the snow was suspended dust and fuzz, floating.

Right, right. That's what this is. All this was nothing to do with weather or the season of winter and snowfall. It was my foolishness, being delirious and fooled by another delirium. It was dust – not snow – that was falling from above.

I feel an urge to shout out my discovery. But then, why bother with shouting? Nothing was discovered, only rediscovered. The job here remains mine and mine alone.

True, my deliriums are concerning. Yet I look around this place, all around, and can't suppress a giggle. Then another. Before long the giggling erupts into cackling.

Besides me, who else is here to be concerned? About me? Who else is here to be concerned for my sanity, or insanity, my work, or lack of work? And who, after pondering all this, wouldn't start to cackle like crazy?

Dispatch #12

What I try my best to do here is not be distracted from my duties. That's what I was first instructed to do: Stay focused, avoid distractions.

The instruction was easy to give but hard to follow. All the same, I try following it – at least the spirit of it.

Even with little to distract me, it's hard to avoid not being distracted and thus easy to lose focus.

One distraction is that I walk and walk and walk, until all that walking begins to feel aimless and endless.

Of course, walking by itself is healthy exercise. Therefore I can't accuse myself of doing too much walking. It's good for me.

But other times, what I do more than walk is pace – unfocused, back and forth across the main floor, up and down the spiral staircase, first floor to mezzanine, plus up and down on the shelving ladders.

Pacing, and therefore not focused on doing my best job.

Here I must pause. I've just mentioned shelving ladders. I climb those, up and down, but I cannot claim to pace on a ladder.

Ladders are climbed, both ways, and this I also do as part of my duties.

Dispatch #13

I mentioned how I wasn't about to count all the footprints left by all my steps across the dusty floor.

Well, part of my job is to sweep and mop the floor. Doing so removes fallen dust and leaves a sure-footed path for walking.

But all my back-and-forth steps across the floor set off a second distraction – echoes.

As I focus on my work, sometimes that focus shifts to my footsteps. How each step echoes across the wooden floor planks.

The echoing steps that I hear seem sinister. At least they seemed sinister at one time.

When I began here and first heard the footstep echoes, I was fooled into believing that someone was following me.

Yet when I looked behind, no one was ever there. But the fact that I never saw anyone made the echoes even more sinister.

I was always deciphering whether what I heard was another person's footsteps or my own.

Now it's rare that I even hear the echoes. I am so used to them that I rarely hear them – unless I focus on them.

I've already focused too much time on distractions. When I count them up, they're barely worth mentioning.

Dispatch #14

For now I've solved my biggest distraction – the so-called snowfall delirium. Falling snow inside here was merely falling dust.

Case solved – until the next time history repeats.

The next time this delirium happens, I must try harder to recall what is real and not be distracted and delirious. Can I ever do that?

Well, time to refocus on my work duties.

The main floor of hardwood planks has boundless layers of dust that resemble flimsy mats.

A dusty wooden floor equals poor footing. When it's slippery, I have slipped, even fallen.

I have fallen and landed on my ass, yet I have always picked myself back up.

But I don't wish to risk more slipping and falling. And I don't wish to be injured or embarrassed by a fall.

An injury would be worse. Rarely is anyone here to help were I to fall and be injured. I would be left helpless to get by on my own.

Embarrassment is something else. Because I rarely have company, my falling shouldn't embarrass me.

Yet somehow the idea of a fall is embarrassing. I still fear that someone could be watching, someone I'm unable to see, someone following me whose footsteps slip away to report my fallen status.

Report it to whom? I really have no idea. It seems my fears are foolish.

Dispatch #15

My sweeping and swabbing floor planks is by now a routine that drifts, if I let it, into drudgery.

First I use a wide broom with short bristles to push and compress the dusty mats into straight lines across the floor.

 Second I switch to a straw broom with long bristles to brush those lines into dust-bunny piles that get swept into a dustpan.

I smile down while sweeping up the dust bunnies. They're like the backsides of cottontail rabbits. My dustpan full of bunny rabbits is emptied into a waste basket.

I bring a mop and pail to swab the dust-free floors. As I squeeze out the sudsy water, drops drip fast inside the metal pail — a steady dripping that echoes rat-tat-tat-tat-tat...

I resist counting the drops. Little resistance is needed. The drops drip in a stream – far too fast for me to keep count.

As with countless footprints over a dusty floor, sudsy water dripping in a pail is uncountable. Another distraction avoided. I can refocus attention on each detail of my duties.

Dispatch #16

A concern for me – no, call this one a fear – is working with the patrons.

They roam outside in herds. They also come inside. Their coming inside is more of a barging in.

Usually the patrons barge in near dark – same as when they do their outside roaming. Their barging in as a herd is permissible. In fact it's welcomed.

The patrons still frighten me, but that goes with the territory. Handling them is one more detail of my duties.

Though I was warned – no, instructed – about the patrons, fear overcame me the first time I tried handling them.

While my fear of the patrons remains, things are different since that first encounter. As of late, more and more, the patrons come less and less. And their numbers are diminished.

I was instructed that patrons are the existential reason for this place to exist. That was the word used: existential. This place, I might add, stockpiles books. Countless books. Officially these are referred to as print materialS.

My chief duty is to withdraw dusty books, one by one, from dustier shelves, then blow off the dust from each withdrawn book. That's how I prepare for a herd of patrons.

Even now, no matter how prepared, the sights and sounds of patrons in my midst bring fear.

As reported, patrons gather to agitate toward evening. They emerge from long shadows, bobbing and weaving as if to avoid the beams of the setting sun – at least when the sun at that hour is un-inhibited by clouds.

Dispatch #17

To prepare for incoming patrons, I unlock the front doors. For that I turn the door latch counterclockwise, then listen and count – click, click, click – to each of the clicks. After three clicks, each door is unlocked.

Soon you hear (and feel) scratchy vibrations coming from count-less shuffling feet.

Patrons come barging through the unlocked front doors. Their movements are jerky. Doors rattle from being jerked open, nearly yanked from hinges.

The patrons shuffle and often stumble, sometimes tumbling to the floor before clambering back to their feet.

I get dizzy watching this shuffling, stumbling and tumbling. There's also a zigzag to these movements. That gets me even dizzier.

Well, I'm as prepared as ever. I've pulled out books, all sorts, any category.

Books from up high, from down low, from one shelf to the next. I've blown on and wiped these books till they're dust free for readers – any reader, any patron.

Next I pivot to face the zigzagging patrons. I contort my facial muscles into my most welcoming expression.

By contrast the patrons, male and female, some very young, have wide-eyed but vacant expressions. That is to report, lifeless.

They zigzag up and down aisles, careen off tables, chairs, benches and racks. Everywhere they go, books go toppling.

The patrons groan in unison. I would describe the sound as a voodoo chorus.

My arms balance a stack of dust-free books. I post myself in the center, a bullseye in the chaos.

I've confessed my fear of getting too near them, but that's not it. It's worse, call it panic. Here they come now – near, nearer.

I ease a book from under my chin. I reach out to incoming patrons like a quarterback trying to hand off a book to each patron zigzagging by.

Backed up against a pillar, heartbeat hammering, I extend a hand-held book. I hardly focus on the hand-offs before these turn into – I confess – book fumbles. Call them turnovers.

One by one, zigzagging patrons brush my hand, wrist, elbow – my arm – brushing right by me, fumble after book fumble!

Most patrons hold up mobile devices. They stare at flickering blue screens.

Some wear smaller devices like bracelets on their wrists. Others have strap-on devices like a doctor's head mirror with a tiny screen sticking out at eye level. Besides flickering, their devices beep and ring.

The spellbound patrons seem not to draw breath. I'm at a loss to explain the medical science.

As they go brushing by, some patrons spin, shake their heads NO! at me, groan louder, even snarl. Once, well, maybe more than once, a mouth snaps, teeth rattle.

Whenever I am snapped and rattled at, that's it – ball game. I cringe, drop my book stack and crawl off like a crab.

Before long, and it seems very long, off goes the herd. Still groaning and growling, devices flickering, ringing and beeping, the patrons randomly yank and topple more books.

They zigzag past the reception counter. A few bang on the keyboard of a manual typewriter relic – CLACK, CLACK, CLACK – jamming keys.

Finally the patrons shuffle out the front doors. Some misjudge and crash against a wall or the book drop-off bin.

Those rebounding from crashes fall backward on their asses, before rolling to their knees and clambering back to their feet. Hands never let go of devices.

Once back up, they shuffle onward and outward. Outside the patrons dissolve in the haze of another darkening night.

Inside I skitter around to retrieve fallen books that lie across the floor.

With various cover and dust-jacket designs, the books appear garbed in the colorful uniforms of fallen soldiers after combat.

Cyclones of rising dust ring the air. I cough while restoring order and, turning latches clockwise, click by click by click, relock all front doors.

Dispatch #18

I confess that what I lack here is total recall. Some things happened some time ago, other things longer ago, and still others long before those. Overall that's how I recall things.

So it is unclear how I'm to account for the passage of time and seasons. My recalling of what was and what is seems unclear – even to me.

What's clear is that the keeper of books – the old bookkeeper – is, or was, in charge. It was the old bookkeeper who welcomed and tutored me.

From the first I recall that the old bookkeeper reminded me of a cartoonish Merlin – anyway, some wizard version in a knee-length frock but no hat. At the same time, as my boss, his demeanor was often aloof.

Instead of a handshake, he tilted his head at me, then curled strands of a wispy gray beard, or maybe the locks of long gray hair, with bony fingers.

Before our introduction I'd come upon his stooped profile. This was just inside the front doors, near the reception counter with the relic typewriter.

I've no idea of how I got there, which is here, where I still work.

Once inside I recall halting and waiting for instructions. When the bookkeeper finally stood up, not looking at me, I saw he held in both hands a mousetrap. He was peering up at it.

Sticking from the bookkeeper's mouth was a white loop. From a sucker.

I was to learn that the bookkeeper had a sweet tooth. He loved hard candy, especially suckers.

I saw that his lips were purplish. I stepped back, fearing a contagion. Then I saw, as the bookkeeper took the white loop from his mouth and smacked his lips, that the purple came from a grape sucker.

I stepped nearer and realized the bookkeeper also wore sunglasses. Why here, in such a dim place? Someday I would learn why.

With his fingertips, the bookkeeper took out the skinny tail of a gray mouse from the trap. The mouse was either stunned or dead, I no longer recall.

Mice here are many, as are cats. They share a symbiotic habitat, so said the bookkeeper – his words.

Still without looking at me, still holding the mouse by the tail, the bookkeeper spoke in my direction: Friend, you look lost. But fear not. No one else has applied. You seem destined to land the job.

I would never describe ours as a friendship, but the old bookkeeper, my new boss, had a friendly side.

Dispatch #19

The place the old bookkeeper oversaw was and is The Domestic Print Materials Shelter. That's right, its official name.

But the bookkeeper had devised his own name: The Vault. He told me the nickname sometime later, how much later I cannot recall.

Inside The Vault the bookkeeper and I, side by side, began our tour.

My first two impressions: gloomy and drafty. I was squinting in the gloom and shivering from the draft.

Over time, I cannot say how long, I got used to living and working in The Vault. Then I no longer squinted and shivered.

Technology was absent in The Vault – no computers. As we toured, another mouse, this one chased by a cat, darted toward the shadows.

The Vault's dim, gray interior felt medieval. Except for windows, mostly at the upper level, the place had a dungeon-like vibe.

The bookkeeper seemed not the dramatic type, but I saw his chest heave before he sighed. He waved a scrawny arm – like waving a wand – at the rest of the interior.

The bookkeeper's wave directed my squinting eyes to a jumbled array of books – countless horizontal rows packed across towering shelves and piled vertically on carts, tables, counters, chairs, even the few window ledges.

The vast, motley collection was coated by shaggy layers of dust and stringy cobwebs. A fairy-tale tableau, with a wizard character to boot.

I wondered how much the bookkeeper, wearing shades, could see of this dust and gloom. I learned that he saw enough to do a bookkeeper's job.

Dispatch #20

After giving me time to process what was all around us, the bookkeeper pulled me aside – by the sleeve. He meant business.

His bony fingers withdrew a dusty hardcover book, minus its jacket, from the middle of a crooked pile on a table. Book removed, the upper part of the pile wobbled, then dropped in place to fill the gap.

Friend, the bookkeeper began, this is how it begins.

With that he got to work showing me how to blow ever so softly across the book's peeling front and back covers, its loose binding and frayed, yellowing pages.

I was to learn that many of The Vault's books were in this condition – past their prime, decrepit.

Despite wearing shades, the bookkeeper saw what he was doing. He was able to show and tell me what had to be done:

Think of it as following your breath, as in meditation, the bookkeeper murmured. That means natural, unforced breathing. Doing so gives your blowing a healing element. Every blow conveys a breath of life to its book.

With each of the bookkeeper's healing breaths, with each blow, dust and cobweb clouds billowed from the books and sprinkled to our feet.

At this stage of tutelage, the bookkeeper smiled, revealing purple-stained lips under a gray tangle of beard.

Next he showed the correct stance for blowing: how to grip each book with both hands; how to keep that grip firm but less so if the book was badly damaged; how to maintain whatever grip despite the slippery, dusty coating; how to flex and hold a relaxed pose; how to inhale, lean close and how to pucker the lips, like a kiss, before exhaling; and how to exhale for as long as the lungs had air to blow out.

If these instructions are followed, the bookkeeper said, dust and cobwebs would scatter to the floor in wondrous patterns.

Before greenlighting my first book blow, the bookkeeper's brow wrinkled. He drew back gaunt shoulders, lowered the shades on his nose so his eyes gleamed from above, and declared through tangled beard hairs:

Friend – never, ever get carried away by the artistry of book blowing. All that matters, or once upon a time mattered – he harrumphed – is that blow by blow you expose each book for its singular reader.

Dispatch #21

On my own, I later supplemented this blowing technique by moistening a rag with cleaning fluid I found in a closet, then wiping those books caked with grime and gunk. There were always a few in such condition. They needed extra care.

After the cleaner dried on those books, I blew off any remaining motes of dust.

If I focused on this detail, the wiping left a shine, especially when these books were highlighted by slanting sunbeams from the mezzanine windows. The highlighting only happened on days when the sun was uninhibited by clouds.

Dispatch #22

As mentioned, so much of the past here, and before getting here, is unclear to me, beyond recall.

What I do clearly recall is the bookkeeper's saying that I was the one and only applicant. This implied that the job – assistant keeper of the books – was mine by default, unless I blew it.

Apparently I didn't blow it, so the job defaulted to me. At least that's how I see it. It's now my word against no one's.

Why? Because there is no one else here, most often, at the Domestic Print Materials Shelter (aka, The Vault).

The old bookkeeper, my boss, the one hiring me by default, has gone. His going was not my fault. I have no proof that it was anyone's fault. That's all I know and choose to believe.

Is the bookkeeper long gone?

For me, counting the passage of time is a slippery slope. As I try to count back – days, weeks, months – the bookkeeper's absence seems fairly long.

The bookkeeper left without goodbyes, without instructions, without a word. Whereabouts unknown.

Were we a team for very long, working together, me tutored by him, or only for fairly long? Or for not long at all?

Fair questions but too slippery for my mind to grasp and answer.

Dispatch #23

Me, the one and only applicant? I don't even recall my application, my applying for any job – this job included.

So I may not have applied for this one. All I recall is one day appearing here.

The job of book blowing is done manually. There's only minimal power in The Vault, at least of electrical power.

Only a few lights operate. I assume at one time more lights or all lights operated.

And the few operating lights often flicker. These include ceiling and lamp lights. There are also wall outlets. Sometimes when a lamp or appliance is plugged in, by me, an outlet sparks.

At such times, as plug holder, I get a shock. Convulsed, I react by falling back on my ass and yelling.

Some time ago I found a hand-held vacuum cleaner stashed in a corner of the storage closet – the same closet where I found the cleaning fluid.

Without asking the old bookkeeper, I experimented with the vacuum. I wanted to speed up my work by vacuuming dust and cobwebs coating the books.

I wanted covert vacuuming to replace my overt blowing. I wanted the bookkeeper, over time, to praise my work speed.

Ready to experiment, I plugged the vacuum's cord into an outlet and flipped the switch to juice up the battery. I waited an hour or so, but nothing happened – no revving of the vacuum's engine. I didn't even get shocked from plugging in the cord.

After that failed experiment, it was back to the manual job of blowing. Another short-lived experiment came next.

In that same closet as the inoperative vacuum, I found a buried feather duster. I decided to try it. Again, covertly, not asking the bookkeeper.

I didn't ask him because I suspected the bookkeeper would nix the tactic. Why else had he not replaced the vacuum? Or allowed the feather duster to be buried?

True, he might have lost track of them, but my hunch was he would veto using them.

When it came to The Vault's work, the old bookkeeper was a purist. I didn't share this purity – not at first. I sought shortcuts, easy ways out.

I slunk around the aisles using the feather duster to whisk away at the print materials – no, strike that phrase.

Ever the purist, the bookkeeper instructed me to speak and think plainly: *BOOKS*! He detested the bureaucratic phrase *print materials*.

My feather duster experimenting was also brief.

The brevity was not because the bookkeeper caught and reprimanded me. It was the cats' fault.

They found and started playing with the feather duster. In no time they had seized it as a new toy, chewing and clawing it to shreds.

That ended the feather-dusting experiment. Yet I can't fault the cats. Besides hunting mice, they need their play time.

Dispatch #24

I can report no shortage of mice here. I catch glimpses, but they skitter off too fast for me to verify if the sightings are real or a delirium.

Later, after being snagged and mauled by the predatory cats, I come upon the remains. Reality sets in.

For the surviving mice The Vault, with countless piles and rows of books, offers an abundance to consume and colonize.

Lying on my back at night, in the dark, my hearing focuses. Then I believe I can actually hear the faintest patter of falling dust motes. And I know I hear my unseen roommates.

Hands folded behind my head, I listen to their squeaking, chewing and clawing as they burrow deeper through book-made tunnels.

Dispatch #25

Just now I recall more details about the absent old bookkeeper. The recollection halts my steps between towering shelves.

The bookkeeper inspected my book blowing wearing fleece slippers – ones with ridged, rubbery soles. He never wore socks.

The old bookkeeper said his bare feet – soles, heels, arches and toes – felt comfy within the fleecy fabric. And because of the slippers' soles, he was less apt to slip and fall on unswept, dusty floors.

Unswept dust is not the only walking hazard. The bookkeeper pointed to several hardwood planks warped from sunlight and mopping. That warping, like dust, was hazardous to footing.

The old bookkeeper's shoes, slippers in his case, are big ones to fill. Actually his slippers were three sizes too big for me to slip into.

One time I got up the nerve to ask the bookkeeper, Why the sunglasses? Were his eyes overly sensitive to light, even in The Vault's dim interior?

The bookkeeper plucked a green sucker – lime? – from his mouth. He took off the shades, squinting and blinking, and said he was partially, quite likely, legally blind.

Though he likely couldn't see it, I could see his tongue as well as his lips were coated green from the sucker. When he licked his lips, a drop of green juice oozed onto his gray beard.

I fondly recall such details because in his absence, as one can guess, the job of bookkeeper defaulted to me.

As far as I know, there were no applicants for the bookkeeping job. I simply took over. Solo, I oversee The Vault.

Dispatch #26

All books – they all arrive used – are delivered, received and either stockpiled somewhere temporarily or shelved somewhere permanently. None are recorded or categorized. That makes for a random collection.

That's how I found things done here and also not done. That's how it was and how it still is.

The Vault is not about book recording or categorizing – it's about book preserving.

I recall how a certain author revered the texture and substance of print books. While blowing and cleaning, I came upon the author's book at the end of a long row and on a page found this quote:

Don't give up on books. They feel so good — their friendly heft. The sweet reluctance of their pages when you turn them with your sensitive fingertips.

The word heft so aptly describes the act of holding a book. Especially on first contact.

Held in your hands, there's both volume and weight. Then comes the swish of flipping pages as your eyes skim the words for understanding.

What the first author wrote about a book's heft reminded me of what a second author wrote. Now I quote from memory: *A book in your hands has weight, it has its own gravity. Let it go and it drops to the ground. Pick it up and it soars.*

Hardcover or paper, I confess my own bookish attachment. Not only for the heft and content, but for something more practical — for what book pages swishing back and forth at the right tempo can cure.

Like my insomnia

Dispatch #27

I was to be tutored in this curative method. Here's how it works:

Before retiring at night, I inspect The Vault's premises. I verify that all patrons have come and gone. They are always gone but still I verify.

Afterward I lie on my back. The floor lamp over my cot carves a flickering shaft of light in the dark. The shaft flickers because of the fitful power.

Propped up with two pillows, I am relaxed enough to read. I listen to the wind-up alarm clock on the side table. Minutes of another night tick-tick away.

The book I hold before me is slim but not without heft: *Too Loud A Solitude*, by Bohumil Hrabal.

The title's irony speaks volumes. My work in The Vault is solitary. I find the solitude echoes loudly between my ears.

On the front cover jacket of *Too Loud A Solitude*, a bespectacled man drops a normal-sized book into a slot in the spine of a book larger than the man. The normal book will disappear in that slot, absorbed by the oversized book.

After counting off 33 pages of reading from this book, I'm still not sleepy. To cure my insomnia I must animate the book's pages.

My fingertips start flipping the pages of *Too Loud A Solitude* – any book will do. First I insert a bookmark to where I left off reading, then flip.

Like shuffling a deck of cards, I flip batches of pages – back and forth, back and forth – easy does it.

I slide the open book closer to my eyes. At some point the flipping pages distort my outlook. This is when I grow tired and, soon, drowsy.

This may also be where I drift across the border from drowsiness to delirium. Soon the pages cast their spell.

My fingers slowly stop flipping the pages. My hands, arms and whole body go limp. My eyelids close on their own.

Here's the delirious part. In my sleepiness, the pages of whatever book I hold continue flipping – on their own! Even when fast asleep, I can feel them do so.

The pages go swish, swish, swish. Back and forth, fitful but accelerating. Soon the swishing pages settle on an even speed, neither slow nor fast, but very much on their own power.

What I love about this sleepy delirium is that the evenly swishing pages emit puffs of air. Each puff caresses the skin of my face – ticklish but soothing.

It's like being breathed on with a wood-shaving fragrance. Impossible to describe further because I'm either asleep and dreaming, or delirious – or, who knows, perhaps all three!

Breathed on by the pages makes me buoyant, soon without volume and heft. I'm airlifted like a balloon, high and remote, bouncing from one cloud to the next, receding into depths of uncharted space.

I don't recall what heights and depths I reach, but, as everything must, I'm pulled back by gravity, falling like a meteorite.

I become aware of my eyes blinking. Each blink is weighty.

I look around, find myself, my volume, weighted down on the cot. The Vault's sluggish, solid interior is outlined by the dusty morning light.

I look down. The book is closed, lying flat on my chest. I'm awake, back again in this too loud a solitude.

Dispatch #28

Oh-oh, here goes. I'm at it again – feeling delirious. Deliriums drift in, drift out. I've no control of the timing. This feels like another one drifting in, taking control of me.

This delirium has me out walking, as in going outside for a walk

I know, I walk all the time, but that's walking inside The Vault, day after day. Walk, walk, walk until the repetitive walking becomes pacing.

But this time I'm walking outside, out somewhere far beyond wherever The Vault lies. Not a book in sight. Nothing for me to blow on.

Is this outside walking a memory from my pre-Vault days? Or memory spliced with dream? Maybe a delirium spliced with memory and dream?

Except for hauling in delivered books, I never step beyond The Vault. My work here is now my life, my 24/7, my calling.

So this delirium is exotic, as the walking takes me through residential neighborhoods.

I'm wearing shorts, khakis, my favorite material. The air against my bare legs tingles. It may be the season of summer, late spring or early fall.

From time to time, whatever the season, I must have walked these routes. Though I lack total recall, I seem to recall such long-ago walks.

Was my walking back then a way to pass time? Did I walk and walk to empty my mind, to jar loose some torment, a blockage?

The exotic delirium won't explain my state of mind.

Dispatch #29

The residential streets and avenues from this delirium form right angles of a grid. They're named by number and direction: 8th Avenue North; 31st Street West; etcetera.

For walking purposes, I prefer this kind of layout – a grid of straight, intersecting lines, no curves or loops.

The street/avenue grid allows me to navigate with less chance of going astray or, worse, of getting lost.

This has happened to me – going astray, getting lost, especially on foot and while alone.

I've a poor sense of direction. Perhaps that's why I recall, from long ago, being called a lost cause. I've even, while frustrated and swearing, called myself that.

I focus my steps on this orderly, paved grid. It's unlikely I'll go astray or get lost while walking a grid, but I cannot rule out the possibility.

Dispatch #30

Frankly, I've had countless streetwalking deliriums. Each time, each one seems unique and vivid.

During delirious street walks, I meet pedestrians. They're unavoidable.

Pedestrians greet me. With a nod, or a hi there, or a good morning or a good whatever the time of day is. I parrot back whatever the greeting. Doing so seems like showing my good character.

Some pedestrians, with leashes of this or that length, pull dogs of all sizes and breeds. For dogs on long leashes, I step aside, often taking cover behind a boulevard tree or utility pole. Fire hydrants are inadequate cover and set me up as a target.

Even the tree/pole cover strategy is ill-advised. The dogs, at least the males, seek the upright to sniff and lift a hind leg. So I must step aside again, and be swift, to avoid a yellowy squirt.

Otherwise I pay scant attention to pedestrians and pets. With one exception.

Often I spot a young female pedestrian – by herself, no pet, walking ahead. That is, when she's not walking behind, which is less often.

At first, as with other pedestrians, I pay her scant attention. Usually the girl is a block or so ahead, less often behind. Ahead or behind, always the same girl.

I've no knack for guessing ages. From the distance between us, front or back, the girl looks nine or ten. Possibly eleven. I give up on guesses.

She wears shorts, too, but not plain khakis that I wear. Hers are of colorful fabrics and styles suiting her age.

The girl's black hair falls straight down her back. Unless it's ponytailed down the middle or pigtailed on each side.

These are details, those I recall. I also recall the girl, while continuing to walk ahead, turn around while walking. We make eye contact.

But do we? Does one make eye contact with someone at a distance of a block or so away?

If so, these eye contacts happen at least once on each of our walks.

The reverse is also true. When I walk for a while and cannot see her ahead, I grow almost panicky. I have to turn to see if she's there walking behind me.

And yes, there she is, always, walking a block or so behind. For how long has she been behind me? I'm left to wonder.

From such a distance, I can't describe her features. She's a kid, cute for her age, my guess.

Dispatch #31

The problem with eye contact at that distance is that it can distract me. Distracted, I may fail to pick up my feet and trip while walking through a neighborhood.

The tripping is more likely when the sidewalks are cracked or buckled by a gnarly tree root or poor drainage.

I've tripped so badly that I've tumbled, arms out, almost falling. I've yet to fall all the way down but have stubbed my toe, often painfully.

While these are deliriums, the mishaps feel as real as they are painful. I've yelled while delirious, even sworn aloud at phantom toe pain.

Does my yelling and swearing cause a scene? I fear yes. By the time my outbursts have ended, in my delirium, my walking companion has disappeared, either from behind or from ahead.

Her disappearances bring a pang, a longing for something, for exactly what I can't say.

But the girl, thankfully, always reappears on my next delirious walk. I can count on that much, and I do.

Dispatch #32

What a relief, I confess, when my walking companion does reappear.

When we make eye contact, assuming we do, she never trips like me. I chalk that up to youth.

Some form of intuition tells me the girl is leading, even when our walking puts me in the lead. We follow what seems to be a maze of routes before the deliriums vaporize.

Am I being led on for an ulterior purpose?

Over time our walks lengthen. I grow physically tired and mentally lost toward the end of these longer walks. I'm also lost as to where we are.

At times during our long walks, the two of us seem to be walking in circles. Instead of squaring off at right angles when we turn left or right, we turn by cutting diagonally across a property, rounding off at corners. This creates an impression that we're circling something.

Circling what?

I've this theory that it was the girl leading (circling) the way until she led me here. To the entrance of the Domestic Print Materials Shelter (aka, The Vault).

I theorize, on circumstantial evidence, that my entering The Vault's orbit is linked to my walking companion.

I theorize further, again, without solid evidence, that it was The Vault's gravity that warped the spacetime street grid, funneling us closer and closer to its orbit, then locking us in that orbit before my eventual landing.

The Vault's mass – its volume – causing a spacetime warp is similarly explained by Einstein's General Theory of Relativity formula.

Anyway, I came to learn that the girl's name is Paige, and that she's a bibliophile.

I also learned that Paige walks with a slight limp. Somehow I missed seeing her limping during our delirious walks.

The walking distance between us of a block or more must have caused the oversight. Or maybe it was that her limping was too slight for me to see.

No matter. I had so much to learn about the girl named Paige.

Dispatch #33

The Vault is defined in every sense by its stacks and rows of print books. The enormity and responsibility of it all is intimidating.

Was the old bookkeeper so intimidated that he was finally driven out? I lack evidence to say. Our talks were more like monologues. His. They focused on instructions to me and critiques of my work.

In his absence, I walk alone in the Vault, stop at a random shelf, at a random row, extract a book and start blowing – either on the far-left side or the far right of a shelf.

I start working my way across, blowing books from either right to left or left to right. The direction across depends on which side I've started to blow.

I keep a cloth and bottle of cleaner in the back pockets of my trousers. I moisten the cloth and rub away book grime too encrusted for blowing.

I am thorough now, aware of each rub and each blow. I no longer seek working shortcuts.

I'm joyful when my blowing and wiping reveal the cover of what was a dust-grimed book. What joy to grip a book, now revealed, and recognize its title and author.

I'm apt to shiver at the recognition, standing there, still gripping the book, actually still in my blowing pose.

During a shivery moment, I am reminded of what one author wrote about our tactile relation to print books:

Walked in the afternoon's warmest hour down the main pedestrian drag and into a bookstore, to caress, one maybe two books on the spine, because that's why they stand there, they're just like us, they want to be caressed and loved despite it all.

Dispatch #34

After shivering from a joyous book cleaning, I snap out of it and straighten.

Standing erect, book in my hands, I'm sandwiched in an aisle between rows of shelving. The shelves of books, twice my height, do intimidate. They shrink a person.

Far above the shelves is The Vault's lofty ceiling, its crisscrossing rafters. Another grid, I might add, only this one's overhead.

All is hushed except for the squeaks and scrapes of mice burrowing and tunneling. I ask myself: Are these imaginary sounds? Deliriums? Too loud a solitude is an apt description for my state of mind.

The hush stills my delirious mind. How I long for someone to appear and walk down the aisle toward me — that singular patron, reaching for his or her dust-free book.

Nothing would delight me more than handing off, like a quarterback, a book to an eager patron's outstretched hand.

The grid of bookshelves and its narrow aisles are like passageways of a crypt. I'm entombed by these towering walls of books.

It leaves me with a nagging sense of being entombed within the covers of one of these countless books – entombed, somehow, within the pages of a single book, one coated by dust and maybe a strand of cobweb.

This sense, more of a flashback, intimidates me. Do I chalk it up as another delirium?

One author has written: *Leaving behind the babble of the plaza, I enter the library. I feel almost physically, the gravitation of the books, the enveloping serenity of order, time magically desiccated and preserved.*

While another author wrote: *I hadn't realized that being in the library for so many years was almost like being in some kind of timeless thing. Maybe an airplane of books, flying through the pages of eternity.*

Finally, this author's quote came to mind: *A book is always sleeping, always waiting for someone who isn't there.*

All books here, the few cleaned, the many dusty, sustain as well as intimidate. I'm bound by their gravity as I walk the aisles and pass the tables, chairs, counters and ledges where they lay – upright, flat, askew.

The above authors' quotes remind me of the countless repositories from bygone times for book lending. I believe these were named libraries. The Vault, now isolated, I'm sure was one of these.

Dispatch #35

I cringe at the thought – not just for all the bygone libraries, but for how book deliveries at present are made to The Vault.

Once, some time ago, before the present, unofficial deliveries came hit-or-miss – books stuffed any old way in cartons, wood crates, paper and plastic bags, gunny sacks, even suitcases.

Regular folks, homeowners, tenants, students, teachers, merchants, civic club members, even travelers, anonymous donors all, simply showed up and dropped containers of books at the front doors.

Book donors were polite but reserved. They knocked or rang the bell before departing, often calling out a greeting or waving as I came to unlock the doors.

None lingered to chat or, curious, try peering inside The Vault. They seemed embarrassed, even fearful, by where they were and what they had brought.

Over time, how long I cannot recall, these unofficial deliveries became more sporadic before petering out to zero. They were replaced by official deliveries hauled in by dump truck.

That is no misprint.

The dump truck's payload of books was tipped high in the air, one end of the flat bed pointing skyward, the other end dipping to the ground before the hinged rear door slid open.

Then the load of books nosedived, tossing and turning, flipping and flopping across the weedy pavement between curb and front doors.

Dispatch #36

At first Kroner, the short, wiry driver, always honked, staying put in his cab, during an official book dump.

The honking signaled to me: Hey Bubs, here I am with the goods. Time to get your butt out and get picking up.

Whenever I heard the honks, I rushed out to pick up and bring in a new load of books. If rain or snow was in the air, I would rush out even faster. These dumped books came unboxed and unbagged, so unprotected.

Rushing out was daunting. To get anywhere outside, even to official book dumps, took willpower. I had to prevail over The Vault's gravity.

Call it a gravitational pull. It pulled back against each of my steps going away from The Vault. The pullback never let up till I reached a book dump and began bringing books back in, step by step, back toward The Vault.

Over time Kroner lingered. Rather than drive off after dumping and honking, he would get out and help stack the spilled books inside wooden shipping crates. Kroner scavenged the crates from a lumber yard.

Together, using handcarts, we teamed up to wheel the book-laden crates into The Vault.

I valued the teamwork with Kroner. For one, it broke up the solitude. For a second, it was a distance to wheel the dumped books all the way inside to the large, wire-basket bins at the far end of The Vault.

One time Kroner acted to shorten that wheeling distance. Instead of stopping at the front entrance, he drove his truck over the curb for a book dump at the side door.

Long ago, before my time, The Vault's side door was deemed an emergency exit. Using a torque wrench, needle-nose pliers and screwdriver, Kroner disabled the wiring. Now we could open the side door and not trip the alarm.

Kroner made me swear never to breathe a word of the alarm disabling to officials. That was easy swearing. I wouldn't know any official if I bumped into one, and where would I ever bump into an official?

Kroner doubted if the emergency exit alarm even worked. But, he said, why risk it? Why, he added, would we put our jobs at risk?

After wheeling in a dump load of books, via the side exit door, Kroner was lingering even longer.

Still breathing heavily, the two of us would relax on cushioned chairs with casters in a so-called conference room. We swiveled at our table as we sipped tepid coffee from Kroner's thermos. I brought out my chipped mug, and he poured and refilled for both of us.

Kroner kept up a torrent of banter: So Bubs, how's it going at this old dump?...Hey, would anyone know if you and me switched jobs?...Ha, I doubt I'm qualified like you to do blow jobs...Can you catch a disease doing that to a book?...Wonder if you've got enough reading material here?...Me, I'm no book reader...Nah, makes my eyes water and see double just staring at all those lines zigzagging down and across page after page...Yeah, my free time, give me the old boob tube or mobile screen any day...

Kroner's bantering could get crude and lowbrow but was harmless. When he bantered his face reddened, as if blushing, as if he knew what he said was mere bluster.

I was fine with the bantering. And the blustering. Kroner, for me, counted as fellowship.

Still, I breathed easier when he left. Alone again, I had my crates of dusty old books in the wire bins to select, one by one, grip, blow, sometimes wipe, then shelve.

Dispatch #37

The days of Kroner delivering books and lingering for fellowship seem to have ended. How long was our time together? Was it just another delirium?

All I hear now is a truck barreling up to the curb by the entrance, not over the curb to the side door. The brakes squeal, engine back-fires as hydraulic arms lift the hinged load for a dumping.

No friendly honking. This dump truck is rusty, grating, reeking of oil and gas.

If I rush to the front-door windows, I may glimpse taillights as the truck rumbles from The Vault down the road toward distant traffic.

But of Kroner, no more glimpses. I doubt he's still the official driver. Did he linger with me too long at The Vault? Did that put his job at risk?

After this other dump truck's hasty exodus, what's left to deal with – alone – is a massive book spillage amid oily, gaseous fumes.

Coughing, I start scooping up, piling, crating and wheeling the spilled books from the front to the far end of The Vault.

Back to my solitary ways.

Because of the side-door's disabled alarm, I cling to the belief that Kroner was no delirious figment. I remain grateful for our fellowship and teamwork.

Dispatch #38

Slinking here, scurrying there, the cats inhabiting The Vault, like the mice, keep a low profile.

They rarely follow me since I rarely feed them. Exceptions are for saucers of water and milk plus scraps of fish or meat from my dinner plate before emptied as garbage. That won't sustain many cats.

So they make do with an entree of mice. Mice here are countless. While in bed I've tried with no success to count all their squeaks as another cure for my insomnia.

The mice population serves up an endless food source plus an existential means of survival. To survive and breed, the cats hone their hunting skills.

Only one cat here ever took to me, even letting me caress her glossy coat.

Though I had no reason to, I right away assumed she was female. I gave her a name. Two names, actually, because of her transitional colors.

In the daytime, in natural light, the cat's coat had a silvery color. So then, during day hours, I called her by that color: Silver.

When natural light was absent at night, replaced by the artificial, the cat shaded a darker, deeper color, an indigo blue. So at night I called her by the nocturnal color: Blue.

Dispatch #39

Most of my dust blowing is done by day. Daylight makes it brighter to navigate The Vault's dim interior and spot the dustiest rows of books.

That's when the day-named cat Silver follows, though at a distance. I am never certain which of us is ahead, which is behind, following, being followed.

If I'm blowing books in an aisle, Silver may drop to her haunches in another aisle and lick her paws. I watch her tail twitch as she sits there, grooming herself before looking up to watch me back.

Sometimes, after a book is blown and, if needed, wiped, I am unable to resist. Standing there holding the open book, I read a passage or two, even three or more, often a whole page that turns into several pages or even a chapter...chapters...

When next I look up to resume blowing the row of dusty, cobwebbed books, Silver is gone, probably hunting mice. Following me is one thing, waiting for me to stop reading and resume my duties is another.

Waiting may remind her of hunger and a survivor's instinct to hunt.

It's futile to resist browsing books that I have blown free of dust. Those covers with titles, authors and blurbs revealed, and those pages inside with countless rows of sentences – they hypnotize me.

So I give in to hypnosis and dip inside the book covers and get lost within those pages.

My book-by-book browsing distracts from duties as a blower of books. So yes, to anyone reading this, I confess, it's a mark against my employment record.

I recall Kroner's complaint that book reading was tiresome.

His negativity reminded me of what another author wrote about reader apathy: *On the bus, I see all these zombies. One with his iPod, another on his mobile, number three fiddling with his tablet. None of these morons reads a book on the bus. Never. That would be too much effort.*

Dispatch #40

That author's zombie reference got me pondering the outreaches to the patron herds.

As long as there is air filling my lungs, I am duty bound to keep blowing, to keep revealing books for their singular readers – even if, as of yet, no one out there has come in to claim a book.

The mission statement for books and readers was drilled into me by my tutor and predecessor, the old bookkeeper.

I often wonder where he has gone to. But then, other distractions intrude.

Like the brushing against my trousers. I look down: Blue. It's nighttime now, so that's her name.

Blue is twisting around my shins, purring and looking up. But is she looking at me?

Her tail twitches like a whip. Her gaze is straight up, traveling beyond me.

I turn to follow the gaze and look up there too. Up there, where I look, a skinny gray tail dangles between a row of books across the top shelf.

For dust blowing I would need a stepstool to reach that top shelf. One folded up is within my reach.

But such a stool is not what Blue needs. Before I can breathe the word mouse, she leaps upward.

It seems an impossible vertical leap. Either I am wrong about her leaping ability or I am delirious – again.

Blue's leap falls just short of the top shelf of books. But she snags the tip of the mouse's tail by her teeth and, suspended in the air, swings back and forth like a clock pendulum.

The bitten mouse's squeak amplifies to a piercing squeal.

Yet Blue cannot hang and swing for long. While swinging by the teeth, her claws fasten on the books from the shelf below. Once she has a paw-hold, her teeth part. At that instant the tail above her disappears behind a row of books.

Now comes the chase. Contestants: One cat, one mouse. In an instant both pursuer and pursued are out sight.

I hear the thuds of falling books, then slashing, scraping, yowling and screeching before all chase-related sounds recede and go mute.

And, sad to report, that's the last I ever laid eyes on my Silver/Blue. Count that as another disappearance.

Dispatch #41

Yet I did not give up on this unique cat. Not right away I didn't. After not seeing her or having her follow me for some time, I don't recall how long, I launched a one-man search party.

My work ethic, now second nature, drove me to probe both visible and invisible spaces.

I overturned and upended dusty stacks of books and tore apart sticky cobwebs. I crept on my knees down one shelving aisle after another, even crawling on the floor on my stomach under tables and chairs. At first I whispered before finally shouting the cat's name – both of her names.

Shouts of Silver and Blue echoed back slowly. One after the other, each Silver and Blue echo came back to me – soft, softer, before muting.

It had darkened during my long day of searching. At night, it was almost as dark inside The Vault as it was outside.

Only a few electrical outlets operate, and I have only a few good light bulbs for the few lamps. Most of the overhead lights stopped working before I came. None got replaced.

Soon night would transition to dawn. Blue, wherever she was, would transition to Silver.

Later that night, fatigued, I gave up my one-man search for Blue. I checked and locked the front doors. There were no waiting or stray patrons.

Besides fatigue, I was saddened by my failed search. I shuffled and stumbled around aimlessly, tripping over an object on the floor near the side door – an upended book. Thankfully I didn't fall.

I recalled having a flashlight stashed in a middle desk drawer. I should have it with me instead of tripping around in the dark. Then I recalled the flashlight's batteries might be dead.

At that very moment a light flashed in my face. Instinctively I ducked.

The light came from a flashlight – the one from the desk drawer? It flickered as if the batteries were dying.

A small, silhouetted figure held and aimed the flashlight at me – at my chest. Now I could see a little.

Seconds later the silhouette spoke: Hello there. Sorry to startle you. My name is Paige. By the way, your flashlight needs new batteries. I locked the emergency side door after I came in. The alarm didn't go off. I promise not to stay for very long and keep you up late. After I go you can relock the door.

Dispatch #42

I confess to the obvious – my solitude here is not total. I may have exaggerated my solitary ways. Such an exaggeration was foolish.

It is accurate to report that I live and work in a state of quasi-solitude.

Paige, the girl who first appeared inside at The Vault's emergency side door, now comes and goes. As she pleases.

I never know how or when she will slip inside and appear. The side door always seems to be unlocked whenever she appears.

I say and do nothing to prevent her appearances.

Dispatch #43

Paige's first appearance seemed linked to the cat's disappearance and my failed search to find her. The cat that favored me, the cat with two names – Silver by day, Blue by night.

It may be a stretch, but I deciphered a second link between cat and girl: In the middle of Paige's brow was a mark, a pointed dot that resembled a bindi. The points gave the bindi-dot the shape of a star.

This was not a reddish, religious bindi. Paige's bindi was a blur of silvery bluish colors. The blurry colors had shifting patterns that varied with the angle of the viewing but sparkled whenever lit up by sunbeams.

Over time, I cannot guess how long, Paige's star-shaped bindi faded – as if smudged. Not long after that it disappeared.

One day when she was older, like a scrubbed whiteboard, Paige's brow was unmarked. While it lasted the bindi was a distinctive mark.

I never mentioned the cat, her names or disappearance to Paige.

Nor did I mention Paige's bindi or my deliriums of walking the grid-like streets and following and being followed by a girl who now resembled the girl in The Vault who identified herself as the girl Paige.

For whatever reason, these and other things were never mentioned. Over time these unmentionables become preserved in our relationship like fossils.

Dispatch #44

What I had failed to see about Paige – if that was her, in my delirium, walking the streets with me – is that this Paige in The Vault walks with a limp. Her limping is barely visible.

I can decipher one, two, three, four, even five explanations for my failing to spot the limp as she walked streets ahead and behind me.

1) It was not the same girl as Paige and so the other girl never limped. Yet the pair seem so alike – that girl on the streets and this girl Paige in The Vault. So I discount explanation No. 1.

2) The distance of a block or more that separated us during street walks was too distant to spot a slight limp.

3) I am nearsighted and in need of glasses. I also need reading glasses since I'm farsighted. Flawed vision kept me from spotting the limp.

4) The curious sight of the following/followed girl distracted me. The distraction blinded me from spotting all physical traits, such as a limp.

5) A mix of explanations two, three and four.

The explanation for why Paige limps is less complicated. By birth defect, one of her legs was slightly shorter.

Paige reluctantly explained the shortcoming. Growing up, she said, it isolated her from playmates. Paige played clumsily because of uneven legs. She was teased and bullied for her clumsiness.

For companionship, Paige turned away from people and found books. She liked their heft and texture as she turned page after page while reading words out loud to herself.

When I met her, Paige read aloud as fluently as any adult I ever recall reading. Books were her companions, educationally and so-cially.

Paige is also private. I respect her privacy. She never mentions social life or family matters. She too has her unmentionables.

Dispatch #45

While private, Paige never withheld useful knowledge she had learned. In fact, she was a sharer of knowledge.

It was she, her first night in The Vault, who tutored me on the page-swishing method, using a book, any book, for curing insomnia.

Paige named this method The Breathing Pages. The name fit.

Paige didn't say how, when or where she became a practitioner – another unmentionable. She said The Breathing Pages method led recipients to uplifting dreams and a deep, blissful sleep.

It didn't take long to learn how right Paige was. As I floated dreamlike, uplifted, the depth of my sleep went ever deeper till I felt myself swaddled by feathers of bliss. As if they too were breathing, the feathers kept lifting and falling back to cover and soothe me.

I quickly learned Paige also had a knack for book blowing. I'd hardly shared my method before she did the blowing better than I as a beginner.

Unlike my first efforts with the old bookkeeper, I never had to blow over books Paige had blown on just once. When she blew, just once, not a single mote of dust remained to re-blow.

Though I strive for decorum in The Vault's aisles, I was unable to resist clapping at Paige's blowing mastery.

However she, finger raised to her lips, gestured as a reminder that book blowing, though an art form, was not performance art.

Here I was, so-called wise teacher, a master, being taught. I bowed my head to her youthful dignity and inherent wisdom.

Dispatch #46

The two of us, Paige and I, stayed up very late that first night. Time passed as we talked about our favorite lists of books, The Vault's operations and what my duties here were. (Regarding the latter, Paige seemed up-to-date and informed.)

As it got still later, I stifled some yawns. Paige noticed. She asked if I was sleepy.

It already seemed as if I had known this girl for much longer than a few hours. With our delirious street walks, if that was her, perhaps I had.

I admitted I was sleepy but likely in for another sleepless night. That's why and when Paige shared The Breathing Pages method.

And that night I was most grateful for a deep, blissful sleep. Upon waking, however, I felt melancholy for what lay ahead of me that morning.

Eyes flickering open, there I was, flat on my back, sagging in the cot.

The Vault's solid shapes and outlines reappeared in the dusty light. A closed book lay flat across my chest.

The girl who identified herself as Paige was nowhere to be seen.

Dispatch #47

Still lying on my back, in the sagging cot, head propped up by two pillows, I reopen the book on my chest. It had closed after its breathing pages stopped emitting the wood-shaving fragrance.

The title on the front cover read *The Book of Disquiet*.

This book was the first that Paige had blown for me. Her blowing, as I recorded, was flawless.

Before disappearing that night, Paige tutored me in The Breathing Pages method to cure my insomnia. We used *The Book of Disquiet*, her first blown book.

I would need help from Paige, more than one time, before mastering The Breathing Pages. Unlike her I am a slow learner.

When I reopen *The Book of Disquiet,* this passage stared back at me:

> *I've dreamed a lot. I'm tired now from dreaming but not tired of dreaming. No one tires of dreaming, because to dream is to forget, and forgetting does not weigh on us, it is a dreamless sleep throughout which we remain awake. In dreams I have achieved everything.*

Like me, the author of *The Book of Disquiet* had insomnia. Clearly he was never tutored in The Breathing Pages method.

Dispatch #48

After encountering Paige in The Vault last night, my mood next morning turns – more so than usual – reflective.

Before starting the new day I sip orange juice, brew medium-roasted coffee and make two scrambled eggs to go with a slice of toasted rye bread with peanut butter and jam. I take my time savoring this modest breakfast.

Outside it's overcast. No sunbeams slant down to add sparkle to the columns of dust in The Vault. Yes, for now at least, I know my dust from my snow.

I walk slowly by tables and chairs heaped with dusty books, through aisles strung out with cobwebs and rows of more dusty books, then past the reception counter with the typewriter relic that I wipe and loosen jammed keys before pushing across its return lever – ding! – to the start position of a new line, at last coming to a standstill at the front doors.

I stand still and look out. Square door windows frame my reflective outlook.

I have failed to mention a central aspect of The Vault's entrance. This was no unmentionable, just an oversight.

Between the set of hinged doors that swing open and shut is a revolving door with four partitions.

Some patrons barging in become trapped in one or more of the four partitions of the revolving door. When that happens, their thrusting forward causes the door's rotation to speed up.

The speeding up door emits a rhythmic whoosh while going round and round. Faster and faster go the revolving door partitions. Soon they spit out tumbling patrons. Some fall back outside, some fall inside to The Vault.

The revolving door's whooshing, with ever louder vibrations, resembles the sound of The Breathing Pages from a nighttime book on my chest – of course, the revolving door whooshing is amplified many times over.

The door whooshing doesn't put me into a deep, dreamy sleep. I'm grateful for that because I cannot fall asleep while trying to welcome and hand off books to zigzagging patrons.

What would happen to me if I did? Well, who knows? Perhaps nothing. Perhaps I only imagine the very worst about the ways of the patrons.

Dispatch #49

Upon further reflection, I step up to a partition window of the revolving door and look outside, way out to distant traffic.

Various makes of autos, trucks, buses, motorcycles, even a moped rush both ways, back and forth. They are remote to me, the size of toys.

From this distance, from inside The Vault, no engine noise reaches me. No braking or horn noises either.

It's like watching action from a quaint silent movie. Before my eyes, the two-way traffic blurs and makes my head dizzy, a tad delirious.

I sway and imagine the pages breathing across my chest from last night's book as I lay propped on the pillows. A passage from another book unfurls before my eyes:

...Her sister read that spiders have book lungs, which fold in and out over themselves like pages. This pleased Isabel immensely. When she learned later that humans do not have book lungs she was disappointed. Book lungs. It made complete sense to her. This way breath, this way life: through here.

I close my eyes and absorb those words, how a book's pages could keep folding and unfolding, emitting breaths of a wood-shaving fragrance to power lungs – like mine.

Inhaling, I breathe in, absorbing The Vault's air. Exhaling, I breathe that air back out – recycling it.

Now then, like that, several more deep breaths. These form a chain of like-minded breaths, and there, I am locked in, where I want to stay locked and how I want to feel.

I am pleased by this sense of belonging. Could this be what led me to The Vault? What keeps me here?

Dispatch #50

With layers of dust and piles and rows of books to blow and reveal, The Vault is not only my place of work but my de facto home.

More so, it is my armor against the outer world – a world that pounds in waves from all directions.

At times I feel the pounding waves pass through The Vault's exterior. They vibrate inside of me. If I pause my walking and book blowing, it feels like the vibrations match my pulse. I wonder: Is this just my heart racing.

I step back from the revolving door and get back to work, focused again on my duties. I cling to the sense of belonging here.

But later that night, lying in the cot, the pounding waves return. Where does the unease they bring come from? And what keeps gnawing at me, mouse-like, also from the inside?

Something, from somewhere, breathes words in my ear, saying I don't really belong, or that I belong somewhere else – somewhere very close.

It's like the Hot-and-Cold children's game. A call of WARM or HOT means a child is closing in on a hidden object or a playmate. A call of COLD or FREEZING means the searching child is going astray.

What I hear in my ear is a repeated word: BURNING – meaning, I guess, I'm so close to some hidden object as to be practically touching it.

I have two books on my chest for tonight's reading. Despite the internal waves, the gnawing and the repeating word in my ear, I want to try sleeping without relying on The Breathing Pages.

Author No. 1 chronicles the story of a woman, mad and delirious like me, recording her travels and thoughts as perhaps the last human left in the world:

Although doubtless all I have in mind is that so many things would appear to exist only in my head, once I do sit here they then turn out to exist on these pages as well...

I'm drowsy by the time I flip open the pages of the second book. Author No. 2's passage is the last thing I recall before falling asleep:

But my fingers too write in other latitudes and the air that breathes through my pages and turns them without my knowing, when I doze off, so that the subject falls from the verb and the object lands somewhere in the void...

Dispatch #51

After Paige's first appearance in The Vault, whenever I hear the emergency side door jiggle, I assume she has reappeared.

I cannot say why I keep making this assumption. Paige never jiggles the side-door handle from the outside.

Her appearances, however, are uncanny. They seem timed for whenever the side door is left unlocked. No door jiggling is needed to get my attention.

I know because, as reported, I do the unlocking as well as the locking. Of all doors, side and front, also the middle revolving door.

For the emergency side door, unlocking and locking was done before and after book deliveries which, as I have also reported, have reverted to book dumps at the curb outside the front entrance.

That means the side door seldom gets used – except Paige uses it. For some reason she prefers that entry. I unlock the side door and soon she appears.

Book dumps are less frequent these days, perhaps once or twice a week.

At one time, don't ask when, Kroner dumped off books almost every day. Except for Sundays and seldom on Saturdays.

Over time Kroner fell into the habit of assisting me. Together we squatted, knelt, gathered, lifted, packed and wheeled crates of books inside. Afterward we settled in for coffee and banter.

It got so there was no more real book dumping. Instead Kroner and I carefully unloaded and crated books right from the open bed of his dump truck to the far bins of The Vault.

It was a humane way of treating and transferring discarded books.

If Kroner has been replaced, his replacement appears and disappears hastily and incognito.

I'm lucky to reach the front doors to see the rear of the departing dump truck, belching noxious fumes and backfiring. Perhaps there is no longer even a human driver, just one of those automated-driving trucks.

Dispatch #52

Evenings are when The Vault's front doors actually get jiggled. Not by Paige, but by Muldoon, as in Constable Muldoon.

The constable patrols his beat on foot. We have that in common – walking beats for our jobs.

Muldoon is gung-ho playing the role of hard-boiled cop. Whenever I hear a front door jiggle, I stop whatever I'm doing and rush to respond.

I must verify that the door jiggling is lawful. That means verifying that the source is not a lawbreaker, not a patron, but in fact Constable Muldoon.

Muldoon won't stop jiggling the outer door handles till I appear and can be seen and verified by him through door windows.

Decibels from Muldoon's jiggling amplify the longer it takes me to respond. He is impatient, and often I have far to go.

I am so used to The Vault's quiet that the amplifying disturbs me, especially the closer I get to the jiggling.

Only doing my job, Constable Muldoon bellows at the sight of me, touching his cap visor. Through the glass, his bellowing is muffled.

Each time Muldoon jiggles the set of front doors, checking locks and forcing me to appear, he always finds each door locked. By me, of course.

Before departing Muldoon salutes. Then he saunters into the darkness, twirling his baton after tapping it against each door frame. The sounds remind me of a xylophone. I count his musical taps.

As he goes off, I hear faint whistling. Other times, more faintly, humming.

Sometimes, before Muldoon leaves, I feel obligated to open the door and stick my head out. We exchange pleasantries.

The constable keeps it jovial. When asked how he's doing, he may joke: Still vertical and above ground, so better than horizontal and six feet under...Ha! At ease, soldier. Sleep tight in there!

Muldoon's pressed navy-blue uniform is unwrinkled. Down his trousers runs a wide black stripe. He is outfitted with bullet-proof-vest, shiny badge, pistol and holster.

Muldoon is bald but his physique shows no evidence of donut snacking. He takes seriously his lawful duties. Snacks would distract.

In cold weather, Muldoon wears a constable's cap and his baldness disappears. In hot weather, Muldoon goes without the cap and his baldness reappears.

Dispatch #53

Once – the old bookkeeper still in charge – Constable Muldoon appeared in the dead of night. This was much later than normal evening rounds. I was already sleeping tight.

At that hour Muldoon's door jiggling was ferocious and amplifying by the second.

Still cinching the sash of his robe, the old bookkeeper strode to the front doors and unlocked the one where Muldoon glowered from the other side.

With no time to put on slippers, the old bookkeeper's feet were bare but barely visible under the trailing robe.

I stayed five steps behind so as not to step on the bookkeeper's robe and trip him or myself or us both.

Muldoon wasted no time with small talk.

Right hand resting on an unsnapped gun holster, his words fired like bullets: Warning…listen up, you two…intruder alert…somewhere in this precinct…suspect on the run…possibly armed…considered dangerous…also…desperate…capable of taking, harming hostages…have you seen or heard anything suspicious in this bunker of yours? …you there, Mr. Merlin?

Those are nicknames Muldoon used for The Vault and for the old bookkeeper. I never heard the old bookkeeper complain. It was same nickname I had dreamed up for him but never uttered to his face.

The first time I heard Muldoon call the bookkeeper Mr. Merlin, I wanted to smirk. Back then I was still a job trainee, so I kept a straight face.

Muldoon had no nickname for me. Joking once, he did call me something goofy like Bubby Boy. Otherwise, he never asked for my real name, first or last. I was nameless.

Oddly, Muldoon was never curious about Merlin's eventual disappearance. Equally odd is that I never mentioned the old bookkeeper's disappearance to Muldoon.

By default, in his eyes I became the new bookkeeper. Case closed, filed away as an unmentionable.

On that night, neither the old bookkeeper nor I knew squat about an armed intruder.

The Vault is an island surrounded by derelict, collapsing buildings. These are remains from a deserted industrial park.

The old bookkeeper told me that, before his time, the Domestic Print Materials Shelter was uprooted from its original downtown foundation and transported here to this forsaken site.

Dispatch #54

Before Muldoon could resume interrogating, with the front door still held open by the bookkeeper, two figures from inside made their getaway.

The usual suspects: cat and mouse. First darted the mouse, second sprang the cat. Neither made a sound.

The distance separating them was perhaps a foot. No more. They raced between Muldoon's spread-eagled legs, disappearing in the night toward the derelict buildings.

All Muldoon had time for was to open his mouth and eyes, both wide, look and bend down, then look upside down from between his legs before exclaiming, Holy mackerel, gentlemen. What in tarnation was that?

The old bookkeeper explained what that was, what the situation was with mice colonies in The Vault. During his explanation I was nodding.

Muldoon scowled, hand still on his gun. He warned us to be prepared – local officials had to be notified. They might send pest control and/or health sanitation officials. Our bunker could be inspected, even shuttered.

Dispatch #55

In the days and weeks that followed we, the old bookkeeper and I, watched and waited. At least I did.

No official from pest control or health sanitation appeared at The Vault's doors, side or front, to inspect and possibly shut us down.

Moments after the cat-and-mouse disappearing act, Muldoon dropped his suspicions that The Vault harbored a dangerous fugitive.

Yet ever the cop, Muldoon warned us to stay alert, to stay on guard.

By all means, my dear constable, agreed the old bookkeeper. That is sage advice.

Minus slippers, the bookkeeper was also minus his shades. His legally blind eyes bulged and watered. Still, he looked proper and wise.

Next Muldoon turned to me. Trying to be compliant, I raised my chin and chirped, Yes, sir, your honor. You can count on me to be just as vigilant!

Muldoon grunted and let his gun hand relax. From the back seat of his cruiser at the curb, window cracked open, came snarling and growling.

Pay no heed to that vicious cur, Muldoon pointed with his baton. I snagged the beast as it chased a smaller mutt, another stray. Taking this one to the pound. Regrettably, the poor canine victim eluded me.

Muldoon left us to disappear inside his cruiser and speed off, his back-seat detainee still barking.

Unfazed by the uproar, Muldoon rotated a roof-mounted spotlight on the silhouettes of derelict buildings. During one flash, his spotlight shone on a fluorescent biohazard barrel, with skull and crossbones, dented and tipped over. No fugitive was hiding behind it.

How odd to see Muldoon behind the wheel instead of walking a beat, twirling his baton, whistling or humming.

As the old bookkeeper relocked the front door, he quipped that if Muldoon made more late-night raids, The Vault might reduce its cat-and-mouse population.

I nodded with a smirk. Before returning to our beds, the bookkeeper sighed, licked his lips and said how he craved a nighttime snack. He mentioned a grape sucker would satisfy the craving.

Muldoon's patrol checkups always disturbed me, especially now that I am on my own. Yet I don't resent them. I cannot explain why because his door jiggling shatters the peace here.

I can only explain by quoting another author, solitary by nature, who wrote on this ambivalence:

> *I long to be alone, but when I am alone I'm desperately unhappy. I can't endure being alone, yet I constantly talk about it. I may preach solitude, but I hate it profoundly, because nothing makes for greater unhappiness, as I know and am starting to feel...*

Dispatch #56

Despite the name, Kitty was not nicknamed for a cat prowling The Vault and hunting mice to survive.

Instead I refer to the human Kitty. When this Kitty first appeared at The Vault, her gender was one I could not verify – not for certain.

Girls are named Kitty, though not often. Kitty can be a first name but more often a nickname, like Kit or Kate, derivatives of Katherine.

Kitty was also the name of an imaginary friend that Anne Frank wrote to in her secret diary. In fact, the diary itself was nicknamed Kitty.

So Kitty's appearance at The Vault reflected gender ambiguity. At least to me it did. Female-like curves were camouflaged by other bulges of a stout figure. The hair was cropped butch; the voice was gravely but not unpleasant.

To make a point, Kitty often turned and spit off to the side. Kitty always wore coarse denim coveralls with a toolbelt held up by bulging hips.

For all of Kitty's appearances at The Vault, I never asked about gender. It was irrelevant, an unmentionable, nothing worth deciphering.

All that counts is that Kitty is and was a helpful, handy person. As with Kroner and Muldoon, we had regular contacts.

In a semi-official capacity, Kitty is The Vault's handyperson. More as an official job, Kitty also delivers supplies.

Beyond The Vault, I have no contact with the outside, official world. Often I am happy this way. Sometimes not as happy and, other times, unhappy.

So, yes, it is a relief when Kitty appears and delivers sundry goods – canned, frozen and packaged foodstuffs, occasional produce, coffee, milk, juice, tea, soap, shampoo, detergent, and odds and ends like toilet paper, pair of scissors, sweatshirts, underwear, socks, batteries, reading glasses, etcetera.

Kitty not only memorizes but anticipates these and my other needs. Without taking notes.

If I drop a hint about getting low on this or that, Kitty is bound to deliver this or that next stop.

Kitty prefers to park and deliver at the back end of The Vault. Kitty can reach the back end by turning on a service road, circling around and then backing in through a garage-like door that rolls up to the ceiling.

Kitty backs a dirt-brown pickup right into The Vault's loading bay. The utility room beyond is quite empty with just a furnace, water heater, and a grid of overhead pipes and ducts.

Seeing how well this delivery method worked, I once asked Kroner to try delivering books for The Vault via the back-end loading bay.

I told Kroner that he too could back in through the rolled-up door with his dump truck – as Kitty did with the pickup truck. Bypassing the side door and using the bay door would halve our hauling distance to the book bins.

As if pondering my request, Kroner paused what he was doing. He said nothing nor did he look me in the eye. At last he looked at the floor before scratching his scalp with both hands as if he had itchy dandruff.

But next delivery, Kroner returned again to the side door instead of trying the loading bay door in back.

The side-door books delivery – emergency alarm disabled – was Kroner's brainchild. I didn't bother making the bay-door delivery request again. Another unmentionable.

Yes, if you count them, these unmentionables do add up.

Dispatch #57

To be frank, Kitty has little to fix in The Vault. A chair leg broken by a patron during a tumble or a defective toilet flusher. All in all, simple fixes.

Simple, yes, but beyond my skill level.

In the bathroom, when I showed how the toilet flusher would only flap but not flush, Kitty gave me a look but said nothing.

An instant later, Kitty leaned over the tank, lifted the lid, plunged both arms in the water and got right to it. Had that toilet flushing in just under two minutes. Didn't even bother with a new part or use a tool.

After the so-called fix, squatting by the toilet tank as it flushed, Kitty looked up at me, waited, then said: You're not very mechanical, are you?

I shrugged and hung my head. Kitty stood and guffawed, then clapped me twice on the shoulders, saying, Don't fret, partner. You're running this joint, right? Means you're not a good-for-nothing. In fact, it actually means you're a good-for-something. Righto!

Besides the toolbelt and denim coveralls, Kitty wore laced, polished brown boots. The boots were the same dirt color as the pickup.

One time Kitty stuck out a left brown boot and pressed its toe to the floor, telling me to step down: Just do it!

I was ordered to step on that boot toe – using both feet and with all my weight and might.

I hesitated but did as I was told. Even with all my weight, might and both feet, I couldn't dent that toe. Ha, ha, ha, Kitty howled, head tossing back and forth.

Surprise – those polished brown boots had steel toes. No denting, no pain.

It made no difference to Kitty that I was not mechanically inclined or that we had little in common. We had our jobs but found time to horse around.

Dispatch #58

I learned that, unlike Kroner, Kitty wasn't a public worker. Kitty's job was privately contracted via unnamed officials overseeing The Vault.

This leaves me ponder how much longer Kitty's contractual duties will last.

Book deliveries to The Vault – now dumps – are sporadic. There must be fewer circulating books, both cloth and paper, to get rid of and dump.

When it's time for goodbyes after a stop, Kitty and I are not hand shakers. Kitty's way is to clap down, with callused palms, on my shoulders.

Kitty claps me goodbye this way seven times. The number never varies. I count each shoulder clap – each one feels like I'm being downsized.

After the shoulder clapping, Kitty pulls me in for a hug that lifts my toes about an inch off the floor.

Then Kitty playfully releases and drops me backward, saying, Take care, partner. Till next time. Hold down the ol' fort!

I like those words – the ol' fort. Maybe a new nickname? I could rename The Vault, The Ol' Fort, but I won't. I will stay true to the old bookkeeper's nickname.

Yet I wonder: Was it he who nicknamed it The Vault. Or was that a nickname passed on by a predecessor? Did he even have a predecessor or was he the first bookkeeper?

If so, does that make me the second bookkeeper or one of a lineage of bookkeepers? If a lineage, how far back in time and number does it go?

I ponder the lineage question while watching and waving goodbye to Kitty – waving at the head and shoulders in the driver's seat – before the brown pickup winds past the derelict buildings and around to distant traffic.

Then I yank down the overhead bay door. It closes and locks with a clang. Again, locked in, secure from the outside – inside here where I must belong.

Dispatch #59

Other than herds of patrons, people rarely appear at The Vault. Once people appeared on their own – to drop off books. That was the extent of the personal appearances.

As bookkeeper and before that the bookkeeper's assistant, I never once checked out a book – not to a single patron or, if there's a difference, to any single person.

I've had no checking-out requests and, frankly, I am uncertain what the checkout protocol is. I was never instructed for this hypothetical.

This makes me ponder if the patrons are indeed our last and only hope. At this point my pondering turns to despair. So what, I ask, is the point of all the book blowing I keep doing?

The more I despair this way, the more it seems as if my work here is pointless and hopeless.

But then I recall the vitality and bookish intellect that young Paige shows. With that, my hope for the future rebounds.

All this reminds me of The Bard, his appearances and eventual disappearance. Constable Muldoon was responsible for the latter.

Dispatch #60

The first time The Bard appeared outside The Vault was sometime ago. I cannot pinpoint the time, so let it go at that.

I had been distracted by fallen debris. This was no snowfall delirium, but debris was falling inside from the mezzanine-level railing and shelves.

Burrowing mice up there had dislodged dust bunnies, even book fragments. The scraps spilled out, some over the railing and down to my level.

On the first floor, I happened to be looking through the showering debris and beyond to a small window. Outside I spotted a lone figure leaning against The Vault's solitary tree – our one scraggly tree with three yellow leaves.

This was a most unusual spectacle bordering on the miraculous. Someone out there, outside The Vault, and not with a herd of patrons.

I stutter-stepped forward. I leaned my forehead against the windowpane. I was unable to decide my next move.

Job training instructs that I stay inside the Vault and welcome patrons who enter from outside. Was this person, leaning against our solitary tree, a potential patron? A solo patron, rather than a herd patron?

If so, was it my duty to go outside and recruit him to come inside, to look at books, maybe to take and read one? I had to decipher what the best option was.

Dispatch #61

By the feet of the lone figure leaning against the tree lay two items – 1) a frayed, discolored shoulder bag; and 2) a clear glass jug half full (or empty) of a dark red liquid.

The figure, a man, went from leaning to slumping against the tree, slumping lower and lower. Soon the man was sitting with back and head slumped against the trunk.

He groped inside the frayed shoulder bag, taking out notepad and pen, placing these on the ground and raising the jug to his mouth. He tipped back his head, Adam's apple bobbing.

After a gulp the man picked up and flipped open the notepad, holding up the pen as if to write. He stayed posed that way, writing nothing before dropping pen and paper to the ground and raising the jug to his lips.

I couldn't take my eyes off him. He wore high-top black sneakers with holes and untied laces, faded green jeans and a tan corduroy vest with a fringe of tassels. The unbuttoned vest exposed a bare hairy stomach and chest.

His receding gray hair hung down to his shoulders. Rimless glasses drooped on his nose. When he lowered his head, his chin doubled.

The man reminded me of the Ben Franklin image on rare $100 bills that long ago circulated.

I almost gasped when he groped in his bag and extracted not one but two hardcover books – possibly a dictionary and a thesaurus.

Displaying such books, any books, by someone other than me or Paige was a first. Could I get a witness? Who was this character? Were the two books to be used or gotten rid of at The Vault?

The side door exit was near. I unlocked and clicked it open, stepping outside. The man had the jug tipped back again, gulping. Red liquid dribbled from his lips and throat to his bare chest.

He screwed the cap back on and lowered the jug until it tilted against his bag, next to the notepad, pen and the two books.

I crouched – to reduce The Vault's gravity – and took baby steps to reach my mystery visitor slouching against the tree.

Dispatch #62

As reported, my stepping outside The Vault triggers a force, as if I were trudging through mud-thick air. Having to trudge like that, out in the open, left me feeling vulnerable, as if I were a fugitive character.

With each step beyond The Vault, I met that force pulling me back in, back to the books. It took all my strength and then some to advance. The gravitational pull eased the farther I got from The Vault.

Now came another issue. Talking to so few people, for so long, often left me dumb when the time came to talk again.

So I merely raised a hand to greet the slouching visitor. He peered at me over rimless glasses and shook his shoulder-length gray hair.

I finally stood up straight but took care not to seem menacing. This was a potential patron, not someone to spook.

My visitor was more focused on the jug and what it held. He said it was a semi-sweet cherry wine. When I told him that sounded good, he held out the jug for me.

Whoa, this was moving too fast. A potential patron shows up on the The Vault's grounds — with books and booze. This was too much, too little time to decipher.

I waved off the offer but told him to please, keep indulging, whatever suited him. I wanted to roll out The Vault's welcome mat for him.

The man said he was a poet/teacher. Or once was. He taught humanities — literature — at an institute of higher learning. His class of pupils, only a few in the best of times, had nicknamed him The Bard.

The pupils whispered the nickname at their desks while tapping away at personal devices, staring down at them, never looking up, never making eye contact. He heard their snide whispers: Bard this, Bard that.

The man didn't object to the nickname. Actually, he was rather fond of it.

But over time there came a day, because of zero enrollment, when The Bard became jobless.

Not just too few pupils enrolled for his class — here, he slapped a palm on a thigh before reaching with his other hand for the jug — but zero pupils. Zilch! Nada!

One day, start of a new semester, no more pupils sat at desks for his literature class, glued to their mobile devices, whispering his nickname.

That left no one for The Bard to teach.

Next semester, the zero-enrollment phenomenon repeated. Next, The Bard's job was terminated.

Dispatch #63

It hardly matters that The Bard's real name, his last name, was Thorn. I didn't learn of that name until the night when the constable showed up to bring him in.

Of his current whereabouts, where he was at this moment, The Bard was clueless. Not a clue of what The Vault, looming next to us, was about.

He was a starving writer, jobless, walking for inspiration, weary, with a stuffed bag on one shoulder weighing him sideways. He had to rest and felt inspired to stop somewhere, anywhere and scribble down something poetic..

But The Bard was wearier and thirstier than poetically inspired. He liked scratching his back against the tree trunk. It hit the spots, getting at his aches and pains.

With a poet's eye, The Bard sighed after seeing how the tree he slouched and scratched against was not only nearly leafless but likely dying.

Between sips he declaimed: Your tree symbolizes my declining health and fortunes, yet here I drink and keep on drinking, hastening my decline. What else is there for a poetry teacher with zero pupils to do? My literary fate is sealed.

Dispatch #64

When I asked The Bard about his poetry, he hemmed and hawed before admitting he was unpublished. He declared he was more of an aspiring poet.

I told him to hang in there, to keep writing every day or as often as possible and not be put off by rejection. The Bard said if he ever got around to submitting a poem, even finishing one, he'd follow my advice.

Having settled that, I asked if The Bard was curious about the building beside us. He was very slow to react, so I turned and waved my arm – like a wand.

The Bard struggled to swivel for a peek, then said: Oh my, my, what can it be – an ancient fortress? In the middle of nowhere! Who knew?

I spoke of the old bookkeeper's nickname for it, saying The Vault stored countless print books for safekeeping and lending but lacked active patrons.

At the news, The Bard hiccupped before declaring: What a coincidence: No active patrons for you, no more pupils for me.

I told The Bard that this could change. For starters, might he want to come inside and look for himself, browse the book collection?

I was gazing at The Vault's outline as I spoke. The Bard, with his poet's eye, got it right – the outline resembled an ancient fortress. Or, as Kitty had quipped, an ol' fort.

When I looked back to The Bard, his head had tilted on his right shoulder. He was snoring.

I saw again that his fringed corduroy vest was unbuttoned, exposing his chest and stomach. Dressed so poorly, I wondered if The Bard ever got chilly.

The wine jug had rolled from his grasp across the cracked pavement. Ants were making their way to the jug's lip.

It often went like this with The Bard, though it wasn't often he appeared.

He never came to the doors, side or front, to try opening them, even knocking or jiggling the handles. It was always me seeing him, from a window, as he scratched his back up and down or side to side against the tree with the three yellow leaves before slouching to the ground.

Only once did The Bard agree to follow me in to inspect The Vault. Already tipsy from wine, he draped an arm over my shoulders.

As we lurched hip to hip toward the entrance, I got the idea of steering him in via the revolving door.

I don't know where or why I came up with such an idea. The Bard's coordination had gone rubbery. He was dead weight.

Instead of pushing through to The Vault's interior, we kept revolving in a loop inside one of the door's partitions. Round and round we went, spinning, until the centrifugal force finally spun us back out.

There, outside the entrance, The Bard tripped over his feet, or mine, and we both fell.

I stuck out a hand to break our fall but we landed painfully, panting and groaning – my palm scraped, his pants torn, one knee bloody.

Dispatch #65

The Bard always appeared with the same shoulder bag jammed with notepads, pens, markers and dog-eared books slung over his left shoulder.

Once a book spilled out of the jammed bag. I picked it up and before handing it back read the title: *You Get So Alone At Times That It Just Makes Sense,* by Charles Bukowski.

The Bard nodded and said the book's author had been nick-named the lowlife wino poet – or something along those lines.

On The Bard's right side he carried the jug of semi-sweet red wine. Sometimes the jug held only dregs for a last swig.

His held the wine jug by hooking the handle with a forefinger. The jug's weight on his right couldn't balance the heavier weight of the jammed shoulder bag on his left. Thus his torso sagged to the left.

The leftward sagging stayed even after he dropped the bag to the ground. The weight imbalance left him misshapen.

There must have been times when I missed seeing The Bard. Focused on book blowing, I couldn't be expected to look out for him all the time.

Just as I did for getting to the book dumps outside, I would crouch and rush against The Vault's gravity to get to The Bard slumped against the tree.

Each time we met up – that is, when he came to – he was unable to recall who I was.

So each time, I would reintroduce myself. We would chat about his notepads of unfinished poems, his teaching termination and former pupils, about books, other poets and writers, including Bukowski, the lowlife poet.

If I invited him in to browse The Vault's collection, The Bard shrugged and yawned, saying he needed to rest up first, needed his nap time.

After giving him his time and space, I returned alone to the inside of The Vault for book blowing. When I looked outside later, he was always gone.

I don't know where The Bard disappeared to. He never mentioned where and I never asked. So between us, an unmentionable.

Dispatch #66

One night The Bard ended up disappearing for good. Before that disappearance came an evening appearance, which was late in the day for him to appear.

This time The Bard's shoulder bag overflowed – but not with reading and writing materials – with more wine jugs.

The Bard had really tied one on. Soon after appearing beside the tree, I heard him babbling. The evening air had a bite. At least The Bard wore a black T-shirt under his fringed, corduroy vest that was buttoned.

To be sociable, I trudged out against The Vault's gravity and hustled over to join him for a few sips from the jug. The mild wine warmed and mellowed me.

After a while I excused myself and let the same gravity escort me back inside. I didn't even bother inviting The Bard.

I left him crooning some kind of folk song. I didn't recognize the tune or lyrics. Perhaps it came from one of the unpublished poems.

Three minutes before the strike of midnight, I was locking the side door when I saw the shifting beam of a flashlight. I thought I could make out the swaying figure of The Bard. Facing the tree, now leafless, it was if he were blowing in the wind.

Then the flashlight beam lit up squirting water – urine – as it splashed off the tree bark. The Bard's jeans were unbuckled and unzipped.

Constable Muldoon, chest badge sparkling in the night, led with his flashlight. He was not walking a beat this time, he was running it.

Muldoon bellowed for The Bard to buckle and zip up and to halt his unlawful act: RIGHT THIS INSTANT, PERVERT!

Lost in his loony tune, The Bard kept crooning. He yawned and swayed as Muldoon, kicking aside empty jugs, charged.

Before Muldoon could react, The Bard, still unzipped and dripping in the flashlight's beam, turned and reached out his arms, drawing the constable in for a bear hug. The two men merged into one large mass. The sparkle from the constable's badge disappeared.

Muldoon writhed and bellowed still louder. It seemed to take him forever to escape from The Bard's embrace.

The last time – no, make that the second last time – I ever saw The Bard was when Muldoon dragged him off by the collar that night.

Cuffed, still crooning, The Bard was buckled up but his zipper was still down. His privates, thankfully, were covered.

The constable chided: For shame, Mr. Thorn, FOR SHAME! Even out here, your perversity is on exhibit.

Then Muldoon said that Mr. Thorn was under arrest – AGAIN! – for exposure and disturbing the peace.

Dispatch #67

Guilty as charged, that's me. Time and time again, I get myself distracted. Some distractions are big, others small. One by one I try to overcome them.

Take my echoing footsteps. Of course I came to realize the echoes as mine, but they also reminded me of the ticking pendulum of a wall clock.

Each tick reminded me of each passing second and minute, and that the hours and days pass by as well. Weeks, months – seasons – all jumbled and tick-tocking away.

Pausing between towering bookshelves, much of the lighting, both artificial and natural, is blocked out. As I pause, so pause my echoing footsteps.

I reach for a book, take it from its row, get a grip, assume the right pose, breathe in and blow on the book by breathing out.

The blown dust sparkles if caught in a shaft of light and sprinkles to my shoes. Then comes the bliss of holding that dust-free book.

Yet sometimes, something comes over me. I cannot explain it, but I don't want to let the book go. Or is it the reverse – the book not letting go of me?

Somehow I summon the willpower and let go. Unless it's the reverse, a letting go of me by the book. One or the other, somehow the dust-free book is returned to its place on the shelf.

Often, between the aisles, I get dizzy after blowing row after row of books. Is that from inhaling too much of The Vault's dust? Is there a limit of how much is too much to inhale?

My mind drifts. I'm hardly aware of the drifting until later – when I snap out of it.

Sometimes, pausing as I do, aware that my echoing footsteps have paused, I come to a standstill, all dusty and dizzy. I may rest my head on top of a row of books and use them as pillows.

Then, yes, I feel it, drifting toward delirium – possibly a familiar one. If so, I'll feel not only pleasure and fear but, ultimately, solace.

Dispatch #68

So this delirium – familiar because I've had it before – begins with the interior of my head filling up like a pool of water with delicate vocal tones.

The first tones have a foamy texture, grazing in and out of my ears. I hear the lilting Gregorian chants of Benedictine monks and, ahhh, my eyes close as my head rests on a pillow of books.

After a time, the full pool in my head drains off the lilting chants. Empty silence pervades. After this brief intermission, the musical pool in my head slowly refills with a second wave of vocal tones.

This time the tones have deepened. It's the tantric chanting of Tibetan Buddhist monks. Big bubbles of sound from their guttural voices rumble in and out of my ears.

Still drifting, I listen to both forms of chanting. The harmonies vary in length and pitch, but the rest of the delirium is unvaried.

Next I find myself walking gingerly as if crossing a pool of ice. For balance, my arms extend like wings, touching rows of books on either side of the aisle.

Invariably my fingers touch and poke the crumbling spine of a mice-nibbled book. My fingertip pressure caves in the spine.

A book so crumbly is beyond preserving. Even so I have a stab of guilt. In my head, between my ears, the chanting pool of voices has drained again.

It is unbearable to describe the second half of this delirium. Not without doubting my sanity, which of course I do.

Dispatch #69

Insane or not, here goes...I begin seeing letters of the alphabet, micro letters. These letters have the size, shape and color of black ants. From the pages of crumbling books, the ant-letters scurry out.

Where are they scurrying? Across the air and before my eyes.

In no time the ant-letters assemble in batches that form virtual words. Within seconds those combine and lengthen to form clauses and phrases that lengthen again into sentences of various lengths.

The sentences evolve, taking form as centipedes. With their itty-bitty legs, these centipedes swarm up and down shelving and along rows of books. The swarm too fast for me to read anything they might be spelling.

I cannot take my eyes from the swarming sentences. As they swarm all around me, the centipedes hiss. Their hissing replaces the chanting of monks still echoing in the drained pool between my ears.

I grow dizzier trying to eyeball all the centipede-sentences. It is hard to hold on now, to hold myself up.

I try taking a step or two down an aisle of books. When I do a random sentence flings itself out and – yes – lassos me by the neck.

I gag as the lasso tightens around my Adam's apple.

Dispatch #70

I swear this is only the beginning. At least not the end.

More delirious is when the towering bookshelves begin revolving and I lose my footing, almost falling forward, backward, sideways. By this time I've totally lost my bearings.

I'm reminded of The Vault's revolving front door, only the revolution of these shelves is vertical – not horizontal like that door.

After the shelves have revolved vertically into place, I find myself walking not on floor planks but on the spines of hardcover and paperback books.

I walk gently so as not fall through gaps between the parallel book rows. Under foot, my full body weight upon them, several crumbling books break apart.

Their creased pages squeeze out still more ant-letters. The letters assemble into words before lengthening into hissing, centipede-sentences. Some pages loosen, detach, glide out and up, rising around me like miniature kites.

Here is my skewed position: While I stand or walk on a floor of book rows, overhead are other rows of books that have revolved into a ceiling. Between this floor and ceiling of books, I must stoop.

Rising pages keep bouncing off the book ceiling. There they glide along until reaching the end of an aisle, then pass beyond and again glide upward, out of sight.

I miss the chanting harmonies of the Benedictine and Buddhist monks. I clap my ears to muffle the hissing as strands of sentences loop over me.

I have a halo of sentences crowning my head; bangles and bracelets of sentences up and down my arms; sashes and belts of sentences cinching my hips and waist; and still other sentences bracing my knees and ankles.

More unnerving are the spiraling sentences that orbit my throat like necklaces, the tighter ones squeezing like chokers.

Fear almost drives me to swear and lash out with my arms and hands at these choking sentences.

Instead I pause, reminding myself to follow my breath. As with book blowing, I breathe out and blow air away from me. Then I breathe air back in.

After some 15 minutes of meditative breathing, the sentence necklaces and chokers loosen and dangle down my chest. My heart beats against them.

More relaxed now, I grin at how fashionable I must look with strands of words, sentences and even paragraphs adorning my body like jewelry.

Delirious or not, there was no need to panic. The sense of belonging in The Vault keeps its gravitational hold on me.

Dispatch #71

Before long, several books not packed tightly above my head fall from the ceiling shelf.

In this still familiar delirium, the falling books never hit me. I observe their crash landings all around, how the covers flip open, how more letters from the printed pages scurry out like ants only to form words and then hissing, centipede-sentences.

After some time, the hissing between my ears drains and refills with harmonized chanting. Ahhh, yes, first back to Gregorian, next to Tantric, then both. Much better. I stoop lower to sit and then lie on my back upon a shelf – a floor – of book spines.

As I lie there something, not another centipede, scurries over my stomach. I lift my head and glimpse the blur of a mouse. The next blur to leap over my stomach is larger – naturally, a cat.

I stare up at the bookshelf that has revolved into my new ceiling. Just then, from that ceiling, strands of sentences and even paragraphs loosen and flutter down to me.

Some fall curling and land like lint or fluff over my face. I spread them out to read what the authors had written:

We dust. And the dust finds a way to return. We dust again. In this way, the sweeping and the dusting of our lives is never finished. It is much the same as our breathing, this going in and coming back.

Although they've shredded the paper towels – I suppose to pad their nests with – the Clam Lake mice seem to have nibbled at only one book in the whole cabin – the old cookbook in the kitchen. The pages of recipes must have been flipped with my greasy fingers.

Another fallen sentence dangles from my earlobe – a small earring. I peel it off, unravel the creases and read what this author wrote:

A book you touch/ Begins/ Reading itself

From the other earlobe, a larger earring sentence to peel off and read:

I learned that books are never finished, that it is possible for stories to go on writing themselves without an author.

And so I start pulling off and smoothing out, then reading sentences that were looped up and down my body...

I know it sounds strange – you might conclude that I, and not my father, was the one suffering from delirium, but I have occasionally tried to take the perspective of the books on the shelves, imagining that they choose their recipients as much as they are chosen.

I was happy to be in a room that smelled pleasantly of old books, where it was warm and quiet, where the pages rustled as they were turned, as if the books were sighing in their sleep.

I also thought of the playwright who, as he lay dying by the window, confused the passersby in the street with the characters of his play.

I cannot recall for how long this sort of reading business went on. I may have fallen into a trance or even slept and dreamed.

Snapping out of it later, I find myself back up on my feet, leaning against an upright shelf and holding a book — one with heft but in need of blowing.

Everything has revolved vertically back to normal positions. Earth's gravity holds the soles of my feet to the planks of The Vault's floor.

As I resume the job of blowing and take more steps, the planks echo, each step like a ticking clock

Dispatch #72

There came a time when the sound of my footsteps — and their echoes — changed.

The change was caused by my switch to wearing clogs. I had little choice about switching my footwear.

After walking here day in and day out for countless days, the heel of one of my well-worn shoes loosened and finally broke off.

Surely Kitty could easily have reattached the broken heel. Yet I was too embarrassed to ask Kitty to do all my fixing, especially easy fixes.

So I junked the old shoes, both, even the shoe with its heel still attached. That left nothing for Kitty to fix and nothing for me to be embarrassed of.

If I had not junked both shoes, tried walking in them, I would've walked unevenly, limping, because of the missing heel.

To verify this I experimented by walking in both shoes, good heel and no heel. As expected, I walked with a limp — similar to Paige with her short-limping leg.

Walking in clogs changed the quality of sound my footsteps made across The Vault's floor. With clogs I sounded like a clip-clopping horse.

I chanced upon the pair of clogs while tidying up the storage closet. The clogs were not an exact fit but close enough.

When I first laid eyes on the clogs, I exclaimed: The old bookkeeper's fleecy slippers! But no, he must have taken those when he took off.

Listening to the clip-clopping of my clogs caused me to lose track of time. When that happened I wound up pacing the four corners of The Vault.

Call it for what it was — another distraction. I failed to pause between aisles and do my book blowing. I swore as these and all my failures added up.

As I clip-clopped and paced, I pondered my recent delirium — the one with chanting, hissing, falling words and swarming sentences. If I didn't resist them, I enjoyed deliriums, particularly this one. Why not induce this particular delirium more often, and on my terms?

With that an idea came for a new experiment. First I needed to find a few items. For one, my old pipe. For a second, The Vault's wheelbarrow.

Dispatch #73

I am eager to set this, my newest experiment, in motion.

In the pantry nook that doubles as a kitchen, I take only quick sips of black coffee with plain toast — skip the peanut butter and jam, juice and eggs.

I grab the long-handled barrow and wheel it to the freight elevator. I press the power button so the creaky lift goes up to the mezzanine level.

Going up to the mezzanine is slow going. As reported, power here is spotty. It's not far up but by my count it takes almost one minute – 56 seconds.

After reaching the mezzanine, an operator must tug down on a flat woven cord to open the two halves of the freight elevator's thick steel door.

One half of the door goes up and disappears through an upper slot. At the same time the other half goes down and disappears through a lower slot.

The split steel door gives off a metallic echo while opening. And closing. While unwieldy, the freight elevator is useful for heavy hauling.

At mezzanine level, I gaze down over the entirety of The Vault's ground floor. From up here, the towering bookshelves are like an archipelago of rectangular islands flattened across a map.

I lean over the railing to survey this map. Some islands are splashed by sunbeams slanting in from the vertical windows. Atop these islands are shag carpets of white dust sparkling in the sun.

From my back pocket, I take out and open a chapbook, browse the pages and read this poetic passage:

I prefer the skyline/
of a shelf of books

As I continue reading more short poems by the mezzanine railing, the sun is warming my back. In The Vault this passes for sunbathing.

Dispatch #74

Under the row of mezzanine windows, built-in wall shelves house what are reputed as The Vault's earliest book collections.

The old bookkeeper once confided that this is where the collection began. He offered no clues to its beginning age.

I have walked parallel to the mezzanine's sagging shelves before and spotted row upon row of splintered, imploding book spines. The plight of these books, while grave, connects to my newest experiment.

Many rows of books in the mezzanine have deteriorated to a mishmash. What is left inside of their spines are misshapen lumps.

As I reach into this mishmash, my fingers penetrate wads of pages, bindings and covers that crumble by the handful. My hands come away smudged with mouse droppings – brownish pellets, the oldest chalky and dry.

The first time this happened, I withdrew a grubby handful and jumped back. So surprised, I swore and let the wad drop to the floor where it plopped in a puff of dust.

I had expected to find such papery wads, but still, how very sad to actually touch and see these bookish remains.

Less visible are the habitats these remains provide – for the larvae of beetles, moths and silverfish. The latter, nicknamed bookworms, eat carbohydrates and love the starches in paper and glue from book bindings.

Anyway, I regain my focus and dig in, scooping out more handfuls. Wads plop from the shelves, down into my barrow.

After a time, under all the weight, the barrow's wheels are wobbly. I labor to roll that weight between shelves and railing, back to the freight elevator.

Going down, I ponder my experiment: What is my goal? Is it pleasure? Escapism? Enlightenment? Delirium management?

My back pocket bulges with an old pipe. For smoking weed. The pipe followed me all the way from somewhere, I cannot recall where, from long past, to the here and now.

A dusty haze hovers right along and over the brimming wheelbarrow. Even by air, dust in The Vault cannot help trailing after me and my books.

Dispatch #75

Back at ground level, I wheel my load into the central office next to the storage closet. For whatever reason, that closet has a rusty spade hanging by a large nail in the wall.

This is the same closet where I found the wheelbarrow and, of course, the clogs I now wear and, before that, the feather duster and the hand-held vacuum. Those add up if you count them, which I do.

The spade is a garden tool. Perhaps gardening was once done on the grounds of The Vault.

Perhaps at one time there was more green space and more than one scraggly tree. Perhaps gardening was another duty for a past bookkeeper or for an assistant to that bookkeeper to do.

It matters not why or who left the hanging spade. What matters is how to use it now to advance my experiment.

The metal blade has a sharp, curved edge. In the office, I raise the spade and thrust the blade down. That is how I begin chopping up the bookish remains.

Before long the thrusting has tired me. This work is harder than dust blowing, which inflated my lung capacity but did not inflate my arm muscles.

Dust keeps rising as I chop the bookish remains into small and smaller chunks and then, smaller still, into chips and flakes. I wield scissors to do more cutting up and fine slicing.

Even with inflated lungs, I am panting in the dusty air. I'm also lightheaded, which I believe comes from inhaling all the rising dust.

The lightheadedness seems to confirm one aspect of my theory related to the pipe-smoking experiment.

So I wheel the barrow with its hacked and sliced-up contents out of the office. As I do, I notice the color of daylight slanting down from the mezzanine's windows.

The color has changed from glowing yellow to solid white. Curious, that change.

Though still lightheaded and panting, I return to the freight elevator. For 56 seconds I elevator my way up.

Back at mezzanine level, I grab the mobile stepladder hooked by rails — one atop the bookshelves and running parallel on the floor track. Rung by rung I climb.

At the top of the stepladder I peer over the last row of books, some with collapsed spines, and stare out a window. I smile at what I see: Snowfall.

This must be real snow falling outside, not snowfall inside The Vault, as past deliriums fooled me into seeing and believing.

To verify the sight, I extend a hand and press palm and fingers to the windowpane.

Yes, snow is falling outside, beyond the pane, not inside, on me. My pressing hand touches only the window's cold, transparent glass, leaving a handprint.

Snow falls outside, coating the derelict buildings and abandoned machinery surrounding The Vault. The fallen snow resembles a shaggy coating of dust on discarded rows of books in The Vault.

Seasons are passing. This one must be winter, season of whiteness.

Dispatch #76

As I climb down the mobile stepladder is shaky. Is the ladder shaking from my weight or do I shake from the lightheaded feeling?

Taking the freight elevator back down to ground level, I drag a chair to the side door and look out its upper window. Here, I will toke on my pipe and behold the whitening landscape outside.

The winter evening whiteness, even with the snowflakes, is giving way to grayness.

I strike a match, watch the flickering flame, then use it to light the contents of the pipe bowl. My first toke.

I exhale smoke from a kindling of ground-up book remains not much larger than motes of dust. Ash forming in my burning pipe bowl turns charcoal gray.

Not once all day did I blow a single mote of dust from any row of books. Nor did I blow dust from any one book stacked or lying on a table, ledge, cart, desk or anywhere.

I cannot recall very far back, but I don't ever recall missing an entire day of dust blowing. It is my job, and I confess to a dereliction of duty.

The number of books in need of blowing here is countless and accumulating. Yet where are my reading patrons? I count none.

So I confess a second time: Instead of blowing, I have distracted myself from despair by toking on a pipe packed with ground-up book remains.

The experiment is to replicate and manage what I've reported to be a random, repeating delirium. Call me totally delirious. Why not, I do so myself while striking another match over the pipe.

Dispatch #77

The bowl's flaming remains glow orange before changing to gray, powdery ash. I inhale smoke and fumes through the stem and exhale.

Outside a breeze has picked up. Through the side-door window I stare at falling, slanting snow.

I cannot help but second guess myself. Is this another foolish experiment? To try to induce a familiar delirium by toking the powdery remains of the oldest, most decrepit books stored in the upper regions of The Vault?

My raid of book remains up there filled an entire wheelbarrow. And, should I wish, the mezzanine wall shelves hold a countless supply of raw materials for me to chop and ground for even more pipe smoking.

Am I merely smoking to blunt my despair? Is that what my deliriums here add up to? Or are they an outlet, a reminder that I must return to something else? But returning from what and to where?

Somewhere within The Vault – hot/cold –must lie the answer to these questions.

Only a fool would be delirious enough to conduct this experiment. With each toke, I count my second guesses. Over time I lose track and stop counting.

Dispatch #78

With each toke, I recall that it works best to inhale air until the lungs inflate to capacity – holding each breath until bursting – before exhaling the smoke. At some point, in that smoky air, I catch a familiar whiff.

Weed? Yes, I recall the odor. The old pipe bowl must be caked with a weedy residue that mixes and burns with the bookish remains.

So, in the end, what did this experiment add up to? My history is one of appearing at The Vault, for whatever reason, becoming delirious and being tutored in the fine art of blowing dust off discarded books for nonexistent patrons.

Sometime later, after a day's dereliction of duty, here I sit, in a haze, inhaling weed/book remains while trying to conjure up a familiar delirium.

Then I sense something – an uplift. My sense of time is slowing, so slow, perhaps reversing. The chair under me lifts my feet off the floor and takes off backward under an airy carpet.

Dispatch #79

Before long, maybe longer, the carpet of air transports me through a revolving tunnel. Seems I'm traveling back in time – again – to another childhood memory.

Is that all I'm to gain from this experiment? Clearly I have no skill at managing this delirium matrix.

As reported, I have no sense of recalling anything before my appearance at The Vault. On the other hand, these time-travel deliriums point me backward, stirring up memories.

And so I seem to travel back to school-boy days, what appears to be my 2nd grade class. I am sitting with classmates and struggling with, of all things, the basics of reading.

Our teacher is Miss Boyle. My head is bowed, eyes holding in the tears. I'm not really that little boy – am I? I seem to be both feeling and reporting this at the same time. As a bystander, I can report what I see and yet also be there to feel what the boy is feeling.

Miss Boyle flickers like a flame before a grid of students at their desk rows. She explains why the boy (me?) will be better off in the lower reading group.

At the verdict, the boy singled out cannot hold in the tears.

Our 2nd grade is split by two reading groups. The upper, for superior readers, nicknamed the Mockingbirds; the lower, for inferior readers, nicknamed the Bluebirds.

For the boy's reading benefit, he is to be expelled from the upper Mockingbirds and demoted to the Bluebirds. Miss Boyle doesn't use the words expel and demote. The boy – through me – interprets.

All his close friends, popular 2nd graders, read with the Mockingbirds. Demoted to the Bluebirds adds up to an expulsion. He will be stamped with a label of inferior reader. Friendships will fray.

Paul, a super popular boy, is the brainiest 2nd grader, maybe tied for the honor with another girl, Sara. Paul wears large-lens glasses and reads fluently – of course, as the topnotch Mockingbird would.

Through his large, reflective lenses, Paul studies me as if reading about the fate of a storybook character – a forlorn boy, rubbing his crybaby eyes. Paul slides from his desk and sidles up to the head of the class. He cups a hand over his lips.

Miss Boyle bends to hear Paul whisper. I watch their figures, one taller, one shorter. Both flicker like flames being lit over a pipe bowl.

The boy (me) overhears Paul: See how he cries. It's making the rest of the class very sad. Why not give him more time, let him hang on with the Mockingbirds until the end of semester? If his reading hasn't improved by then, tell his parents at conference time, then send him down to the Bluebirds.

As the boy, I see how Paul flaunts his brainy status with the teacher. Paul's flaming image flickers until it blurs.

Other details signal my time-travel memory is distorted: As he sidled up to the teacher, Paul not only flickered but limped; and when he glanced at me while counseling Miss Boyle, a silver-blue, star-shaped bindi sparkled on his brow.

As Miss Boyle straightened after Paul's counsel, she accepted a licorice sucker he handed her, tearing off the wrapper and holding the sucker up for my classmates to see.

After that Miss Boyle took the sucker and licked it before leering at me. Her shiny lips and tongue were smeared black. She held out the sucker and nodded for me to come forward from my desk – for a licking.

The boy (me) resents Paul for butting in but is thankful because he (I) was never demoted to the Bluebirds. He (I) hung on with the Mockingbirds and kept (our) friends, even our friendship with Paul.

Gradually the delirious memory vaporizes. My adult eyes open. The night view outside The Vault's window has blackened. Snow no longer falls but what fell blows in drifts.

Was that a hazy child memory or one distorted by delirium? Both, it seems.

I had failed to conjure up the literary delirium – the one with ant-words and swarming centipede-sentences. So, call this another experimental bust.

Groggy and stiff, I massage my temples, rise from the chair and rattle the side-door handle to verify the emergency exit is locked for the night. It was.

Dispatch #80

In no time winter blows by. At least it does from the inside looking outside, blowing by at speeds no meteorologist could forecast.

Is the speedy passage because I'm discombobulated from always smoking book remains laced with pot residue?

The weather pattern also seems to have discombobulated the patrons. Their herd instincts are diminished. They roam now by the handful or even fewer. Adrift, they appear outside The Vault at all hours, night and also day.

The patrons no longer barge in the front doors around sunset. I never know when to do the unlocking to prepare for their appearing.

As a result, I am unprepared. Instead I must listen closely, at all hours, for their diminished numbers colliding off the locked doors.

When I asked Kitty on the last supply run what was up with the patrons, Kitty turned – as if I'd spoken in tongues – and stared at me, or through me.

Had we never discussed the patrons before? I was carrying in a large box of supplies. Focused on not letting the box slip from my grasp, I forgot to ask Kitty again about the patrons.

Either the pipe smoking, the diminished patrons, or both have distracted and made me lazier. I have not kept up with book-blowing duties. Or I just do a random book blow or two.

By default, I have become a lazy worker.

I justify the laziness by repeating, like a mantra, that there's only one book – ONLY ONE – for me to blow and reveal. I cannot recall how or why this mantra appears, but it echoes in my head with each of my footsteps.

The floor planks need sweeping. They need mopping. Dust coats them and thickens as my lazy days accumulate.

In some sections, the dusty coating is thick enough to muffle my clip-clopping clogs. Twice I have slipped on a thickness of dust. Once I even fell, legs going out from under me, landing on my ass.

That one pratfall was so painful I could not sit for some time. I wound up spending days on the cot, lying on my stomach, reading, napping, drifting in and out of deliriums, waiting for the pain in my ass to diminish.

Of course the accumulating dust took no days off.

Dispatch #81

My recuperation gives me ample time to ponder. I designate the time off as sick time.

Like dust here, my sick time must accumulate. Yet I was never told I had that benefit. On my own – by default – I have claimed sick time as a benefit. Go report me – if you can find anyone to report me to.

During my sick time, I keep pondering the ultimate purpose of this job. More pondering finds there is no purpose.

Even when they barged undiminished through The Vault, the patrons shunned my outstretched hand. Not one accepted a dust-free book.

No one has ever come to The Vault to browse our collection. Before his arrest Mr. Thorn, The Bard, came and went without showing a hint of interest to set foot inside. And this from someone calling himself a poet.

The exception is Paige. A singular young reader, she's a sparkling star, a guiding light to the future.

Day after day the dust and cobwebs accumulate. I'm tasked with blowing the covers and spines while the books, dusted or not, go unread.

The very oldest of books, in the mezzanine, are forfeited to mice and bookworms. Only now I slice and pulverize their papery remains for pipe smoking.

So the outlook here appears hopeless. Absent hope, I take more and more time off, calling it sick time. Except I've stopped lying on my stomach and started shuffling

I shuffle around The Vault in my socks, clogs left under the cot, puffing on my pipe like an addict, off and on delirious. I stare out a window, up at the ceiling grid, down at the floor, anywhere but at the piles and rows of books left undusted.

Dispatch #82

At times the toking deliriums take on a form I've nicknamed pipe dreams. These are not time travels but they do project me beyond the shelving of books, even beyond The Vault.

Delirious projections, these are my guilty pleasures, since the very thought of leaving The Vault brings anxiety. I feel both exhilarated and anxious, even fearful, to imagine taking part in a life beyond The Vault.

In one pipe-dream delirium, I found myself projected aloft over a middling town in, of all things, the gondola of a hot-air balloon.

Ah, what a crisp, sunny autumn day it was. Driven by gusts of wind, the few clouds surged from one end of the pale blue horizon to the other. Blowing foliage on the skyline hinted at seasonal colors.

I toked on my pipe, watching the puffs vaporize. The gondola pilot looked familiar. He cranked a lever up several notches to release more gas, igniting a larger flame. His other hand fiddled with the buttons of a peacoat uniform.

We had to hang on tight because of the wind. Our swinging gondola crested low over the rooftops of offices, shops, stores and cafes.

People below, whether holding briefcases, shopping bags or, in most cases, mobile devices, stopped to look up, even pointing their devices at us to take pictures and videos.

Some shielded their eyes from the blinding sun. Others waved and blew kisses. One clasped hands under her chin, as if praying for our safe flight.

How very odd to be among people again, even from above. At this distance I could watch them all day, but the balloon's trajectory was onward and downward.

As we crested still lower, we became a distraction. People on foot or bike rushed after us, as did motorists, some making U-turns. A teenager's skateboard went out from under his feet and he landed, where else, on his ass.

Our balloon sailed on past the bedlam, past the outskirts of town, but our presence went on distracting. We skimmed across a highway, forcing drivers going both ways to honk, break and swerve.

We bumped once on a gravel shoulder, knocking me and the pilot to our knees, but avoiding the traffic and just clearing a culvert before landing with a thud at the edge of a cornfield.

Even with skinned knees and thumping heart, I was impressed by how the pilot, also on his knees, handled the controls. It was a dramatic, poetic landing. We staggered to our feet.

When he unhinged the gondola's door to let me out, the pilot tipped back his peaked cap and mumbled apologies for the rough landing. At his feet an empty wine jug rolled across the tilting floor. That's when I got a proper look.

Why, it was The Bard, in the guise of a hot-air balloon pilot! Even in the windy, higher altitudes, he had done right by his piloting duties.

I looked closer at this pipe-dream version of The Bard. His bare chest and stomach showed under the partly unbuttoned peacoat, but at least his pants uniform was buckled and zipped.

This version of The Bard beamed at my recognition. Arms outstretched; he reeled me in for a bear hug.

I counted 30 seconds on the dot before The Bard pilot released me. I stumbled down the gondola stairway and into the cornfield, doubling over and wheezing for air.

I felt around for it but found my pipe was gone.

Dispatch #83

After weeks of more delirious sick time – I am only guessing at how long – I chanced upon these words by an author describing what it truly feels like for books to be held and handled...*because that's why they stand there, they're just like us, they want to be caressed and loved despite it all.*

That's all it took, that spark! That simple, fragmentary passage. Like an electric current, a Zen koan, it shocked every ounce of laziness from my system. Flushed it right out.

I read and reread the fragment, but one reading, the first, was the only shock it took to get me back to my old work habits.

Those words lit up the spirituality of the old bookkeeper's pithy instructions: If nothing else, fool, just blow for the well-being of each book you're able to lay hands on.

Thus enlightened, I wasted no time resuming my dust-blowing duties.

Dispatch #84

But right after being shocked out of my apathy, who shows up? Paige, that's who. Talk about timing. As in bad.

Just as I was gearing up, feeling all enlightened, to resume my duties, Paige tore into me for...what else?: Dereliction of duty!

My old words, her new words. Her tone of voice was more of a growl. Coming from a teenage girl, the growling tone shook me.

Before Paige showed up, I was rushing like mad to make up for lost time – all that sick time off. I rushed way too fast and lost control.

I yanked books by the hand- and armful from shelves. I blew on them willy-nilly. I even blew on more than one book at a time.

Multiple book blowing is taboo. Blowing must always be done one book at a time – for that singular reader.

Still worse, I blew on multiple books with barely a single blow, more like half blows, before jamming them back in their row on a shelf.

Sometimes the jammed books didn't line up, tipping over any which way, even falling to the floor. Many rows of books were left askew and dusty.

I also left spheres of dust on various shelves that were dislodged, falling and whirling across the floor like tumbleweeds.

Worse yet, I was mopping the dusty floor without first sweeping up the dust. And I mopped in a rush. That left soapy, filthy puddles.

The leftover water stagnated, and that caused more warping while the floorboards stayed filthy.

Dispatch #85

It is Paige, by default, who now inspects my work and proclaims that what I've been doing – mostly not doing – is shiftless and inexcusable.

It is Paige who now seems to call the shots here. She condemns my prolonged apathy, my so-called sick time, my, yes, my dereliction of duty.

While Paige is not the old bookkeeper, her commanding tone and words echo like his, like that of a boss.

As I stand before her, my face blushes, then pales. I bow my head.

Even with a shorter leg, Paige has grown taller. Her hair is cropped short and curled above the shoulders. No more pony- or pigtails. Some pimples dot her cheeks.

I keep my face lowered, avoiding eye contact.

Where is my pipe? I panic, not wanting Paige to find it during this compromising time. Then, relief: I pat my back pocket, trace the pipe's outline.

Upon Paige's arrival, I slipped on my clogs again. I had to restore a semblance of decorum.

Paige says nothing about how the clogs echo. Odd, but with her walking beside me, the clip-clopping diminishes.

Paige stays for hot tea. She selects two bags, organic green, no flavors. She prepares and serves the hot beverage from a kettle in the pantry nook.

The table's a bit wobbly for one but with the two of us on opposite ends, elbows pressed down, we stabilize the surface.

We sip our green tea from steaming mugs. My hands and insides are relaxing. My shame and panic ebb. I feel the tension between us ease.

Spring is finally here, Paige murmurs.

Call it small talk, but Paige is at least smiling as she speaks. With the tea sipping, her growling tone has evaporated.

She continues: As you surely must appreciate, the work here requires backbone and commitment. Can we count on you, again – count on you to keep nurturing the health and welfare of these books?

Paige uttered the word we – plural. I'm sure I heard her speak that very word.

We? I ask. Who else?

She deflects my question by replying in the singular: Let's just say that I am the one counting on you. We go way back, you and I. In my book that counts for a lot.

I nod and breathe in the more of the steam's warmth. I take another sip.

Knowing that I'm a counter of things, I know exactly what to say: Paige, there are no ifs, ands or buts. This dereliction of duty won't be repeated. I'll never again let you down. Continue to count on me to keep doing this job to the very end – whenever that is.

Dispatch #86

After teatime, after rinsing our mugs, Paige and I set off together to focus on one aisle of bookshelves among many for dust blowing.

Togetherness, teamwork. There is so much catch-up work to be done. Two blowers are surely better than one.

Paige begins on one end of an aisle, I on the other end. Our eyes meet. She nods to start.

Inwardly I still marvel at Paige's blowing technique. Mind and body, she is so fluid, so Zen-like.

We begin at the top row of each shelf. Those books are hardest to reach. We use footstools. Even I need one to extend my reaching.

On her stool, Paige reaches for those upper books on tiptoes. She uses her longer leg, by itself, as a final extension. Somehow she balances. The one-leg reaching fails to slow her speed or disturb her balance.

One book after another is pulled out, spines, covers and pages blown on, then replaced on the shelf before the process is repeated in the same manner and speed.

Book covers caked by grime get a special wipe with a rag dipped in cleaning solution. As reported, my idea. Paige approves – Yes!

Having such a gifted coworker inspires me. Book by book, I try to match Paige's technique but her speed exceeds mine. Our stools slide closer. I meet her one third of the way down the first row of books to her two-thirds.

No matter, still inspired, I press on. We return to starting positions on opposite ends of the same aisle, still on our stools, and, after her nod, begin blowing again, beginning on the second highest shelf.

After we finish the multiple rows of shelving, both sides of the aisle, Paige goes. I wait. She returns with broom and dustpan. I go and return with bucket of soapy water and mop.

We work as teammates that way too, all day long. Book blowing, row by row, up high, gradually going down low, both sides of an aisle, followed by sweeping and mopping of the floor between.

We blow and clean an even dozen sets of bookshelf aisles and sweep and mop the floors between those. That is only a fraction of The Vault's ground-floor area but, all and all, a productive day's work.

I cannot recall how long since I worked this hard. But working with a teammate, one as gifted as Paige, makes my workday pass quickly.

Dispatch #87

So there, work's done, at least today's work. Now I have to go, Paige announces. I have schoolwork to prepare for at home tonight. A finals test tomorrow. I should've brought my things here so I could study and keep you company, make sure you get your sleep before getting back to work.

I tell Paige not to worry, that my work ethic is fully recharged. For good. I have that spark to persevere with my duties. I also tell her that I sleep like a baby – thanks to her tutoring me in The Breathing Pages.

To reassure Paige, I add: And listen, come back again, anytime. Check on my blowing progress, sit for tea. As I've said, you know you can count on me.

Paige laughs and sticks up two fingers in a V – for victory! Then she sniffs the air and says, Whew, smells smoky in here! Reeks. That odor's been with me all day. I'll leave the side door propped open when I go. Place needs a good airing. And that also goes for the book collection.

I watch Paige go limping, just a bit, out the propped-open door. I stand in the doorway, watch her depart and call out: Ace that test, girl!

Paige turns once to flash me another V. Her short black hair makes her look grownup. Did she skip school today to check on me? How long ago and where did we first meet? Was that meeting another delirium?

Outside, heaps of soot-encrusted snow are melting. I hear faraway traffic. I inhale the mild, spring-like air. For once I'm reluctant to step back inside, but I feel The Vault's pull, unyielding, and know that I must.

I forget to keep the side door propped open. Instead, out of habit, stepping back inside, I shut and lock it.

I consider throwing away my old pipe or maybe stashing it away – somewhere I'm likely to forget where, like buried somewhere in the closet. Let another bookkeeper, one from the future, stumble upon it and ponder.

That night, after the long day's work, I am so tired and my muscles ache. It was tiring, our mutual day of work, but the outcome filled me with renewed purpose. I hope Paige noticed my renewal.

Lying there on the cot, my thoughts revolve around Paige. I admire her can-do attitude. Already I miss her spark. I wonder what her future holds as well as mine. There's so much to keep me awake pondering that falling asleep becomes impossible.

So lying on my back, I do The Breathing Pages. And soon, on their own, pages from the book on my chest swish back and forth.

Though my eyes have closed, I visualize those pages. They breathe fitfully at first, then accelerate before settling at an even tempo.

I inhale their wood-shaving fragrance. I breathe in, breathe out. Before long I'm gliding off to sleep, trailed by words from this author's passage:

...I had wanted to learn what places appeared in the mind of one or another fictional characters whenever he or she stared past the furthest places mentioned in the text that had seemed to give rise to him or to her; what places such a character thought of during the hours of the days that were never reported in the text; what places such a character dreamed about — not only in sleep but during those waking moments the strangeness of which can hardly be described by the dreamer, much less suggested by a writer of fiction.

Dispatch #88

Kroner? Not possible! Can it be? No, can that really be you, Kroner, out there that I see? That isn't possible, is it? That cannot be you I am seeing. Can it? Kroner, is that you?

Real? Delirium? Which? I shake my head, rap both temples with my knuckles, pull on my eyelids and lift them as wide open as they can stretch.

Moments ago I was distracted during book blowing, so I detoured to the emergency side door. I was curious to peek and see how much snow was left.

In fact, all snow has melted. The cracked pavement is streaked from the melting remains. The branches of our half-dead or maybe dead tree are still without buds.

But there, atop a mound of dumped-off books, sits...Kroner? He is sitting there now, up high, at the very top, as if he's king of the hill, a delirious vision of book-dumping royalty.

How long has it been? How long since Kroner last drove and delivered discarded books to The Vault? I won't even guess.

I must have missed the latest book dump that created the mound for Kroner to ascend. That happens. Dump-truck deliveries are so rare that I rarely look for them.

Now those dumps are done via drone. These hover over The Vault and automatically drop a load of discarded books — like bombs — to the ground. Sometimes drones fly over in pairs or even triplets to drop their loads. The chopper blades slash the air as the drones hover above before veering off.

And now Kroner is at the top of the latest book bombing. Sitting there like that, legs crossed in a lotus position, he also reminds me of a reincarnated Buddha. I pull on my eyelids again to see if I can see any better

The Buddha's lips move. Is that chanting? I cannot lip read to decipher his words and, besides, Kroner is holding a book up that blocks his lower face. He wears reading glasses with half lenses. These are attached by a chain around his neck.

I unlock and fling open the side door and holler: Kroner...son of a gun, where the hell have you been keeping yourself?

Kroner lowers the book, revealing a meditative expression. He looks to have somehow transformed into a serious reader. How did this character transformation occur?

I step outside. Kroner hollers back that the book in his hands, like some oracle, has spoken to him, revealing secrets of what his life too often feels like. The revelation of what it's like, he says, is mind blowing.

For emphasis, Kroner whacks his forehead with a hand while holding the book open with the other.

He shouts – Here, just to listen to this part – before reading aloud:

> *People say you can never be certain that you're not in a novel, and if, while you are in this uncertain place something strange happens, you should begin your own novel.*

Kroner nods and rises, standing atop the shifting mound of books to declare: My good friend, do you ever feel that way? That life's been written out for you, line by line, that it's someone else's script that steers you, that the steering takes you places you might never choose to go or do things you might never choose to do? But, no, what choice have you? It's already written out.

Kroner whacks his forehead again and waves his free hand. His footing on the book mound is unstable but his voice is steady: Listen to this, from the same author:

You begin to feel like you were the page of a book and novels were being written and erased on you all day...

Kroner presses the open book to his lips. Now he speaks in an undertone: Where is this thing called our life taking us? We zig and zag like characters being written, deleted and rewritten by a mad scientist. We have no idea what it means, how it adds up. Do we ever get a say in steering our own lives?...Well, now that I've started reading on my own, that's what I've been pondering. And my friend, it's taking me a long, long time because, have to admit, going back to grade school, I'm still a very slow reader. Haven't had much reading practice in the life written out for me.

Dispatch #89

When I beg Kroner to please come down from the book mound and talk face-to-face, man-to-man, he shrugs but obliges. He slides down from the summit as if riding a sled while still holding the book.

In his wake, streams of books tumble down. By the time Kroner lands and staggers back up to his feet, the book mound behind is partly flattened.

Kroner brushes himself off, whistles and steps forward: Whew, dusty sons of bitches. Man, these books sure need a helluva blow. Know anyone in these parts qualified for such a job?

Kroner opens his mouth for a big silent ha, ha before bending to slap his thighs. After the outburst he straightens, squints and gives me the once-over.

Holy moly, my dear old friend. What's happened – budget cutbacks? Have the authorities rationed your razor supply? Cut off your toiletries?

I dab at but can barely feel my chin, cheeks and throat. My whiskers are long. And bushy. Have I neglected my appearance, my hygiene? What will Paige have to say? How long since her last checkup here?

Kroner keeps on wisecracking. He says I'm starting to remind him of his honor – the old bookkeeper – the one who ditched me. Before I can decipher the quip, Kroner changes the subject for a personal update.

Yeah, yeah. Well, I'm sure you guessed. Lost my damn job. Got sacked for idleness, for taking too many coffee breaks. That's the official version. Truth told, I wasn't dumping the books and other junk I haul fast enough, couldn't make the higher-ton garbage quotas.

Without work, Kroner enrolled for jobless benefits. Then, with more time on his hands, he gave reading a go and slowly got into it. He had to waste valuable time sounding out syllables and then words before deciphering their meanings.

I ask where Kroner found his reading materials. He admits to spotting the airborne drones and trailing them to The Vault. Then he would sift through the piles before borrowing a book discarded from the sky.

I dug this one out from your pile last week, Kroner says, raising the book with the passages he had read aloud. You didn't cart those books in right away, mister. Anyway, you got a problem with my borrowing books? I return whatever I borrow to your precious Domestic Print Material Shelter.

Print Materials, I correct Kroner on the official name – plural.

I encourage him to take all the time he needs, to read the book, any book, from cover to cover before returning it. As far as I know, no policy on return dates was ever established. The focus was on checking out books, even one book, and that never happened.

Since last seen, Kroner has lost weight. His clothes are saggy, the collar loose around his neck. He attributes the weight loss to walking more, while eating and driving less. Without a job he cannot afford to buy as much food, especially junk food, or to repair and gas up his car.

Kroner has on a stained windbreaker, but I'm in short sleeves. Even with springlike weather, it's too chilly to stand around outside.

So I invite Kroner in to warm up with a kettle of tea, black or green, or a pot of freshly roasted coffee. He declines, claiming he must go look in on his frail mother who recently entered an assisted living facility.

Before walking off through the industrial park ruins, Kroner points to the flattened book mound and says, Friend, your work is laid out in front of you, plain as day. It's part of your script. Be grateful it still includes you having a job. Enjoy while it lasts.

I wave goodbye, even flash Kroner the victory sign. Walking away, he kicks at the skull-and-bones biohazard sign before whack-ing his head, calling back to me: If only I could figure out how to rewrite the script for my life instead of having it written out for me by someone else's hand...

Dispatch #90

Before long, but way too soon, snow is falling again. That's much too fast. Another seasonal anomaly?

I stop at the side-door window, my eyes fixated on the blur of blowing snow. Looking out from The Vault is like looking into a snow globe after a vigorous shaking.

And so, all blurry, seasons here are passing. They no longer pass as distinct seasons but as a mishmash.

Earlier today, a white glow of natural light – there was no sun – slanted down from The Vault's mezzanine windows. It got my at-tention. Since I had nothing to haul up, I took the spiral stairway instead of the freight elevator.

At mezzanine level, I scaled the rungs of the mobile stepladder, going all the way up until I could peer over the top row of books, quite a few collapsing and decrepit.

I peered out a window until verifying that, yes, it was in fact snow falling outside The Vault, and not inside where dust falls and accumulates.

I stood still on the ladder, feeling relieved. This must count for something, this verification of falling snow outside. Again, proof, perhaps, that I am still of sound and clear mind.

But was I?

Consider what occurred even earlier today, at dawn, when I woke to caterwauling. What were those predatory cats up to now? Their screeching clawed my sleepiness to shreds.

I splashed water over my face. As it dripped, I looked in the mirror. My watery reflection was...what? Well, like some alien character's face!

The looking glass reflected a bushy bearded, ashen man. The beard was not only long and wiry but gray, not all-gray but streaked with white. Same with the matted hair and cowlicks on my head.

No wonder Kroner wisecracked about the old bookkeeper and me. Not that long ago that was — wasn't it? Or was that back in early spring? Or was that way back, countless seasons ago?

Come to think of it, had Kroner ever returned that last book he was reading? The one he swore to return?

Hard to recall and so long since I last laid eyes on Kroner. I believe he was thinner and out of work. Technically, the book he borrowed was to be returned and shelved as part of The Vault's collection. But if the book wasn't returned, perhaps it was destined to belong to its singular reader — and perhaps Kroner qualified as that reader. If so, that pleases me.

Dispatch #91

I also recall how, soon after dawn, the caterwauling went on unabated. The noise distracted me from further pondering about Kroner and his overdue book.

As I listened closer, I felt the hair rise on the nape of my neck and along my arms. No, this time it wasn't screeching I heard, it was more like wailing.

Before I could turn from the sink, I glimpsed another reflection in the looking glass: A line of nine cats – I quickly counted – tails erect, one after the other. The cats shot around the corner of a distant shelving aisle.

I was about to turn from this reflection and look with my own eyes when I heard a chorus of squeaks. Except it wasn't squeaking this time but lower pitched, more like grunting and snorting.

Then I saw, also reflected in the looking glass, what must have been dozens of gray mice – by my quick count – running as a herd in pursuit. All shot around the same corner, pursuing those nine cats.

Then came more wailing, followed by more grunting and snorting. Over time and distance these noises waned. I pulled anxiously at my bushy beard, keeping my eyes looking straight into the mirror.

Did I really see what I just saw in the looking glass? What about those cat and mice noises. Mirrors don't reflect noise. So then, that much was real. What I heard and, by extension, what I saw. Did those two add up?

I reminded myself that I am The Vault's latest and only bookkeeper. Yes, no doubt, I am that. But, always the question, am I a bookkeeper of sound and clear mind?

If I am, then why did the looking glass show a herd of mice chasing nine cats? Did I really hear all that wailing, all that grunting and snorting?

Was I seeing with my own eyes? Or was this looking glass fooling me? Am I both a bookkeeper and a fool? Was this some new, grotesque delirium?

That night I shut off the few operating lights. Every single one. In the blackness I lie with eyes opened wide, on my back, on the cot, black hour after black hour. All I do is stare up into the void, listening, pondering: Reality, delirium? Which?

From unseen depths, still under attack, sound the wailing cats. Their wails echo distantly. Mouse grunts and snorts are softer, their echoes reaching my ears only if I focus on them. And I do.

If all the cats retreat after the mice offensive, how do I find reinforcements for a stand to save the books? Scattered mousetraps aren't enough. The newly liberated mice will annihilate The Vault's collection.

My sleepless night crawls on and on. I am too distracted to practice The Breathing Pages. Still wakeful, morning brings more snowfall outside but, blissfully, utter silence reigns inside The Vault.

Dispatch #92

And then, on some other day, call it another today, I find myself dripping sweat from the heat and humidity of the next season. Next? No telling what comes next, let alone what passed before.

Seasons no longer pass, they warp. Just now, maybe overnight, it must have warped to summer. I cannot recall what season came before, if there was even a spring.

I have The Vault's doors, everyone, front, side and back, opened wide. The stuck windows will not budge and stay shut.

Even with wide-open doors, it is stifling and stale inside, barely breathable. No fresh air circulates from outside. Nor do any patrons barge in.

I splash rust-colored water to rinse soapsuds from my face, beard, upper body, underarms. The looking glass reflects a snow-white beard dangling to a scrawny bare chest.

So I am, as always, the bookkeeper, like the one before me who may have resembled a fairy-tale wizard. My own appearance is evolving.

Sunbeams slant in to brighten the gloom and shadowy recesses. I raise my hands to shield the glare. Without sunglasses, my eyes squint and water from the beams of bright natural light.

The other day, while blowing and tidying up a row of books, I chanced upon a pair of shades. My predecessor's?

These were smudged and dusty. I wiped them, brushed away a cobweb and blew off dust, using the book-blowing method before putting them on.

Long used to The Vault's inner gloom, my eyes are keenly sensitive to light. Wearing sunglasses blunts that sensitivity, which may be a form of blindness.

All electric lights, even my flashlight, are inoperable. I do nothing about them. My light-sensitive eyes have evolved. In fact, away from any light, my vision penetrates far into the gloom.

I have not bothered asking Kitty to bring new light fixtures, bulbs and batteries. Kitty, yes, I believe that was the name. I have not seen Kitty in... well, don't recall when.

I seem to recall that Kitty's character was strong, helpful and handy. Or was Kitty just another kitty cat? Once there were so many kitties roaming here. Their job was to hunt mice. But the mice offensive drove out the poor kitties.

Anyway, true or false, that is what I am reporting. For now. Does this report typecast me as a foolish character? Delirious to boot? Does the typecasting undermine the soundness of these dispatches?

Fair questions, but for those making that claim, come show me where all the kitties have gone. Like the number of book readers in The Vault, show me one kitty cat...Right, I thought so.

Dispatch #93

I swear, somewhere around here, I have a partial box of candles. It's important for my sleep that I find where that somewhere is.

For the life of me, I cannot recall where I placed that candle box. I also have two books of matches — again, somewhere, not sure of the where.

Without lighted candles, even with my evolved vision, I cannot read well, not at night. And that stops me from doing The Breathing Pages to cure my nighttime insomnia.

These days, during daytime, I prolong book-blowing rounds by pausing in aisles between the shadowy, towering shelves. I pause there, even if I have finished blowing all rows of books on both sides of an aisle.

Even while pausing in the shadows, I keep the shades on, the ones that may have been my predecessor's. They shield my hyper-sensitive eyes from slanting sunbeams.

Sadly, I have again allowed my book blowing to diminish. I am lucky to blow one row of books per day. Rather, I just wander about The Vault. The slow wandering does not even add up to pacing.

Wandering or pacing, all my movements have turned aimless. The floor is slippery with dust. A number of warped planks protrude. I could count them. If I am not slipping then I'm tripping on them, stubbing my toes.

Pausing again, I ponder the fearful shock I got last time, whenever that time was, when a band of patrons barged inside.

Dispatch #94

When was it that those patrons last barged in here, with the sight of one of them taking my breath away in fear and panic?

What I recall, and will not forget, is that these patrons no longer held flickering devices. And they no longer roamed as a herd.

Such herds had long ago vanished. This time I counted the patrons but no longer recall the exact count. Call it a handful, six or seven at most.

Their hands were empty, arms dangling. The only flickering came from their eyes — it seemed their mobile devices were implanted there, in both eyes.

These patrons still growled and snapped at each dust-free book I held out. Only now, free from holding the devices, they swatted at me with their arms and hands — as if their appendages were flyswatters and I a fly.

Even with the implants their eyes, behind the artificial flickering glow, were vacant. The shock came when this band of patrons zigzagged over for a book hand off.

I shrank back, then groaned as if I were a patron myself. What I saw, unless it was delirium, was the long-lost old bookkeeper among them!

My former boss, my book-blowing tutor, had mutated into a patron.

I stared for as long as I dared, not long. Then I dropped my book pile and retreated as he zigged and zagged in my general direction. I could not bear the sight of him swatting and even snapping at me.

Still bearded and gaunt — my mirror image — the old bookkeeper gave no sign of recognition, either of me, his apprentice, nor the place he had nicknamed The Vault.

Wormlike, I slithered across the floor to hide behind the reception counter, in a cubbyhole beneath the typewriter relic.

Had I known, I might've tempted him with a sucker, orange or maybe mango, instead of merely a dust-free book. Would that have reconnected us?

Long ago I learned that the old bookkeeper was legally blind. Perhaps like me, his eyes had merely evolved – devolved? – during his time walking and working in The Vault's dim lighting.

What did he see now behind the eye-implanted, flickering device? Did he see anything of our old book shelter, see that it was me, that once we toiled on behalf of any and all singular readers?

Dispatch #95

After that, well, next thing I recall, is being unable to resist staring at the star-shaped bindi between the eyes of Paige. Her bindi fills the air and is all I can see.

In the various tints of light between towering shelves, the color of her bindi flickers – less blue, more silver; then more blue, less silver. On and off, that coloring.

Was there once a cat by that name here in The Vault? Yes, had to be, with alternating colors for names.

When did I last see that cat? For that matter, any cat? And what about mice? When was the last time I came upon their telltale pellets or even glimpsed a live mouse?

Unchecked by the cats, I feared the victorious mice would annihilate The Vault's book collection.

Yet they have not done so. Not at all. Perhaps all the mice did was chase all the cats right out and keep right on chasing them on the outside – both species never to reappear again inside The Vault.

Oh, that Paige, she's had a growth spurt. Standing before me, straight and tall, she and I see virtually eye to eye. Am I shrinking or has she just shot up? Both, I'm sure.

I tug the ends of my bushy beard and stare at her bindi star. Finally I ask Paige questions – personal ones. These pour out, the unmentionables.

What has come over me? Indeed, this feels like putting my affairs in order.

Paige listens patiently while snatching away cobwebs that stretch halfway across a row of books.

Do you have parents, Paige? Tell me, what do they do for work? What are they like? Are they avid readers like you? What about your home? What's it like there for your family? How is school going? Do you have any close friends? What are your favorite subjects. What are your plans moving forward – for your education and career?

Strands of webbing stick to Paige's fingers. She flicks at them. The strands are sticky, having snagged flies and unnamable vermin.

You know, most everyone has parents, more or less, at least one parent, and a home, Paige says. Why should I be any different? I'm an only child. Home is home, just like it is for other kids and my classmates. You get used to wherever you live and grow up in. At high school this semester, my last year, I've been swamped with homework. Practically all subjects, especially the advanced ones. That's why I haven't been here as much – which is a shame.

Before I can ask more questions, Paige changes the subject. Her tone of voice reverts to that growling tone. It reminds me of another cat species, maybe a cougar.

She throws up her hands, fingers out like claws, points one here, there, and accuses me of neglecting my duties. Another reprimand for dereliction. My chin drops. My neglect is impossible to conceal.

Paige brushes at more cobwebs until exposing an iridescent spider. As if guarding a dusty row of books, or one book, the spider swivels to face us, lifting and whipping out thread-like legs. I see shades of colors, including blue and silver.

Before Paige can flick the spider away, it retreats up and over the top of a thick hardcover book.

Tentatively, Paige extends a hand before pulling the book from its place on the shelf. Behind it there is no sign of the guardian spider.

Paige holds the book up in the air. She puckers her lips to blow the dust off before examining the title. She riffles pages, reads, nods every so often, then hands the book over to me – a hand off for that singular reader?

Without looking at it first, I can feel the book exerting a grip. On me? And I can see it's some kind of novel, very long title, with front and back covers caked with grime. It will take more than blowing to clean.

Though not shelved in the mezzanine, this book is old and worn. A filament of cobweb is coiled diagonally across the peeling front cover.

At last, Paige says, pointing to the book in my hands and clapping once. I'm so relieved to have finally found it. It's the book I've been searching for. I knew it had to be in here somewhere. Well, time for you to read what's inside the covers. The story will hit home, I'm certain it will. Believe me, reading it will bring you a lasting sense of closure.

Dispatch #96

So after Paige had gone, I blew and wiped until the book she gave me actually gleamed. Then I peeled back and separated the brittle pages to begin my required reading. I felt obligated to. I also felt the book's physical grip glide over my hands. Unless I was imagining it, the grip was getting stronger.

Just enough of the day's natural light filtered in for me to read almost all that was printed on the pages of the book. Luckily, I had earlier found the missing box of candles and matchbooks. I struck a match and lit one candle to help me read.

Adding to its palpable grip, the book's warped storyline seized my attention until, after a while, I lost track of time. I was unable to set the book down, even if I had wanted to, or even glance away from the pages.

Only when it got too dark to keep reading – the candle by my side had burned down – did my mind drift and I dozed. While still barely awake, I reminded myself that when I woke, I had to finish reading to the end.

The novel began reading like this:

Wham!

A solitary man, a reclusive writer, takes what might be described as a walloping – to the back of the head.

This happens too quick to hurt. The assailant, if there was one, is unknown. Maybe it was merely a fall, a backward fall. Either way, having been knocked out by the walloping, the man is unable to decipher what follows.

The knockout wallop sends him somersaulting – in his head – down through an opening like that of a trapdoor.

Whoosh!

It feels like a long way going down but he quickly somersaults the distance. Being knocked out, all that follows seems like a delirium.

On the way down he feels an updraft of stale, dusty air. Someone, some blurry shape, passes him going up as he goes down. Or is he the one going up at the same time as he's going down?

Never mind, too delirious to know what's what.

When he hits bottom, lands on his ass, the man bounces, once, then lands again on his ass but doesn't bounce as high the second time. His eyes shut tight. He grimaces. The bouncy landing gives him a pain in the ass.

Next the man has a coughing fit. He begins counting each cough. Shaking his head as if to loosen mental cobwebs, he spits out a gob of saliva mixed with dust. He rubs his eyes before they reopen on their own.

Even with eyes open wide, it's too dim and dusty to see anything clearly. But wait. He cups both ears: Hear that? Those sounds? How peculiar.

Knees raised, he bends forward on his painful ass, ears still cupped: Can the sounds be ID'd? First, a sort of clacking – from a keyboard, maybe a manual typewriter? Second, is that groaning? Chorus of deep groans? Human? Then, something else, something animal-like: Some kind of meowing maybe...and finally, another sound, small animal, high-pitched and faint: Squeak-squeak...squeak, squeak, squeak...

Dispatch #97

Deafening concussions jolt me out of a dream, one that had movers with packing crates. My eyelids flutter open. More startled than awake, I blurt: Where am I? What is this? What is with this noise, all this crashing?

Since I live and work in near solitude, there is rarely anyone in The Vault to answer me. As usual, no one answered this time.

At my side, a yellow candle has burned down flat. The burning candle came from a partial box – a box I had finally found from somewhere, along with, from somewhere else, matchbooks.

The melted candle had spread across a white plate on the footstool by my cot. The remains left a waxy yellow pancake.

The novel Paige assigned for me to read – the one I had not quite finished – leans against a leg of the footstool. The fingers and palm of my right hand are sticking to the book's spine. The din of engines and machines blast away the remnants of my dream.

Like some sort of apocalypse, each jolt to The Vault shakes me to the core. I roll over and scratch my head with my left hand. What in hell can all this mean?

OK, I recall something – imagine that – yes, it's coming back to me now, the storyline from the book guarded by a spider that Paige found on the shelf for me to read.

I had read most of the story, nearly to the last page, before dozing off as the candle burned out and darkness snuffed out further reading.

The plot revolved around this guy, some tormented writer, one unable to finish anything he tried to write. Because of torment over these failures, he was losing his mind, or possibly had lost it.

Piece after piece of writing the writer started, then stopped. He aborted writing drafts as short as a few words; others only sentences and paragraphs long. Some got to be as long as a several chapters. But every one, no matter how short or how long, remained unfinished.

The writer's resume was a paper trail of unfinished stories.

What kind of writer was he, unable to finish anything, not one thing, that he began writing? Finally, the writer faced the writing on the wall, and it spelled out, in big block letters, that he was no writer at all, just a hack. The realization devastated him. He curled up in a ball and fell into a psychosis.

During this time, from one of his unfinished stories, a main character revolted, hatching an escape plan – at least a way to end the endless captivity – for him and for his fellow captives. These were desperate characters.

Somehow the writer had to be lured into giving up or ending his life. That death, or surrender, would mercifully end everyone's torment, including even the writer's.

This main character, a detective, was shrewd. He probed the writer's consciousness – digging for clues, for vulnerabilities.

One vulnerability: The writer's habit of binge drinking after his failures until blacking out. During one drinking blackout, the detective character forcibly exchanged places with the writer. He did this by prying open a trapdoor he discovered leading to the writer's consciousness.

After the forcible exchange, the detective character found himself inside out – so to speak. He was somewhere out there, outside, no longer captive inside the writer's mind.

But having reached this frontier, the detective's own persona began decaying. Nothing was clear to him anymore, including his mission and identity.

Having taken control of the writer's consciousness, the detective character was unable to recall what brought him from the inside, what his mission to the outside was.

Outside, where he would walk to the point of pacing, the detective found little else but objects veiled in dust. The setting where he paced was walled in by towering aisles of books.

Meanwhile the writer himself was outside in — so to speak — a captive of his inner psychosis. There, in a haze, he found himself impounded with moldy, pent-up story characters from a stagnant plot he had long-ago created, aborted and forgotten.

The writer felt as lost and bewildered on the inside as the escaped detective character felt on the outside.

Dispatch #98

Well, what does all this information possibly have to do with me — that corkscrew plot of a story? How does it affect my blowing duties in The Vault? And how is it meant to hit home for me, to bring lasting closure?

Yes, I am feeling far too delirious to go on reading the story to its very end.

Paige — help, advise, reprimand. Are these all my clues? So, am I like the detective character? Or, am I a writer who aborts, never to finish?

Or am I still a bookkeeper? The latest in a lineage of bookkeepers? The last one? The second one? Here to preserve a dusty, decrepit storehouse of unread, unwanted books?

Am I on the outside, or am I stuck inside someone's head, maybe my own, my psychosis, captive to a stagnant, unfinished story?

Or is all this made up, mixed up, a never-ending spiral of deliriums? Perhaps all of the above?

I am reminded of what one notoriously tormented writer confessed in a diary about his ongoing curse of unfinished writing pursuits:

I can't write anymore. I've come up against the last boundary, before which I shall in all likelihood again sit down for years, and then in all likelihood begin another story all over again that will remain unfinished. This fate pursues me.

Dispatch #99

The mechanical concussions amplify till I cover my ears and press hard, then harder, but I cannot block out the amplified pounding and vibrations. I am being jolted out of mind and body. And still, hands pressed to my ears, I can feel the book's grip, at least its imprint, over my right hand.

Barefooted and draping the cot's blanket over my shoulders like a shawl, I get up and slink to the emergency side door for a peek.

What mayhem! Bulldozers, backhoes and skid loaders are slashing through and ramming the derelict buildings surrounding The Vault. In the midst of these maneuvers comes a crane with its wrecking ball.

The site is being flattened and cleared. Trucks rumble in to haul away the wreckage. Black cyclones of dirt, ash and smoke rise skyward.

So far the Vault is unscathed, but its walls, roof and floor vibrate with each direct hit against a nearby structure. During a lull I hear other sounds – voices! – coming inside from way in the back.

I drop the blanket from my shoulders and slip into whatever clothing is handy. I cannot find my clogs, so I run in my socks, without tripping or falling, toward the voices.

Far back in the utility room, the garage door has been rolled up to the rafters. The rear of a semi-trailer now fills the frame of the open bay.

Paige and...yes...that's Kitty, are hustling up and down a ramp that leads to the interior of the trailer. Both are huffing and panting while carrying up wood crates loaded with books – the movers and packers from my dream?

Kitty's attention is focused on the crate in her – his? – arms and not dropping it. Kitty's without a toolbelt and does not notice me. Same with Paige. Both go up and into the depths of the trailer with more crates to add to all the others.

Next, from inside the trailer, I see Kroner emerge, looking fit as ever. He is followed by The Bard and Muldoon. The latter is in civilian clothes. The former looks dapper wearing a tucked-in flannel shirt under a buttoned-up denim vest without fringes.

They're all hustling their butts off while going down and coming back up carrying crate loads of books. They remind me of a human conveyor belt.

At the sight and haste of their activities, I holler out the first thing that comes to mind: DOES THIS MEAN I'M OUT OF A JOB?

Dispatch #100

The Bard half turns and gives a thumbs up, but he's bopped on the head, from behind, by Muldoon and so he keeps on loading. Both do.

Muldoon's baldness shows now without a constable's cap. He nods to me but barks out orders. Perhaps he is overseeing The Bard under a work-release correctional program.

Paige finishes carrying up another crate into the trailer, comes back out, leaps over the side of the ramp and limps over. So, she saw me after all.

What a sight for sorry old eyes, and how she has grown! With seasonal warping time flew, and Paige has soared into adulthood, becoming a young woman. Her forehead and cheeks are smooth and clear. The bindi is gone, so are the pimples.

She hugs me, lightly, not a bear hug.

Oh, I'm afraid we've little time, she breathes, her hands rubbing my upper arms. We're saving what books we can save, transferring them to another shelter. Time to move on. We've done what was written for us to do here. So have you. Kudos for your tireless work – for hanging in there when things got tough, for blowing, for preserving.

Kitty, Kroner, The Bard and Muldoon are now wheeling up hand trucks piled with the last crates of books. These are stacked inside the trailer. Everyone's movements have accelerated. The trailer's interior is filling up.

Paige, about to return to the crates still to be wheeled up the ramp, looks me over – my stocking feet; my glum bearded face; my hunched posture. She hesitates and lowers her head before speaking.

Hey, this is what we were brought here to do, what you do – you, and your dispatching. We're at the end now, so finish what needs doing, she says, flashing me the victory sign. Someone, somewhere, someday, is going to read some of these books. You've played a part. Reading may seem a lost art, but really not all the patrons are as lifeless or hopeless as you fear. So go – be fearless.

Paige folds her victory sign into a fist and pumps the air. Next she blows me a kiss before turning to grab a hand truck and wheel its load up the ramp.

Well, perhaps after all I must come to accept this, whatever this is. And this must be the home stretch, the finish line. I've almost fulfilled my role. As a story character, what more is there to ask?

Dispatch #101

After the semi-trailer doors are swung shut and latched, I wave, then keep on waving. Why stop? I'm positive the will to do so is out of my hands.

My associates, one by one, climb up to the truck's front bench seat or go back into the extended cab. Doors on the left and right sides slam shut. I flinch at each of the slams.

They take turns, each of them — not mere associates, my dear friends — leaning out the cab and front windows to shout and laugh and wave goodbye. I wish I could follow them, join them, but apparently that's not my role.

Kroner settles behind the steering wheel. He seems thin yet healthier. He takes his time, delaying the inevitable by adjusting the seat and fiddling with the side mirror. Then he leans on the horn, honking away.

Two, three, four honks. With emotions welling up, I lose count after four. I blink back tears and resist counting as they drip to the floor.

The semi's trailer is packed, front to back, top to bottom, with crates of books. Still, I can only guess at the countless books left behind in The Vault.

The waving and honking goes on as the gears grind and the truck sputters out from under the overhead door to the outside. At that instant, from the direction of The Vault's entrance, comes the boom of a wrecking ball. The booming feels like an earthquake tremor.

I turn away and stumble back to my cot. So, this is it. No more waking to begin my daily rounds of book blowing. Instead, I rotate on my heels, looking all around. I try to preserve this panoramic picture in my head.

But there is no picture worth preserving. Shelving units have given way and fallen, even falling on top of other fallen units. Most shelves are laid bare. Like fallen comrades, books lie littered far and wide across the floor.

By the footstool, I stoop to pick up the novel bestowed from Paige. I reread the title: *From the Vault: The Bookkeeper's Dog-Eared Delirious Dispatches.*

My fingers caress the pages. Before long, on their own, those pages breathe. They really do. They swish back and forth, fitful but accelerating, then settling at an even tempo like natural breaths.

I catch the fragrance of ink and paper. These sensory impressions, like acupuncture needles, perforate my skin and go deep into my bones.

I trace the book's cracked spine and covers, even blowing away freshly accumulating dust.

Standing at the side of the cot, my stocking feet have stiffened. What is this? I cannot even wiggle my toes, not a one.

As if glued on, my fingers bond to the book covers. They cramp if I try letting go.

I give up trying and simply give in. My hands and arms have gone numb. There is no separating my hold on the book from its hold on me.

Next I hear, zeroing in, the ramming and pounding that collapse walls and chunks of the roof.

A black bird I have never seen inside The Vault – no, a bat? – is exposed by a wedge of sky while stretching web-like wings and flapping away from The Vault's demolition.

I feel that familiar wallop. To the back of my head. Shortly after, an updraft but also a down draft. Did someone just pass me by? Am I that someone? Writer? Main character? Bookkeeper? All three? Others perhaps?

Oh yes, I am delirious but hardly alone. All too well I know where I have landed.

And I land painfully hard – of course on my ass. I pick myself back up, stand.

Moldy characters, like the patrons, surround and mingle with me. They groan, shuffle, kicking up dust. I imitate the groaning, the shuffling, heck, I even get in my kicks. No fears. We all go way back.

Call it unfinished business.

Now my view narrows, getting narrower and narrower, down to a slit: Imagine peering out from within the dog-eared pages of a fallen book. See how the pages swish back and forth, as if breathing. See how we all breathe.

THE END

Postscript

*Footnotes, from the order in the story as they appeared in italics, from the quoted authors:

1. Peter Handke, **The Weight of the World**, Dispatch #1
2. Bud Smith, **Random Balloons**, Dispatch #11
3. Kurt Vonnegut, **If This Isn't Nice, What is?,** Dispatch #26
4. Joseph Musso Jr., **Apartment Building**, Dispatch #26
5. Dorthe Nors, **So Much for That Winter**, Dispatch #33
6. Jorge Luis Borges, **Dreamtigers**, Dispatch #34
7. Richard Brautigan, **The Abortion: An Historical Romance,** Dispatch #34
8. David Connor, **Oh God, the Sun Goes**, Dispatch 34
9. Sophie Divry, **The Library of Unrequited Love**, Dispatch #39
10. Fernando Pessoa, **The Book of Disquiet**, Dispatch #47
11. Alexis M. Smith, **Glaciers**, Dispatch #49
12. David Markson, **Wittgenstein's Mistress**, Dispatch #50
13. Samuel Beckett, **Malone Dies**, Dispatch #50

14. Thomas Bernhard, ***Extinction***, Dispatch #55
15. Gary Thorp, ***Sweeping Changes***, Dispatch #71
16. Edward Lueders, ***The Clam Lake Papers***, Dispatch 71
17. Yoel Hoffmann, ***Moods***, Dispatch #71
18. Paul Auster, ***The Red Notebook,*** Dispatch #71
19. Tim Horvath, ***Circulation***, Dispatch #71
20. Michal Ajvaz, ***The Other City***, Dispatch #71
21. Jung Young Moon, ***A Most Ambiguous Sunday***, #71
22. Jim Harrison & Ted Koosner, ***Braided Creek***, #Dispatch 73
23. Gerald Murnane, ***Barley Patch***, Dispatch #87
24. Renee Gladman, ***Houses of Ravicka***, Dispatch #88
25. Franz Kafka, ***The Diaries of Franz Kafka***, Dispatch #98

Book II

Machines of Loving Grace

What I do is just lie here in bed, our bed, not sleeping, not at first, just waiting for sleep to come over me, just lying on my back, waiting and waiting, just breathing, trying to be aware of each breath before, finally, with sleep not coming, getting up and hitching the dog to its leash.

The two of us, dog and I, we only walk late at night. When I don't sleep, which I never do, not at first I don't. That's every night I don't sleep at first, or at least nights I can recall.

My insomnia keeps me up on nights that I recall. I end up throwing off sheet and cover, swinging my legs out, getting up and going for a walk outside – but only after the woman beside me is asleep.

First I check the woman's breathing to see I've not wakened her before getting up out of bed to go out.

Before even getting up I wait to make sure she's asleep next to me. I bend close and listen to hear if her breathing's light and even, like the breathing sleep brings.

That's my routine for the lie-in-the-bed-still awake-not sleeping-time. Only if she's asleep, which I can tell by her breathing, do I get out of bed and leash the dog. The woman is always asleep when I check. Before I leave the house I check again to make sure. She is.

Once outside the house, which way do we walk? Simple. If the dog pulls left, we walk to the left. A pull right, a walk to the right. Either way, that's the way the dog and I start to walk.

There is another way, a third way, a way neither left nor right. If the dog pulls me over the curb, across the street, the way we cross is not left or right but between the two – so straight.

After crossing the street to the opposite sidewalk, taking the straight way, it's back again to the old left or right way. Unless the dog pulls to recross the street back to where we started. Then it's straight backward.

Enough with these ways to walk. Say the walking ways are simple but multiple.

I simply follow whatever way the dog pulls. That way there is no need for me to think about it. As simple as walking whatever way the wind blows, that is, if there were a wind blowing.

Before pulling this way or that, almost right away, we stop. The dog lifts a hind leg to mark territory – curbside tree, no-parking sign, fire hydrant.

As for the woman back in the house, I never know if she wakes in my absence. She has never said. I have never asked. I don't know why this is so, but this unknowable defines us somehow.

Much later, when I get back from walking the dog, I fall asleep as soon as my head falls on the pillow. Without waking, the woman throws an arm across my bare chest and we hug, snuggle, then sleep, every time, even me. I am finally able to sleep after walking at night.

After the walk and the unleashing, the dog jumps and curls up on the living room sofa by a pillow, licking himself, maybe sighing or snorting. He too must sleep, but I never know since I'm snuggling and sleeping with her in the bedroom.

On our walks I use a shoulder harness with the leash to pull the dog. I never use a collar, would never pull the dog by its neck.

Rarely does much of anything happen when we walk at night. Safety is not really a concern. I'm not concerned about our safety.

And yet, vaguely, not often, I have felt unsafe while walking at night with the dog. A better word for this feeling might be: unsettled.

During walks I've sensed things coming for us, but only vaguely and not that often. The sensing is more of an intuition, and I just live with it. I never know if these things, whatever they may be, are coming for just me, for the dog, or for us both.

If I sense a thing coming, no matter how vague, I pick up our pace. I walk the dog a little faster or just plain faster. I don't want to be caught off guard.

Walking even a little faster, I pull a little harder on the leash hitched to the shoulder harness. At least the harder pulling does no harm to the dog's neck.

For these night walks I stay on sidewalks with the dog. Not all neighborhoods have sidewalks, but closer to downtown they do. There is little traffic at night but I still prefer walking on sidewalks.

The few drivers at night tend to be more reckless and drive too fast. Sidewalks are raised, more level and provide safer lanes for walking.

Even so I've tripped where some sidewalks have cracked and buckled, and nearly fallen, but not often. I've also stubbed my toes and pulled too hard on the dog's leash while tripping on the cracks and buckles.

So sidewalks aren't safety-proof but, overall, they are safer for walks than walking in the streets.

The dog normally keeps me from walking too fast. As a pup I named the dog Chi (Chee). Out of nowhere, yes, the name just popped in my head.

I know traditional Chinese philosophy spells Chi as Qi, defined as a circulating life force that binds and propels the universe.

The dog Chi prefers sniffing to walking. I have to pull Chi away from sniffing objects on the ground, also anything upright that other dogs have marked, so we can return to actual walking.

Not often have I pulled too hard on Chi's leash. When I do, it's more like jerking than pulling him. Those hard pulls make me feel like a jerk, though at least there's no chance of harming Chi's neck since I use a shoulder harness.

When we first start walking late at night, pulling either left or right or even straight, a thought often pops up — *this is all in your head.*

Like the origin of the name Chi, I have no idea why this thought of mine keeps circulating. Or where it originates. Or what it means. I also don't know why the thought disturbs me. I shake my head hard as if it were possible to shake out the all-in-your-head thought.

My head shaking circulates through my body. Then my arm and hand, as if by reflex, give a pull that's more of a jerk on Chi's leash. The jerking yanks Chi in a circle, lifting his front paws off the ground.

I swear at myself for doing this and for any harm I may have caused Chi. I blame the disturbing thought in my head for what I may have done.

In the end all is forgiven. Or at least forgotten. By me at least. I can't speak for Chi. Anyway, we go on into the night with our walking.

With little happening on our walks, I often focus on my footsteps echoing on the sidewalks. Chi's paw pads don't echo.

By bringing my heels down softly, I can make myself walk softer so I can no longer hear my footsteps echo. But first I have to think about it, so the intent to walk softly is all in my head.

The only aspect of Chi's walking that echoes are his nails. But only if they are long enough.

Chi's nails don't echo as much as clack — like clacking made by tapping an old keyboard. But his nails only get that long if I've neglected to trim them.

So little happens on our walks. Except, you might say, for happy endings. After walking and coming home, my insomnia ends and my snuggling and falling asleep with the woman begins. For me that adds up to happiness.

At times, I am unsettled by my memory gaps. What memories do I even recall? Really, very few, except for ones from my insomniac night walks.

I do recall squatting to pick up Chi's turds with a plastic shopping bag. I grab and stuff an empty bag in my back pocket before each walk.

Avoiding hard surfaces, Chi poops on grass and weeds or on soil by shrubs and flowers. He hobbles forward while pooping, leaving behind a trail of turds like fairy-tale breadcrumbs.

I am not at all fond of picking up these crumbs. The warm turds reek in the plastic bag I carry as we go on walking. Over the course of our long walks, if no trash can is found, the stench can make me retch.

Not often, only rarely, do I squat and graze my bag right over the turds, pretending to pick them up – in case I am being watched.

It would mortify me to be caught and cited for violating some pet excreta removal law. I might be stereotyped as a lawbreaker. No, that's not for me.

For a while on our walks a discarded toilet bowl sat at a curb, presumably for garbage pickup. The toilet's flushing lever was missing. Raising the lid, I would drop a bag of Chi's turds in the empty bowl.

After a few weeks the garbage haulers took away the toilet – and the turds. That was a handy outlet for dog-turd disposal. I wished more people would throw out their toilets.

At the late hours Chi and I walk, it's rare to meet passersby. Drivers, yes, always a few at that hour but not that many.

I watch for them, these late-night drivers, and I wonder: Why out so late and not home snuggling and sleeping next to someone dear in bed?

Some of the drivers are maybe long-distance, overnight truckers. Others, perhaps, have no one back home to snuggle or sleep with. No doubt others stay out late drinking, fishing for a partner to catch and bring home and go to bed with.

As for me, a confirmed insomniac, staying out late walking is what I seem made to do. Not by choice, but by instinct.

Of most drivers all I see are their winking taillights, or blinding headlights, going by one way or the other way on the street. What I stay on guard for are when drivers reach intersections when Chi and I do. These bring close encounters.

Even when marked intersections are lit up, I stay on guard. I've had close encounters while crossing intersections – marked and lighted or not – with Chi, from one curb to the next.

Once as we stepped off a curb at an unlit but marked crosswalk, the tires of a large, dark SUV rolled up. The grill of the black vehicle nosed out and reached the middle of the crosswalk just as Chi and I did.

Startled, I pulled hard, jerking Chi's leash. I glared through the tinted windshield at what looked to be a female driver. She was looking left, preparing to turn right, not even seeing me or the dog straight in front of her.

As she looked away, her SUV kept nosing more and more into the crosswalk. That gave me just a second to step aside, jerk Chi back again to safety while pounding with a free hand on the SUV's hood.

The vibrating hood noise redirected the driver's attention. She braked, stared out the tinted windshield, saw me, or maybe didn't, smiled faintly, shook her head and shrugged – meaningless gestures.

I glared and hollered for her to start paying attention before she harmed someone. I jogged across to the opposite curb with Chi and resumed walking, not looking back.

And so we walked on, past nighttime-shuttered storefronts, shops, offices and cafes. Sometimes we approached bar patrons spilling out and milling around to smoke and gab. When I spot a knot of smoking, gabbing bar patrons, I normally pull Chi over and we cross to the opposite sidewalk.

Chi is apt to bark at people, at animals, too. Sometimes, hard to tell the difference, people act like animals. His barking gets people's attention. So I say, No bark, Chi, no bark! And rarely, not often, to get his attention, I jerk Chi's leash and repeat the no-bark command.

Normally people take no notice of Chi's barking. They do notice Chi – smaller dog but not a toy, muscular, short-haired, black-and-white colors with bulldog blood and a swelling mug that calls to mind Popeye the Sailor Man.

People normally smile, grin and coo, calling Chi cute or sweet, as we pass. Some even stop to bend and pet him, but with his jumping and barking the hands quickly withdraw. Me, the owner, as if unseen, they ignore.

Bar patrons are less predictable and more reckless. I recall one incident when I didn't take time to cross to the other side and avoid the rabble.

A male bar patron in a black trench coat leapt from the crowd and landed right before us, booted feet planted far apart. Chi stopped in his tracks, but I jerked his leash so we could detour. I wasn't quick enough and Chi had a barking fit.

That got the leaping patron's attention. Whipping back the tails of his trench coat while holding a longneck beer bottle in one hand and a cigarette butt in the other, he waved his arms overhead like a referee, woofing back at Chi and shouting – Easy there, Big Boy. Easy, Killer. I'll do anything you say, anything, but pwweeease, pretty please, don't hurt li'l ol' me.

Beer suds sloshed out of his bottle from the overhead waving, splashing his hair and trench coat. His cigarette butt went flying.

The outburst animated the other bar patrons. They closed in from all around, baring their teeth, woofing, growling, whistling, hooting, howling, clapping and chanting out the nickname and a plea: KILLER, KILLER, oh, please let us go, please KILLER, please KILLER...!

The Killer chants amplified to an outright chorus. Me, they mostly ignored, even as I murmured the dog's real name was Chi. Someone with beer breath got in my ear and hiccupped, Hey Bubba...hold on tight...don't let Killer boy go...or...you'll lose little poochie forever.

I turned a deaf ear to Beer Breath and jerked on the leash. Chi – living up to his Killer nickname – pivoted to bark, even standing on hind legs like a boxer and swatting with his paws and then snapping at the rowdy patrons.

I wasted no time jerking Chi's leash and shouldering through the rabble. We scooted ahead for several blocks until the jeering behind us faded.

All in all, these were still minor episodes. Part of our night-walking routine. The norm. What came next were major episodes, anything but normal.

While random, the abnormal episodes also seemed like connect-the-dot messages. The last one buried anything that remained of my so-called life – nightlife and otherwise.

This first such episode was during yet another night walk, a quiet one. We had paused on a corner next to a used-car lot. That time of night, the paved lot was bathed in a yellow glow cast from tall light poles – the shining glow a deterrent against car thieves and vandals.

As Chi and I were at this corner, the overhead lights reflecting off the metallic autos seemed to activate another kind of light – this one, inside of me. Somehow I could feel it spreading, this light. It felt warm and it kept me waiting longer than I would at just any street corner.

One block up the street, not far from a postal box, a lone pickup truck driver signaled to turn though there was no traffic. As the truck turned, its axle screeched, the noise receding as the driver straightened and drove off. The quiet of night resumed.

I then saw a bunny on the opposite street corner from the car lot next to a bank. It hopped up and over a mulch-layered berm with small shrubs. Chi saw it too and woofed but didn't strain on the leash. The bobbing white tail was the last either of us saw of that bunny.

But the bunny sighting put Chi on alert. He sniffed, turning his attention to a wire-mesh trash bin. Moments later he still wouldn't budge from sniffing this spot. His refusal redirected my own attention to the trash bin.

I looked inside. Just the usual jumble of debris, cans mostly, cardboard and paper scraps. What was unusual was this — a few of the scraps were charred, as if from fire.

What further drew my attention were the carbonized remains of a spiral-bound notebook. I reached as far down as possible and dug out the notebook. Except for the spiral-ringed spine, most of the sooty pages crumbled to ashes.

The ash-crumbly pages were filled with lines of a handwritten scrawl. One page was maybe three-quarters intact.

Chi was still sniffing and now licking the outer rim of the trash bin. I held the partial page up for the car-lot lights to shine on. Then I tried reading the scrawl.

The charred notebook's nameless narrator described being in a room of people at a lively party. Partygoers mingled and embraced, laughing and boozing it up. Then, like a bomb set off, the hostess burst in their midst. People stepped back fast as she took center stage. Someone whispered, *Take cover, Katrina's on a rampage. Get ready for the fallout.*

Katrina leaped onto a coffee table that wobbled under her weight. She pumped a fist out like a home-plate umpire calling strike three and demanded everyone listen up. Now! She yelled that the party woke her from a fitful sleep, one with a disturbing dream.

A quote from the notebook's charred page: *Katrina took aim by pointing at all of us, one by one, wagging a finger, scowling, yelling that her dream was a vision, that it revealed there was a single person at this party, in this very room, someone who didn't belong — for emphasis, she stamped her left foot and the wobbly coffee table almost collapsed — someone who had no business mingling with the other guests, and that, further, this person wasn't a real person and that, in fact, this unreal person didn't even exist.*

While the accusation and mood felt staged and farcical, the guests in that room acted petrified. The notebook narrator noted expressions of panic and fear, that no one dared even whisper, that a sense of dread coiled around the partygoers, causing them to huddle closer and press back into a far corner.

The only other words I could read on the next charred page were these...*I had the urge to step forward, raise my hand, get it over with, just confess. Didn't we all have this same...*

With the other notebook's pages crumbling and unreadable, I tossed them back in the wire-mesh trash bin. Ashes on the bottom fluttered up like confetti before floating back down and settling.

I don't know why but I ripped out and folded the two readable pages, stuffing them in the left front pocket of my pants. Was it a confessional diary fragment? Rough draft of an unfinished manuscript?

Unsettled, maybe unhinged, I hurried off with Chi at my side. I regretted jerking his snout from the trash bin's burnt odors. As if afflicted by nervous twitching, like a puppet, perhaps from what I'd read, I had to stop myself from jerking even more on poor Chi's leash.

My upper thigh began itching through the pocket fabric where the charred notebook pages were folded and stuffed. For relief, the return way home, I kept rubbing over the fabric on that part on my thigh. But no relief.

Nothing else happened for the rest of that walk. Except that I was unusually tired. Yet I hadn't walked that far, not as far as usual. With no stars, the night sky must have been cloudy. As if reflecting the cloud cover, my head felt woolly.

I fumbled with the key trying to unlock the front door. It took forever. Had I left the door unlocked and now, unwittingly, locked it?

How abnormal, to take so long fumbling with this familiar door. Chi, from below the key and lock, looked up and barked.

Hey, easy Big Boy, easy there, Killer, I murmured, smirking as the front door finally swung in and we were again safely back home.

Inside, in our bedroom, I saw the noise I'd made unlocking the front door had not wakened her. Her sleep sounded normal but she was spread across the mattress as if reaching for something. This wasn't her normal posture.

As I squeezed onto my half of the bed and nudged her sleeping form over, her arm swung out and whacked my nose.

I turned away and sneezed twice, covering my mouth to smother the noise. Then I kept nudging her until we were side by side, middle of the bed, soon face to face, back to snuggling and then joined in sleep.

The next time I had insomnia, had to be the next night, my head still felt packed with wool. At least my body didn't feel as tired.

So Chi and I walked briskly along. I didn't jerk or even pull his leash. The two of us glided in sync.

The summer night air was mild but still overcast. After a breeze blew away a cloudy patch, a full moon shone before obscured again by more clouds.

Instead of rubbing, I had to scratch my itchy, inflamed left thigh. The charred notebook pages remained folded in the same pocket. I had wanted to change pants but the pages in that pocket were so brittle and crumbly that I didn't want to pull them out and risk more damage.

As we walked I kept peering into the night, as if trying to make out ill-defined or concealed shapes.

Even with me peering everywhere but at nothing specific, Chi and I kept gliding along, putting the city blocks behind us one by one. It seemed we returned to the front concrete stoop of our house in record time.

Again, why oh why didn't my house key work? This time I figured I must've left the door unlocked – it opened without the key. I never recalled making this blunder before. Now, two times in a row – door left unlocked.

After I removed leash and harness, it was Chi's turn to act unsettled. He didn't jump on the sofa or seek his doggy cushion on the recliner. All he did was sniff out and explore the floors, walls, nooks and furniture – in the dark.

Fine, I muttered, whatever gets you through the night, Killer. Meanwhile I tripped over a stool and bumped against the door frame going into the bedroom. Luckily the noises didn't wake her. I was quiet slipping out of clothes and crawling in on my side of the bed.

She didn't fling the usual arm across my chest. I missed that arm, prelude to snuggling and sleeping.

When I reached my arm out to her instead, she grabbed it and jerked me close. Very close, closer than ever. This was beyond our normal snuggling.

Her face moved closer and her lips closed over mine. Her tongue came out and flicked against my teeth. My mouth parted. Her tongue wiggled in.

Her eyes stayed closed. I closed my eyes too.

The hand that grabbed my arm dropped to my inflamed thigh, brushing it like a feather duster, before grabbing my dick. It got instantly hard.

Before I could react, she rolled on top. Our bodies were soon flopping up and down. We shrieked in darkness, our voices echoing off the walls. Every so often, most unsettling, she shrieked names: Rob...Oh Robby! Oh...Oh...

Our sudden coupling was beyond snuggling, beyond our norm. For me it tapped a hidden lode. Afterward I fell into a dense, dreamless sleep. Our sleeping bed felt enclosed as a coffin.

The coffin lid of sleep lifted when a silvery beam of light sliced through a crack in the bedroom curtains. I looked at her, so close, still in my arms. Then I pulled away – more like jerked away. No, this was not her! This was some other her. A different her. What had I done? Where was I? Was this dreaming?

I panicked, squirming out of this one's sleepy grasp and over to the opposite side of the bed. I yanked the curtains shut to blot out the revealing slice of predawn light.

After pulling on underwear, socks, pants, belt, shirt and shoes, I found Chi. He was already at the front door, as he normally is when he has to go out and do his business. Only this time Chi was yipping and whining, clawing the door, leaving scratch marks.

And so we walked home. Slowly. I recalled the correct way. The walking felt more like trudging over sand dunes. The predawn sky was hazy and gray. Or maybe silver. A few drops fell by the time I unlocked the front door – indeed, this time it was locked.

Once inside, Chi right away jumped and curled in a ball on the living room sofa. No sniffing around. That seemed a good omen.

Ever so gently I closed and relocked the front door. I stripped for the second time, trying to make not a sound, and crawled into bed so the mattress wouldn't creak or sag.

Still asleep, she didn't throw an arm over me and snuggle but faced the other way, toward the doorway. I waited but all I saw was the silhouette of her back and hips. Not a bad view, but still, not like snuggling face to face.

She stayed that way, on the bed's far side, her backside to me. It seemed to take me forever to get sleepy. Maybe because it was already morning and hadn't I already slept? And done more than sleep?

It was upsetting to think she might be upset with me, for my absence, let alone for what I had done. I missed our snuggling. I felt like a dick, and I was, literally. I don't recall if I ever slept but I must have.

On the next walk, or the next walk I recall, I found myself looking behind me. My intuition button had lit up: We were being tailed.

My intuition proved wrong, or at least not entirely right. The menace came from the front, not the rear.

Before us a hulking, slobbering dog had burst through a porch screen window, leaving a gaping hole. The dog's body landed with a thud on the sidewalk before rising on all fours and charging at us – straight at Chi.

With rock-sized bulges on its back and shoulders, the dog resembled a grotesque, mythological beast. I guessed the bulges were tumors.

I was stunned by the sight but recovered enough to take aim and swing with my foot at the lunging beast. Too slow, I whiffed.

As a result, Chi and his attacker collided at my feet. Both went down on the pavement in a furry swirl – Chi yipping, his attacker growling and slobbering.

Wedged between, I did what I could, slapping and kicking, but the canines were a swirling, sliding mass of furry hair. I whiffed more often than I hit the other dog.

Fortunately Chi is fit and agile, partly from our nightly walks. Still yipping in pain, he at last squirmed free and darted off, outracing his clumsy attacker.

I too raced after Chi, block after block, as he grew smaller and smaller to me. I shouted and pleaded for him to return, assuring him that life would be safe again. No use. I finally lost sight of him, the other dog, too.

Head down, I slowly retraced my steps until returning to where the attack had begun. There I saw a stumpy figure in an oversized hooded sweatshirt standing behind the ragged hole left in the porch screen window.

Presumably, the attack-dog's owner. He spat out some name and hollered for the beast to get his ass back home, and before long the animal did, stomping in through the propped-open front door. The dog's name was a common one like Spot or Dot but to me it sounded like Snot or Rot.

From across the street I stared at where the owner still stood behind the torn porch screen. He gave no sign of seeing or acknowledging me.

So what was I to do now? I wanted to shake my fist and cuss the owner but couldn't work up the nerve. Instead, I took off and dashed up and down the deserted blocks of houses, calling out Chi, Chi, here boy, come on Chi, be a good boy, everything's all right, it's safe now, I'll protect you, let's go home.

Ever more desperate, I even called out Killer, Killer, come back, Killer. Considering what just happened, using the nickname seemed in poor taste. Really, the things we say, as if words were put in our mouths.

One time, from a distance, I glimpsed Chi zigzagging at the end of a cul-de-sac. Near the boundary with Sunset Park.

I glimpsed what looked to be another cottontail bunny hopping across the street, go through a side yard and into the park. Then, what looked like Chi's silhouette in pursuit.

Chi had transitioned to becoming a pursuer, maybe even a killer, to survive on his own. Another thought, that was, one that just came to me.

Anyhow, that was the last I ever saw of him, Chi that is. Much later, as I recall, after another major episode, I heard what sounded like his barking – several more times, in fact, I heard the same barking, but always far off.

So it was with hollow heart that I eventually gave up and trudged home, minus Chi, and unlocked the front door. Only it was never locked again to begin with, so there was no unlocking to do, only a door to open – the new norm.

I hung up the key, crossed into the living room and stood with my head bowed in the bedroom doorway. Because of Chi I was in tears. Then, right before my teary eyes, I saw two bodies flopping together on our creaking mattress.

There she was, on her back, getting fucked. There he was, someone, on top, fucking her. They were flopping as if on a trampoline, panting and making noises more beastly than those of the tumored beast that attacked Chi.

My need to cry more tears for Chi dried up. Now the need for tears came for another reason: Here she was, after all our nights of snuggling, fucking someone else.

But who? When I forced myself to bend nearer and see who, what I saw from the side was some fucker who might have resembled me, at least who did in the shadows of our room.

If not me, who could this fucker be? Nearing their climax, he yelled once, more than once, something, some word. Yes, he was yelling a color: *blue*!

I turned, left them and stepped to the front door. I clapped my ears to block their beastly noises. The two climaxed with fury. Ears clapped, I could still hear it all. They had seemed oblivious to my presence – and now my absence.

I sat slumped over outside on the front stairs until before the crack of dawn. By then several cars drove by in both directions. No one glanced my way. Normal folks, you might say, drivers and passengers setting off for work, school, a store, cafe, gym, going off on vacation.

Once or twice I heard distant barking. It might have been Chi but likely that was wishful thinking. It could have been any number of neighborhood dogs.

I climbed back up the stairs and went inside, pausing before the bedroom doorway.

What's this? Here she was now, sleeping, alone, on her side, facing the doorway where I stood. Her rumpled nightie was back on, the hem down to her knees. Figures, I thought. All proper and prim but drained from the fucking.

Had my look-alike fucker – my doppelganger – slunk out the back door like a thief in the night? No sign of him.

I stripped, dropping clothes and underwear to the floor, then stepped around the corner of the bed to my side and climbed in. I lay on my back, conflicted, waiting to see if she would make the normal move with her arm.

She did and she didn't. Yes, she reached for me, but no, not for my chest. Her hand reached lower, found what it wanted, jerked.

Snuggling, hell no; fucking, hell yes. Here we go. Apparently I just had to wait for my turn.

After it was over, we were beyond drained. I felt like I had – we had – done it twice. Somehow even I had. We fell asleep, as usual, snuggling in each other's arms.

Following the fucking episode – once, twice? – I recall that my nights of insomniac walking grew more forlorn and aimless. Surely more forlorn without Chi by my side to walk with.

And so I began to stray from walking on city sidewalks with curbs and gutters to walking on suburban roads with fewer sidewalks, curbs or gutters. Traffic there was geared for the wheel, not the foot.

Other nights I strayed still farther and walked on exurban roads, still paved but with no sidewalks and with only the occasional car, motorcycle or truck speeding by. Some roads were gravel.

Solo I went, walking on and on, heading farther and farther out, heading out beyond exurban to rural – into the boonies.

As I did I recalled how revolted I was by my sexual lapse – the one possibly occurring in another house, possibly with another woman. Or, and this made little sense, was that spin-off from the original house and sleeping woman, a figment of an overactive imagination?

Imaginary or not, I'd felt guilty for behaving like a dick, even cursing myself for being a dick.

My guilt was eased by the way the sleeping woman and I had gotten back to our snuggling routine after my insomniac walks.

But as I walked through the boonies, where artificial lighting was sparse, all roads unpaved and gravelly, houses and outbuildings far apart, where there were rolling meadows, groves of trees and dense underbrush, fence posts tipped and splintered, I thought, Well, maybe in fact that's what you were meant to be – a plain old dick – but no, not just a dick in the slimeball sense, but a dick in the slang sense, meaning, yes, a detective.

That idea of being a detective/dick hit me like a wallop to the back of my head. My footsteps stopped, my shoulders slumped forward and I nearly fell – in a somersault – all the while laughing so hard at the detective label that I sneezed equally hard.

That's when, after the sneeze and before my eyes, I saw stars zigging and zagging. They weren't real stars, but stars of my making, from sneezing.

The solitude so far out in the boonies was calming, even liberating. But I still couldn't fathom what or who I really was, nor what my future plans were. Therefore the idea of detecting for clues, seeing where they led and might mean, was appealing. Working as a dick. Why not? My new calling. Who hired me? Well, ha-ha, me.

It was easy to get lost walking in the boonies. Finally I did just that. Lost my bearings, found myself lost. At a four-way junction I stopped and began, on a whim, turning round and round, looking in all directions. I held my arms straight out and spun like a spinning whccl.

Soon the spinning had me dizzy enough to fall but I chanced to glance up at the black sky splashed with stars – real ones this time. I stared at those sparkling atoms all lit against the blackness till my spinning slowed and slowly my dizziness did too.

When my spinning came to a stop, I looked down from the sky, looking straight ahead, at road level: And, what was this? A dark van, no side windows, had pulled up, engine idling. The junction where it stopped had no stop signs.

The van had stopped diagonally opposite from where I stood. I was still swaying slightly from all the spinning.

The van's sliding door swung open. Gentlemen in dark smocks, funny hats, white painter pants and shirts with bowties lowered their heads, hands folded to their chests like paws. They hopped out the doorway to the road, hopping down like big bunnies.

Was this a mirage brought on by dizziness? Like a real dick, I had to verify what I saw. I rubbed my eyes, also my forehead, then planted my feet squarely on the gravel till I felt as rooted as a pylon.

From my position and it being night, it was hard to identify these gentlemen, especially with their hats and uniforms. Why did I call them gentlemen? Perhaps because of how they were dressed? Anyway, I counted and they numbered six.

One of the six leaned through the open passenger-door window, conferring with a driver on the other side who I couldn't make out in darkness through the windshield.

Then the one leaning on the passenger side door stepped back to the road, saluting and bowing. His movements were mechanical. The unseen driver made a U-turn, tires crunching over gravel as the van itself melted away in the gloom of the boonies.

In no time the van passenger who'd conferred with the van driver spotted me. We had a stare down, like Western gunslingers, across the deserted four-way junction. Finally he raised a hand and waved for me to come across.

When I crossed over and came up he bowed, saluted, doffed his hat and said: You appear to be lost, sir. Most unfortunate but perhaps not for us. Might you care to join me and my associates for a work shift? I am certain our labors will be optimized from the efforts you can bring as an apprentice.

His hat of woven straw was from another era and quaint, at least for me it was. I believe the hat was called a boater. It resembled a sunhat. It made the rest of the uniform seem less, well, less uniform, more playful and comical.

Anyway, the work offer was unexpected. Since I had no better way to kill time before returning home – except to do more aimless, forlorn walking – I said, OK, why not? I'll give it a shot. But then I added, embarrassed: That is, if the work's not too hard for me to be taught.

The gentleman chuckled, straightened his boater, lifted my hand, shook it, then said, No, no, no. The work is not so very hard, sir, but it does take practice-practice-practice to approach a level nearing perfection. If you are willing to practice with us, diligently, that is all we will ask of you.

Right off I was amused by how our gentlemanly group marched off like toy soldiers. We were marching single file over a sandy, curving path toward some kind of manor building that I had not detected. The estate was set back a ways but within view of the four-way junction.

Since I now considered myself a dick – in the detective sense – I paused to examine the exterior. While the manor's outline struck me as Victorian, even Gothic with the towers, I noted how the jutting roof ends curled up like a pagoda's.

Painted letters on a shingle hanging from two chains above the veranda read: *The Institute for the Greater Fasting Mind.* A lullaby breeze rocked the sign back and forth.

As we were poised to reach for the handrail and mount the three stairs to the veranda, the lead gentleman, my contact, saw me reading the sign over. He elbowed me lightly in the ribs, which tickled a bit but I didn't laugh.

Good sir do not take the grandiose name too seriously, he said. Indeed, we do serious and even intensive work here, but The Institute's nickname is more charming and witty. When we whisper it amongst ourselves, not too often, say at the end of a work shift, we refer to it as *The Forgetful Inn.*

My contact hunched over to cover his mouth, as if clearing his throat or muffling a chuckle. Whatever the mannerism was for, it left me smiling and more relaxed.

Next the six uniformed crew members from the van stopped before the institute/inn's massive, square, front door. My contact carried a duffel bag. From it he got out a dark smock, white shirt, bowtie and pair of painter pants.

I always bring spare articles of clothing for contingencies, he said, handing me the uniform garments.

I do not, however, bring an extra hat and cannot say why, perhaps because the hat is window dressing, so to speak. Anyway, we doff our hats before entering The Institute. We place them right here to store and to air out.

He dropped his hat in a wicker basket by the square door. The other five fellows, short-haired and clean-shaven as he, followed his lead.

Upon closer detecting, I saw my smock was charcoal-colored and the painter pants had tan-colored knee patches. After buttoning the top button of my dress shirt, the clip-on bowtie snapped on easily.

I hesitated about unbuckling, unzipping and dropping my own pants – as I did before going to bed and snuggling with her. I didn't like stripping in front of others, especially strangers like these, my odd, new coworkers.

I also didn't like exposing the itchy rash on my upper left thigh. The rash that began itching the night I stuffed the charred notebook pages in my pants pocket.

I made myself strip while my contact offered me a shoulder to lean on as I wiggled into the legs of the painter pants. He noticed my rash and reached as if to touch it, but then withdrew his hand and mumbled tsk, tsk, tsk.

My working getup was completed once I slipped on the smock over the dress shirt. My contact tugged at my bowtie ends so they were even. After that he patted my cheeks and nodded with a faint smile.

Upon even closer detecting, I noted the group's uniformity. Not just their uniforms, but their features and grooming. All so alike. Eerie. I tried not to be obvious as I stole looks at them. One at a time. Somehow it left me with the sense of looking at myself in a mirror.

Then I noted shiny name tags pinned to the breast pockets of their smocks: Robby 1; Robby 2; Robby 3; Robby 4; Robby 5; and Robby 6.

The one doing the talking and bowtie tweaking wore a Robby 1 name tag. He smiled broadened and he brushed his hands, saying, For the moment you are the apprentice, our intern. All that is self-evident. No need for tagging you.

Robby 1 then rapped thrice using the brass door knocker but saw my puzzlement, so added: Sorry for our robotic tendencies. The name-tag numerals set us apart. They also lend each of us a hint of character.

The massive front door rumbled inward like a boulder sliding from a cave entrance. Six set of eyes, plus mine, seven, slid along with it. A young woman stood revealed in the doorway, facing and blocking us.

Running a wee late tonight are we, gents, she said, frowning while holding the door open just enough so we could file inside one by one. Lifting our heels, we marched in. As a clever dick and practicing intern, I fell in lockstep, the last one, filing in like the others had.

Once inside, the young woman pushed a shoulder against the massive door, rumbling it shut with a boom. Robby 1 tried justifying the late arrival:

Madam Silver, we were detained by this poor soul. No, strike that. Permit me to rephrase and clarify: To be fair, it was I detaining this poor soul. Then, after doing so and analyzing the data, I took the liberty of asking him to join our ranks. He exhibited an abstract potential that merited an internship offer.

Really? Care to clarify what potential he exhibited, asked the young woman called Silver without looking back, leading us down a corridor lined on both walls with books. I watched Silver's rotating hips, for some reason expecting her to limp. She never limped.

Allow me to process your request, said Robby 1, as if calculating sums. Then he resumed: I observed that the man was out on his own, here in this unpopulated region. He appeared lost, perhaps untethered, perhaps on a quest, and, visualize this, he had been spinning, like a top, and then stargazing – as if seeking signs from the cosmos. I audited these traits and found them to be beginner qualifications for employment at The Institute. Am I wrong?

Silver stopped and spun, stopping to face us. The group of Robbys, myself included, also stopped in unison, behind and now before her, one long file of us. I brought up the caboose.

We had reached the arched doorway of a spacious, vaulted-ceiling room. Inside the room, towering over all our heads, I could see walls of built-in shelves filled, every inch of shelf space, with still more books.

With a tilt of her head, Silver gestured for the Robbys to pass under the arch. Robby 1 hesitated before going first, followed in numerical order by Robbys 2, 3, 4, 5 and 6.

Except for the speaking done by Robby 1, the other Robbys had been mute this entire time. They seemed interchangeable. Their shoes clopped horselike and echoed on the hardwood floor.

Then, like a railway semaphore, Silver's arm thrust out, blocking me, the caboose, from following the file of Robbys. Wait here mister, she said. For you, first, some job training is in order.

Silver looked me over. I looked her over back.

Her getup was youthfully casual – loose, coal-black sweatshirt with wavy fabric patterns and a mini-skirt length; navy-blue yoga pants; black athletic shoes with fluorescent red shoelaces. The sneakers caught my eye – the bright laces half untied, holes in the shoes from wear or fashion.

Unclear if hers was another variety of uniform – a boss's – distinct from the uniforms worn by the worker Robbys.

There was no missing Silver's colorfully beaded headband. It looked Native American but without feathers.

On the lower left side of her neck was some sort of birthmark. The pattern, like a loop of tiny ocher stars, trickled down to the top of her sweatshirt before dipping under the collar.

Silver opened a door in the corridor. I assumed it was to a storage closet. Instead it was to a cramped office.

Inside on a wheeled cart and a large desk were more books, rows and piles of them – laid out horizontally on the cart shelves and stacked vertically on the desktop. All seemed to have a crust of fuzz or lint.

Without my asking, Silver enlightened me about the crust, exclaiming: DUST! She seemed so horrified I stepped back.

She splashed the palm of her hand on a row of book spines on the cart's top shelf. A dust cloud mushroomed in the air before sprinkling to the floor.

Silver pushed aside stacks of books on the desk to make room to sit. A blue jean vest with a fringe of tassels hung over the chair behind the desk.

Above the desk chair on a beige wall, side by side, hung two framed and matted photographs of young women.

Both portraits looked very much alike. Both, in fact, looked like Silver, but the one was very hard to look at.

I leaned closer, squinted, twisting and tilting my head, back and forth, up and down – the first, the second. It confounded me to look at both because one woman's portrait hung upside down.

To regain my attention, Silver snapped her fingers. I recoiled, then looked straight back at her and not at the portraits.

If you're curious, as you appear to be, then yes, that's my twin sister, Blue, in one of the pictures, Silver said. Blue's portrait is the one hanging right-side up. She's wearing a white sweatshirt. Mine, black sweatshirt, is the one hanging upside down – like a bat, if you will, which signifies that I work here at night, when it's dark out, which is when bats emerge from caves and trees using echoes to pursue sources of food.

In Silver's portrait, the starry birthmark on her left was now on the right side of her neck and shoulders – because her portrait was hanging upside down. Whereas with the other portrait, Blue's birthmark – she had one too – was on the opposite side from Silver's, the right, and with the right-side-up portrait, Blue's birthmark stayed on its proper side, also the right.

Silver paused for these impressions to sink in, then continued: We twin sisters oversee The Institute – as keepers of all the books, and as therapists for our clients. I oversee the night shift; Blue oversees the day shift. Blue is sleeping right now. And, I might add: She's an incredibly sound sleeper.

Our staff, consisting of the Robbys, often privately refer to us sisters as bookkeepers. Blue and I have overheard these hushed references. It's uttered without malice, and it's literally true. We act as bookkeepers here, though we have our other duties.

The Robbys, meanwhile, toil as client attendants and as book blowers. For the latter, their labor is valuable but repetitive, for which they're ideally suited.

As the intern, that's what I'll expect from you – to blow and blow, and to keep blowing books, like a bona fide Robby. But first, I'll demonstrate how to do this before assigning you duty as the intern book blower.

I listened to Silver's tone after taking a seat on a round metal stool. She had a certain presence. As she went on speaking, the office around us seemed to close in, get as small and confining as a closet, yet I wasn't alarmed.

No knowing exactly what was expected of me, I didn't move from where I sat on the stool. Or ask questions. Silver was in charge. She turned and withdrew a cloth-cover book from the very middle of a tall stack behind her.

Her timing was as flawless. The lower half of the stack of books remained stable and upright. The upper half dropped to fill the void of the withdrawn book.

I wanted to ask Silver to repeat that, that trick, but she, all business, had moved on. No distractions for this young woman. A spiderweb thread clung to the bottom of the book she held. Silver ran slender fingers over the cover, then held up a finger with the thread coiled on the end.

Not too much dust on the covers, she nodded. Most of the dust is caked on from being tucked between other books. This one may also need wiping with a moist cloth. Even so, look at the spine.

I did look. In the ceiling light, the book spine glinted with specks of dust.

It's dusty but it was even dustier before I pulled it out, Silver said. The spine was exposed for a long while to air and, from the disuse, gathered a layer of dust. Part of the layer peeled off when I pulled the book from its stack.

The minutiae of book-blow training hardly interested me. Silver then explained how one of The Institute's two main services was the stockpiling and preserving of discarded books:

All kinds of books, in all conditions, often battered and falling apart from neglect. The stockpile fills every available wall niche and shelf in the rooms and corridors of The Institute's vast interior.

This detail was a tad more interesting, but then Silver got my attention by bending, in a crouch — as if to wrestle a foe. I hoped that wasn't me.

I saw the book, still in her hands, extended straight out from her face. She murmured like a prayer: This is it...the beginning act...of blowing...

I stared at how the wave-patterned black sweatshirt, a bit tight over Silver's chest, stretched tighter as she inhaled for a deep breath.

Silver held this pose before puffing her cheeks and pursing her lips. Only then did she slowly exhale and blow. Her blowing was a long gust of air...going on and on...

The air from her pursed lips sent dust tumbling across the cracks of the spine and coalescing into dust bunnies before going over the edge and free-falling to our feet.

Watching such a spectacle, I held my own breath. I could no longer restrain myself. Dazzled by Silver's artistry, I clapped and shouted Bravo! Her book blowing was potent – the biggest breath of life I had ever seen.

Silver replaced the dust-free book at the top of the stack. Hands and lungs emptied; she caught her breath.

This is not about showing off, she said, placing a hand to her heart. These books, while neglected, still exude intellectual and imaginative content that beckon to discerning readers. Always handle them with the dignity and empathy they deserve. Remember that, please, as you blow and wipe.

It pleased me that Silver used that word – *please* – in my training. Her plea was just the incentive I needed to satisfy her wishes by blowing the way she taught, to the letter.

My reverie ended when Silver reached out with another dusty book. The one in her hands now was for me to try blowing on – my first blow.

But I never got the chance. Not this time. Before I could begin blowing, a Robby appeared behind me in the office doorway and spoke.

At the sound of this voice, a Robby voice, I turned and looked at the name tag. This time the Robby speaking was not Robby 1 but Robby 2. I had entered The Institute earlier in the night escorted by six Robbys. Now I'd heard two of them capable of speech, Robby 1 and Robby 2.

We have a problem, ma'am – possibly escalating to crisis stage – with one of the clients. The client in question is on the verge of losing control and spiraling into breakdown mode.

Robby 2 spoke to Silver in a voice sounding about as different from Robby 1's as Silver's appearance did next to the portrait of her twin sister, Blue. In other words, minus the sweatshirts, hardly different.

Despite the brewing crisis, Robby 2's voice, like Robby 1's, was deadpan. Silver stepped around me and followed Robby 2. I stepped after Silver and followed them both, though no one said I could follow.

Following them through a web of narrow, crisscrossing corridors was like navigating a maze. I lost track of where we had been and where we were going. So many doors did we pass. They all looked alike. All were shut. Almost all had Do Not Disturb signs dangling from porcelain knobs.

Somewhere in that maze we stopped so abruptly I nearly collided from behind with Silver. Robby 2 stepped aside, Silver stepped forward, held up a ring of large iron keys and leaned against the door frame. Listening.

Robby 2 and I, right behind her, did the same, leaning in and listening. I know I listened. What we were listening for, I didn't know, not at first.

From the other side of the door came muffled grunts and groans. Soon the grunting and groaning amplified. It sounded like someone constipated on a toilet. Were we outside a lavatory and someone inside was sick?

After more of these sounds, Silver inserted one of the antique keys and flung the door open.

The room we entered had the feel of a prison cell. I was to learn that this and the other rooms were designated as dens – not cells or lavatories.

Inside this den sat a rail-thin, red-faced, mid-aged woman wearing only a discolored white slip, one strap hanging off the left shoulder. Her forehead and neck were sweaty; her short hair stuck up in unwashed tufts.

My eyes were on the woman's arms – gouged with cuts and nicks and what might have been teeth marks. Her fingernails were bitten to the nubs.

The anxious woman was hunched over a circular table, her bottom at the edge of the one chair.

Hardly glancing up as we came in, the woman groaned and grunted loud enough for echoes. Ballpoint pens, pencils, markers and a pair of reading glasses lay at her right elbow. Two fists propped up her chin. Tears dribbled from both cheeks to the table and formed twin puddles.

Before Silver hand signaled for Robby 2 to guide me back to the little office, I saw flames flickering from inside a potbellied stove in a corner of the den. Reams of writing pages like those of a manuscript writhed and turned carbon black in the smoky fire.

Absent Robby 2's guidance, I never could have navigated my way back. The corridors were too narrow for us to walk side by side. We advanced, if that's the word, single file. Robby 2 walked first, evenly but stiffly, without a word, veering this way and that down intersecting corridors.

Behind him I glanced right and left at doors, doorknobs and Do Not Disturb signs. I heard constipated grunts and groans coming from various dens. None rose to the decibel level of the client in the den we'd just left.

In fact the grunts and groans were so muted that, curious, I wanted to stop outside one of the doors and listen closer. But Robby 2 wasn't stopping so neither could I, not without falling behind and getting lost.

At last, back at the office, I finally got back to blow training. I did so under the guidance of Robby 2 and under gazes coming from the wall portraits of the bookkeeping twin sisters – with Silver's portrait hanging there, bat-like, upside down. From that angle, hers was a discombobulating gaze.

One by one, I blew dust from rows and stacks of books, both hard and soft covers, even wiping several grimy books with a microfiber cloth.

My blowing seemed amateurish compared to Silver's and Robby 2's. I lacked their endurance. I could not, like they, exhale for long and thus blow away each and every speck of dust.

After my first blow, dusty blemishes still clung to the spines, covers and pages. So I blew repeatedly and raggedly. I don't have asthma but the blowing left me winded, breathless, feeling out of shape.

Yet Robby 2 did not find fault with me, not once. Nor did he ever once praise me, which I didn't deserve but probably needed. What Robby 2 did was watch my blowing. Every blow, with each book, not missing a one.

His watch over me became a distraction. It made me self-conscious. I couldn't help but watch him watching me as I blew.

When I took a breather after more than three dozen or so book blows, I asked about the anorexic woman in that den: What had we witnessed there? Were those her manuscript pages turning black and going up in flames?

Robby 2 was about to reply when he got distracted by the sight of Robby 1 standing in the office doorway. Watching us. I squinted to read the 1 on his name tag. How long had we been under Robby 1's watchful eye?

There the three of us stood, watching each other, three sets of eyes, a triangulation of watchers.

Finally Robby 2 saluted Robby 1, or maybe he saluted me, or maybe both of us, and departed. Not a word was spoken between 1 and 2.

What you witnessed in that den is part of The Institute's other, equally vital, mission, explained Robby 1 after the departing Robby 2 was out of sight.

Robby 1 went around to the other side of the desk but did not sit in the chair with the tasseled vest. He straightened his bowtie that already seemed straight and went on explaining:

Writers, established and aspiring, apply and gain admittance to The Institute – to the Forgetful Inn – for consultation, therapy and the healing aura of our stockpiled books. These writer types are typically diagnosed with Block Syndrome. Thus, they become our patients.

However, Robby 1 added, clearing his throat, we refer to them as our clients. We strive for them to forget, to expunge their pasts, to wipe clean their mental slates and to have a fresh start, a renewal, so they feel inspired to write again or even to write fluently for the first time. Of course, nothing in the treatment assures a positive outcome. Our clinical recovery process is ongoing since the syndrome is rarely erased but rather goes into remission.

I waited for more details but Robby 1 went silent, as if his vocal batteries had run low.

Robby 1 must have registered my questioning look. Before we resumed book blowing he came around the desk, faced me, got all wide-eyed, maybe even teary-eyed, and spoke in a hoarse voice:

My fellow worker, as intern, the one thing to remember is this – stay away from trapdoors. For your own well-being, so let me repeat: Never remove or even reposition the throw rugs concealing them, the trapdoors, and especially never be tempted to unlatch and lift up the trapdoors themselves.

After the cryptic warning, Robby 1 clapped me on both shoulders, shook a finger before tapping my chest with it and stepping over to the doorway. He nodded, saluted and declared that Silver would soon return, that I should try to blow all the books in the office so they would be spotless and ready for carting off and shelving.

As Robby 1 was leaving, I felt obligated to raise my hand and salute him back. I can't be sure if he saw me but he may have winked, so I think he did.

When Silver returned – gone longer than soon – I was sweeping the office floor. A straw broom and dustpan had been leaning against a filing cabinet. From all my book blowing and wiping, the office floor had wads of dust bunnies to sweep.

I emptied those bunnies from the dustpan into the wastebasket. Inside the basket was a woebegone hardcover book with a binding detached from its spine and most pages coming loose.

The discarded book was beyond salvation. I buried it under the heaps of dust swept from the office floor. A lump formed in my throat at the sight of that dust-buried, damaged book. Did the empathy come from my brief time here?

Silver seemed pleased by my book-blowing output and office tidying up. She inspected the newly cleaned book rows on the cart with a clinical eye. At that moment my heart went out to her. I can't explain this emotion or why the image of her sleeping twin sister popped in my head.

Yes, I do believe you're learning the trade, Silver said. You must have taken your time and not rushed. That's the way blowing books must be done. That's how we achieve job satisfaction.

I listened but also wanted Silver to know that I was better informed. I changed the subject by asking, And how was it resolved with that client, the one having a breakdown? She seemed to be going out of her mind.

Silver looked down then back up at me. She raised and lowered her eyebrows. The gesture rippled the rows of colored beads on her headband.

I'm afraid that particular client did lose her composure – you saw as much – so she needed remedial therapy, Silver said. That's why I stayed behind. It disappointed me how quickly she gave up, lost her wits and tossed her writing in the fire. Fire tossing is only constructive when a client is ready to start afresh by writing something new so the old can be burned into oblivion.

Silver said that each client's den had either a fireplace or a pot-bellied stove. Both were fueled by wood for heating; both could also be used to burn pages of failed writing samples. The later then doubled as a secondary heat source.

Sometimes, but not often, Silver said, clients lose their composure after gazing at their blank white pages, getting stuck and writing nothing. When this stage is reached, when they snap, they often tear up their blank pages and stuff them into the fireplace or stove to burn. Less often but more destructive are when they stuff handfuls of books from the shelves to ignite something bigger, like a bonfire. Such fires, rare as they are, threaten not only one's den but everyone and everything else, including the books, at The Institute.

Some avoid the bonfire stage and resort to scribbling letters from the alphabet, random words or incoherent phrases on their face, palms, hands, fingers, arms, even their legs, feet and toes until supplied with fresh writing paper. Others, feeling still more hideous, resort to mutilation – slicing themselves with a pocketknife or nail clippers – even scratching and biting their flesh. Such fleshy wounds are illegible.

When I said that the client we saw sounded constipated, Silver said, Yes, this happens. Thwarted clients desperate for inspiration can sound as if they're trying to go on the toilet.

Silver said dens are discreetly furnished with a commode. Often clients constipated about writing are also constipated about bowel movements. They sound off in agony that a movement of the latter will never come.

In the end, it all comes down to inspiration, Silver said. That's what the wall shelves of dust-free books are for. Clients contemplate them, those rows, up and down, one side after the next, contemplating the spines, titles, covers, names of authors; take a book off a shelf, get physical with it, rub its contours, feel its heft, riffle its pages of type and allow the book's swishing pages to emit a woodlike fragrance.

As she continued, Silver's voice and hands grew animated.

At The Institute for the Greater Fasting Mind, we believe our stockpile of books contains, literally, breathing pages, and that done mindfully, for clients who forget themselves by emptying their minds, who meditate and inhale the fragrance of breathing pages, a connection between mind and hand is made, followed by a creative big bang, one that jump-starts the writing current.

Silver folded her hands and lowered her voice: For other clients, for most, it's nourishing enough simply to be here and absorb the vibes of a den lined with nothing but books covering every iota of wall space – they become like infants suckling at their mother's breasts.

I hesitated, trying to take in the entirety of Silver's words. When there was a lull, I spoke: You know, what you're describing comes off sounding like some sort of mystical experience, an occult of sorts.

As if on the defensive, Silver ushered me out of the office say-ing, Well, we are not sorcerers here, if that's what you're insinuating. Now, back to the mundane, are you ready to continue with the book-blowing internship?

I wanted to ask Silver about Robby 1's taboo for throw rugs and trapdoors, but, too late. Time for more of my training. Walls of book contemplation and breathing pages for constipated writers, the so-called clients – this had the trappings of a black-arts fairy tale.

The whole premise of The Institute for the Greater Fasting Mind – The Forgetful Inn – gnawed mouse-like in the pit of my gut. The gnawing distracted from my focus of being a dick – detective, if you will – searching for clues to see what added up, what didn't. Personal, basic math.

Thus distracted, I scratched the itchy rash on my thigh. I fished out the charred notebook pages of handwritten scrawl from my pocket. I had remembered to transfer the two pages from my own pants to the worker painter pants. By now the words on the crumpled pages were unreadable.

What do you have there? Silver came over, curious.

Oh, nothing really. Just scraps of paper I picked out from burned-out litter in a trash can while walking my dog the other night.

Well here, let me put you at ease by taking that off your hands and throwing it away for you.

Reluctantly I dropped the crumpled, charred pages of writing into Silver's palm. Her fingers closed over them, and then they were gone.

The interior of this section of the Institute – the arched hall doorway leading to the vaulted-ceiling room – was vintage and stately. The mahogany wood trim along the floor was high and thick, gleaming of polish. The ceiling was outlined with ridged cornices.

But this was no time for architectural clues. I had book blowing to practice. Yet I couldn't stop practicing basic math as it applied to my situation: How had I landed this job – this internship – anyway? Did I really want it? Had I even applied, or asked, for such work, any work? The job seemed to have found me – by chance, fate? How did all this factor into the equation?

I had to compartmentalize my thinking, be a real dick in the slang, not derogatory, sense of that word. I had to go about detecting, then analyzing.

And so I did, and I recalled that no, I hadn't applied for this or any job, but yes, I had been spotted in the boonies, alone, having lost my way at a four-way junction, I had spun under the stars overhead, and then, still spinning or maybe having stopped, but before I could get my bearings, I was enlisted, or perhaps conscripted, by a robotic crew of six to aid with the job of blowing books on behalf of writing clients at a place named The Institute for the Greater Fasting Mind.

Now who in this world gets a job that way? And a job like this? Who besides me? And then, more unsettling, a color, a name, a mental image with questions zapped in my head: Blue?...my sleeping beauty?...Still asleep? Waiting in bed for me? I missed her, no question there, but what did I really know about her? And what about her did I miss? Falling asleep, snuggling with her? The sleeping habits we shared each night? The sex we had one night?

So, if she were really Blue, then that would make her The Institute's day-shift overseer and Silver the...

As I balanced on a mobile stepladder facing the upper rows of a wall of books, such conjectures put me in pause mode. Odd phrase: pause mode. Was I transforming into a Robby? My conjecturing was disrupted by faint barking coming, it seemed, from right outside The Institute's walls.

I clambered down the ladder, passed under a chandelier and rushed to the opposite side of the vaulted room to a window taller than me. I shoved aside folds of drapery. The window itself was locked.

By then the outside barking had ceased. It was still night. I could only see the outlines of tree trunks across the backyard. Then I glimpsed two smaller shapes zigzagging wildly, one pursuing the other — A coyote, a fox? Or, was that Chi? And, a cottontail rabbit or some other game animal being chased?

The barking and the animal sightings reminded me that I'd lost my Chi, that I missed him, that he could still be circulating out here in the boonies.

Was that his barking or a coyote howling? Had Chi caught my scent in the city, tracked me out here and was barking or howling to be saved? Or to come save me? Yet maybe Chi had moved on and was surviving in the outdoor freedom, chasing rabbits, squirrels, gophers and chipmunks.

Like any good dick, this got me analyzing my walking routine, which I did late at night when unable to sleep, which seemed like every night, nights being my entire life, and how I left home with her sleeping alone in bed, how I walked with Chi, how we circulated back to her each time (before I lost my Chi), how she threw an arm across my chest and snuggled with me again in bed, and how, as with dreams after waking, I could recall little else because afterward I just slept.

I knew nothing about her character, the woman sleeping with me, though we must be two of a kind, with things in common, one surely being our shared bed.

Still stuck in pause mode, this was where my detecting petered out. I knew the math added up to very little. The adding equaled more questions than answers.

Hey, is everything going OK with you? You look stiff as a board.

Silver had materialized at my side. Her presence again brought to mind Blue, the sleeping twin who oversaw The Institute's day shift. The name Blue had earlier zapped in my head. Was Silver's Blue also my snuggling Blue? And if so, where and how did Silver fit in, if she did?

Again, no mathematical answers, only more questions.

My detecting tried adding one and one – meaning the twin sisters – to see what they equaled, but Silver distracted me with a steaming mug of black coffee.

I turned from the window while Silver drew the drapes shut again.

Thought I heard noises outside, in the backyard here, I told Silver. And so I went over to check. I'm worried about my missing dog. I was hoping it was him out there barking – either for help or for me.

That's a shame, Silver said, handing me the mug. A devoted, loving dog, man's best friend. I'm very sorry to hear about your loss, yet it pleases me to see how vigilant you remain while on the job.

Here's some fresh-roasted coffee to help keep you on your toes and doing your best work. Drink up.

Thank you, and cheers, I said, taking a sip. It tasted hot, almost bitter, like espresso. Drinking a mug of this, I thought, should burn away my drowsiness for the rest of the night shift.

Silver flexed her beaded headband and smoothed down her lengths of hair, laughing as she said, Of course, the Robbys don't require a coffee boost.

Why not? I asked between sips. Taking out a scrunchie, Silver knotted her hair in a ponytail before replying.

Because they're humanoids, silly — machines. Factory remainders, actually, charitably donated as a tax write off to The Institute. They go on until their internal batteries need recharging. Just like we do, in some ways, but for us, coffee is our battery recharger.

After Silver left I clambered back up the rungs to balance myself on the bookshelf ladder. The higher I got the more the ladder wobbled. So, at the same time, I focused on two things — balancing, and quality book blowing.

The room I was assigned wasn't like the countless cell-like dens lining the web of corridors and reserved for writing clientele. This one was tall and airy, like an old-fashioned parlor or salon, with upholstered chairs, sofas, settees, ottomans and end tables.

I wondered how clients were allotted time to spend here and how they spent it. Maybe, I deduced, the parlor was reserved for group-therapy sessions or even an outlet for casual socializing.

Anyway, the rows of books on the parlor walls were packed in, floor to ceiling. That left only spines and tops of pages exposed to air and gathering dust. Very little wiping needed. Only sustained, vigorous blowing.

Once I came away with not only a dusty book but a spider and a wisp of web clinging to my fingers. The row that book was in must have been a breeding ground for reclusive spiders.

Instinctively I shook my hand and yelped. The spider held on.

I nearly let go of the ladder to use my other hand against the spider, but then I hung on, regained my balance, emptied my mind, breathed deep, shut my eyes and blew long and hard on my fingers until my lungs also emptied.

When I opened my eyes again the spider was no more, blown away. I caught my breath and smiled. My blowing technique worked to blow away not only specks and patches of dust but an unwelcome spider.

Rung by rung, wobbles and all, I clambered down the ladder to finish the last of my coffee. The mug no longer steamed. I was a little winded from the deep breath needed to blow away the spider, so, on my own, unauthorized, I gave myself permission for a work break.

I sat on a long, L-shaped sofa, stretched out my legs and leaned my head back over the edge of a cushion. My thigh had stopped itching but there was no stop to the gnawing in the pit of my gut.

I should've used my work break to recharge for more actual work. Instead I used the break to analyze Robby 1's cryptic warning about The Institute's throw rugs and trapdoors.

My analysis was distracted by the sight of a streaking mouse — with what looked like a scrap of charred notepaper trailing from its mouth. The mouse shot under the vaulted room's arched doorway and into the corridor maze.

I sat up on the couch and leaned forward. A second later a me-owing kitty-cat darted in pursuit — a brown kitty with three legs, the fourth a back-leg stump — causing it to limp while pursing the mouse.

Thanks to Silver's black coffee and the cat-and-mouse chase, I was anything but drowsy. But I felt like time was running out, that I'd best be on my way — out the door, back to walking, circulating back home, back to snuggling in bed with her. Yet it seemed as if that home and bed were far off and receding.

With the urgency came dread. Like an electric shock. It stood me up. As I did the blood in my head seemed to drain to my feet, to spill out my shoes. With a bang I plunked the empty coffee mug down on the end table.

Yes, now I knew, my work at The Institute had to be over. And done with. Time for this book-blowing internship to end. I had done my time, a little time, did the blowing of books I trained for and tried doing it my very best. But I was not another factory-issued machine programmed to take orders.

And then, one by one, questions amplified till my ears rang: If not machine, then what? What kind of person, character, was I? And the sleeping beauty in my bed – who was she? Together what did the two of us equal? And what about the other bed, the other she, the one I also slept with and who kept shrieking Rob and Robby? And what's more, what about that doppelganger of mine, if it was actually my doppelganger that I saw with my sleeping woman, the woman who may be Blue?

With questions amplifying, the ringing nonstop, I covered my ears and bolted from the parlor. I ran in the direction of the limping kitty and mouse, my gnawing stomach doing flip flops.

I ran on and on, zigzagging through a web of narrow corridors. I ran into some dead ends. For those I had to backtrack and start running in another direction, any direction.

It didn't matter which direction I ran. Running itself was all that mattered, the speed of it, the freedom it brought. Oh, what a relief to run like that, to never stop, only to circulate, to feel somehow unfettered and alive.

I had no idea where I was or where I had started. Further, I still couldn't answer the basic question of who I was. Some dick (detective) I turned out to be.

All doors of the dens I passed were shut. Almost all those doors had Do Not Disturb signs. What did the shut doors without signs mean – total blockage failure? positive/creative jump-start? den vacancy? I didn't stop running to find out.

Then, after it seemed I was hopelessly lost running, I came upon a door ajar and with no DO Not Disturb sign.

I pressed nose and lips to the crack and peered in – first one eye, then the other, taking turns, an eye for an eye. The den inside was in shambles: Table and chair overturned, notebook pages and books from the walls strewn across the floor.

The eye I was using, left, rotated up and down and from side to side before settling on a grayish throw rug. The rug was creased in hilly folds, partly exposing underneath what looked like – yes, no mistaking – a trapdoor.

I heard a voice and readjusted my left eye until it found and zeroed in on a Robby tidying up. He'd been outside my single-eye range. I wouldn't know which Robby unless I pushed open the door, entered the den and got closer to read the name-tag number.

Not that it mattered since, from my limited experience, all Robbys looked, sounded and acted almost alike.

Still, I was partial to Robby 1 – the lead Robby? He'd enlisted or conscripted me for the job internship, though I really didn't want such a job and would prefer, right now, to be out walking, circulating my way home, getting into bed, snuggling with her, our happy ending, instead of being stuck working here like a menial laborer.

May I request to see who that is stationed out in the corridor? the unidentified Robby called out, picking up an overturned commode. One of my eyes, not sure if left or right, was visible through the door's crack. I opened the door wider, revealing myself and stepped inside.

This Robby had been picking up fallen books, blowing and re-shelving them. Now he stood haloed under a ray of light while holding the commode. The commode's cover was latched shut so nothing putrid had oozed out.

How remiss of me to just now notice a small round window – like a ship's porthole – above Robby's head, above the topmost book row and right below the ceiling.

The porthole was too high for looking out, either sitting down or even standing on tiptoes, but it let in natural light. Rays slanting down on Robby and the commode must have been moonlight, since it was still night out.

I deduced that all dens must have these portholes. If so, they would be too high on the wall to be an outside distraction for isolated clients on the inside.

I told Robby I was here to render assistance. I asked what had happened and stepped closer but still couldn't read the number of his tag.

The unidentified Robby replied: This scenario transpires 48.6 % of the time for first-time occupants of The Institute. A client is unable to overcome his or her Block Syndrome – in this case, a he – which leads to mounting frustration, then hysteria boiling over to a full-scale meltdown. Once that stage is breached, the den and its contents become obliterating targets. In the aftermath, we Robbys are summoned for custodial cleanup.

Oh, wow, that's tragic. Well, anyway, I'm here now to do whatever is needed to assist cleaning up, I said, my eyes reverting to the partly exposed trapdoor on the floor.

This Robby was chatty, telling me that clients who succumb to meltdowns and lay waste to their dens are eligible for rehabilitation after a month-long, cooling-off period. Two-time offenders must cool off for a year. Three-time offenders, the incurables, are ineligible for another cooling-off chance.

Well, three strikes and you're out – seems fair and reasonable, I said, righting the table and chair.

I had shifted closer to Robby and read his tag: Robby 3. I wondered if the tag numbers amounted to a Robby-ish chain of command. If so, was Robby 3 serving under the command of Robby 1 and maybe his first officer, Robby 2?

After looking at Robby 3's flawlessly straight clip-on bowtie and touching mine, I could feel mine was askew. I didn't have a mirror so I straightened it blindly.

Robby 3 observed my blind attempts and came over to tug at the bows until both were straight. He nodded at me, bowed, stepped back, and then we both resumed cleaning up.

Later, almost done, I saw that Robby 3 was sniffing the den's air. I did the same and detected, it had to be, the lingering odor of marijuana.

I watched Robby 3 sniffing as he also kept watching me sniff. He muttered that while controlled substances were not officially banned, they were frowned upon at The Institute, that clients, at their owns risk, smuggled them in to use as a creative stimulus and/or for recreational bliss.

Soon after Robby 3 swished his hands and said, Whew, this den is regaining its proper form. He thanked me and asked me to do the finishing touches and wait for his return. He had to track down Silver, update our progress and be assigned the next task.

Robby 3 added that if I finished before his return, there was always book blowing to be done across the shelves of the restored den.

Sort of kidding, I told him that The Institute, with its mechanized workforce, could use a technological upgrade – say, smartphones, even walkie-talkies, and why not cordless vacuum cleaners to hoover along walls lined with dusty books?

Robby 3 halted mid-stride, hand reaching for the doorknob. He turned with furrowed brow and put his other hand to his mouth, as if to cough or clear his throat, probably the latter. I wondered if Robbys actually coughed.

As far as I know, acquisition of said devices has never been contemplated, Robby 3 said, hand resting on the doorknob. The

Institute employs time-proven methods, and these do evolve through trial and error. While resources are limited we maintain a creditable track record. Also, for the record, we Robbys are also evolving. Our robotic evolution has led to performance gains too numerous to itemize without impeding these night-shift duties.

Therefore, sir, if you do not object, enough of the metaphysical chitchat. I will return soon, count on it, Robby 3 said, saluting me this time and again bowing. Until then, do carry on with whatever work remains to finish here.

I relaxed after Robby 3 left. He sounded prideful about The Institute — almost human. I wished I had my regular clothes to put back on. I hung a Do Not Disturb on the outside knob before shutting the den's door and deciding the time had come for another break.

Wasn't I entitled to job-related breaks? Who was here to say I was not? I sat in the straightback writing chair, massaging my face with both hands.

The caffeine buzz from Silver's coffee had dissolved unusually fast. Now, I actually felt I could sleep forever if only I were back where I belonged.

Through clasped fingers, I peeked — and soon stared — at the creased throw rug, calculating. I could almost reach it with my toes if I extended a leg and stuck out a foot.

I felt the gnawing in me again, still intense, like an ulcer. I extended my left leg, stuck the foot out, aimed and kicked at the bunched-up rug.

My kicking flipped it backward. Just enough. Underneath where the rug had lain, on the floor's surface, squarely outlined, was the entire trapdoor, maybe four by four feet. On one side was a silvery-bluish metal ring: The handle.

Of course I knew better, knew I'd been forewarned. And I knew I best get back to work in this den before Robby 3 returned with the next assignment.

But I knew just as well that the work of a Robby, evolved or otherwise, wasn't cut out for me. Not for this, my character, if you will. There was no plot, if there ever was, for me to follow. Something else awaited me. I coughed. The den was dusty.

Yet how was I to deduce my evolving role to see how things played out? Should I even bother with role playing? That's what this dick business was about, but where did that leave me?

I'll tell you where that left me – facing the odds of going it alone, of standing over the exact spot where I was warned not to be and staring at it. Before I could think it through, I fell to my knees, twisted the silver-blue ring and lifted that trapdoor. It was heavy lifting. A bell dinged, and I gulped for air.

At first I just held the trapdoor open, as you might a book cover, gulping and staring into a pit. It reminded me of an abandoned mine-shaft. The murky depths below were unreadable. I could only make out the upper part of a hook ladder for going down – or for going up. Or for both. The ladder was hooked under the trapdoor hinges.

I fell farther – to my elbows, my hands, then flat on my gnawing gut. The pit gave off a stale, decaying odor. From its depths came shuffling sounds, countless feet dragging and scraping. I heard sobs and moans, begging, cries for help.

After a while pale hands bobbed up and down, reaching up at me from down in the gloom. From the bobbing, outstretched hands, fingers clenched and unclenched. I gagged at the odor.

And yet, I crawled forward, inch by inch. I found myself dangling over the edge before finally tipping and losing my balance. I hollered while falling through the open trapdoor.

As I fell, an official-looking document fell with me, unfurling before my eyes. I knew these had been mug shots of story characters trapped underground. Doomed to slow decay because of a client's Block Syndrome, their glassy eyes stared from behind bars. I looked for my own mug but got distracted.

Concurrent with my downfall, someone, another trapped character, perhaps a client, shimmied past me up the ladder and leaped through the opening above – trading places. Had I possibly done the same once?

But I was still falling and the heavy trapdoor clanged shut as I fell. My falling was swift yet seemed to drag on as if in slow motion. Darkness fell too, like the night sky but absent moon and stars.

Still falling, I heard that same bell go ding-ding from above. Had the trapdoor been reopened? A voice like a recording addressed me – a Robby voice.

Ahem, it is me, Robby 7. I never wear a name tag, and I am never seen. You would think I am invisible, but you would be wrong. I merely maintain the lowest of profiles. As warden of The Institute for the Greater Fasting Mind, my duties include burials – figurative burials, such as yours. We have not met, nor will we ever, so, pleased not to meet you. And now, to you sir, a very long, endless and dark good night.

Would Robby 7, any of the Robbys, whatever their number – or Silver, or even Blue – catch the trapdoor escapee? Or would the fugitive elude them, blend in as the intern, later to slip out and replace me on insomniac walks and cohabiting sleep?

As the trapdoor clanged shut again, I swear I heard a dog's distant barking. I might have heard it before my fall. Was it Chi barking for me or just barking while giving chase or being chased across The Institute's lawn. I hoped my Chi would persist, find ways to keep circulating.

But really, what difference would it make? Least of all for me? Here I was, down here, trapped. I had landed, first on my ass, in pain, then bouncing back on my feet, exiled in this pit. I wouldn't bounce back any higher.

I breathed in, out, feeling more and more sleepy, but, oddly, quite safe. With each breath, being down here seemed less and less abnormal. Even the stale, decaying odor, as I got used to it, wasn't nauseating, seemed almost normal.

Standing in place, eyes closing, I found myself falling asleep but soon felt the presence of characters breathing down my neck, hovering and circling, their silhouettes kicking and shuffling, back and forth.

So I got in their midst, eyes wide open, joined in, willingly, I admit it. I even tapped my toes, dug in with my heels, swung my elbows, moaned a couple of times. It was a hoot, mindless fun, and it sure woke me up, kept me up, too. How we kicked up dust, clouds of it, coughing, rubbing our eyes, rubbing shoulders, bumping and grinding hips, dragging our feet, etcetera.

It's all we can do, partying for our lives, to stay awake, hoping, always hoping for a breakthrough from above. Characters like us, trapped down under, oh, you bet we stick together. Forever and ever.

The End

Book III:

Character Assassination

Running for our lives

It turned out, after all, that to run didn't solve one damn thing. Running to stay alive was more like running from the problem – and for us, there was only the one existential problem.

I didn't learn this lesson until later. In fact, not for quite some time later. I doubt if my fellow characters ever learned it before they were gone. By the time I had learned the lesson I assumed I was nearing some kind of truth.

Yet in the end, my end, I learned that it really didn't matter what lessons characters like us learned – or unlearned.

And as for what is true, well, when the end comes, that's it. Isn't it? Curtains? The final exit? The one and only truth? Or doesn't it ever end?

Are these rhetorical questions? Someone else can decide. Right up to the end, my end, the questions I had kept piling up. The answers to them never kept up with the piles.

In theory

For us – and, for a long time, for me too – running wasn't recreational. It was a commitment to peak health but, beyond that, it was a means of survival. The survival theory was laid out starkly in black and white: Run or perish.

In some ways it's not that different from what it is for the average person. In daily life we're all on the go, on the run.

We have places to go to and things to do – friends and family to visit, coworkers and deadlines to meet, appointments to fulfill, supplies to pick up, even some exercising. Characters are no different except, we theorized, for us everything was on the line.

Our theory was that running went beyond staying healthy, going places, and meeting people and deadlines.

The act of running was how we, as characters, maintained our existence. If we ran, especially instead of sleeping at night, so went our theory, there was less chance of being erased, deleted – X'd out.

The origin of our theory is unknown.

Being X'd out is a euphemism for character assassination. No one says those words, not ever, at least not out loud they don't.

All that mattered was this life, surviving it, then waiting to morph to the next life. The concept has been described in religions and philosophies. It goes by the name of reincarnation.

We factored in every move as counting toward our survival. For instance, any body movement, stretching, going up and down stairs, taking out the trash, even having sex, all of it kept the dust off so we didn't look like outdated, obsolete characters – ones unworthy of reincarnating.

Movement was the incentive for our running: The friction with air, while on the run, blew dust from our bodies and clothes. Besides staying alive, after running we felt and looked fresher. Again, so goes the theory, this made us more worthy of character reincarnation, as opposed to the opposite, which was unspoken.

Lights out

Absurd as all this may sound, here's another tidbit, my own little confession: I have this fear, more of a phobia, but since it's already happened, I'm always fearing it could happen again.

What I fear happening again is when I leave only one light on in my basement flat come evening. All at once, that one bulb flickers and burns out like a candle: Poof, all around me, the air turns pitch black.

I know a bulb burning out involves electricity, but the sudden, surrounding blackness must feel very much like being erased, deleted, does – the much-feared Big X-out (assassination).

Being X'd out in the middle of reading, watching TV, using the computer, singing to radio music, eating a meal or looking out the window – it feels like this could be it: The End, My End.

The end-time feeling lasts only a few seconds, but still, long enough to scare the life out of me – figuratively speaking.

Even in the pitch-black air, how fast I go to retrieve and screw in a new bulb so that light around me flares bright again.

Then, poof, just like that, I'm back in the spotlight of existence. I'm also guessing this hints at what reincarnation must feel like for us characters.

I have to say guess because while I've been reincarnated, it's only by hearsay. I can't recall my prior lives. No character can because, like a revolving door, our story roles and names are replaced and written over by new ones – unless it happens to be our very last story, with nothing to follow.

What happens when there is nothing to follow, no new role or name, involves those two words we never speak out loud.

The solution to this fear of mine, that sudden life-and-death scare, is to never leave just one light burning in my flat. Always have a backup light going.

My hat, his device

At this time, the present, it wasn't later but earlier in my learning curve. So I still ran, especially at night, to keep from falling asleep. But there came a night, this one, when I dropped out of running with the pack.

First let me explain this reference to the pack: Characters like us, including me, do our all-night running together, our group activity – as a pack.

On this night, without knowing why, I was about to break that routine and begin to run on my own – solo. No more running with the pack. Fellow characters would soon call me a dropout.

My dropping out happened by accident when, on a night like any other, I set off running very fast – faster, for some reason, than I had ever run before. I was running to join the pack of night-time character runners.

I ran so fast that my hat flew off. I wear a sunhat, though some mistake it for a Panama hat or something called a boater. Believe me, it is neither.

Why I run wearing a sunhat, at night, when there is no sun, I can't really say. Maybe force of habit, a leftover from a reincarnated life. It simply feels right when I have the sunhat on my head, even while running at night.

I don't recall working in a garden with a spade, rake, hoe and trowel, but I've been told I had done so as a gardener in a past character role. Maybe that started this habit of wearing a sunhat.

I've been told about my past-life gardening duties at coffee by more than one fellow character. I take their word.

On this night, I looked and reached backward for the flying-off sunhat while still running forward.

While looking and reaching backward, I ran into a man walking forward but going the other way. While I had looked back for my hat while running, he was looking down at his mobile device while walking.

During our head-on collision, heads bonked – back of mine, front of his. Our bodies bounced a few steps backward, and sideways, before I fell and landed on my ass.

The man's device flew from his hand and landed upright on the sidewalk, tottered there for an instant before dropping face (screen) down.

Meanwhile my sunhat fluttered in the air like a mini-flying saucer before landing right side up in grass by the curb.

The man I ran into and bonked heads with did not fall, as I did. He didn't offer a hand to pick me up either, but instead bent to pick up his device.

Still bent over he checked to see that it still worked and glowed. It still did both.

Only after this did he bother to look over at me, just long enough to say asshole and spit on the sidewalk near my feet.

I scrambled up off my ass, up on my feet, wondering if this meant fighting.

The other man stood there but not to fight, only to look back down at his glowing device. Then he walked right by me, ramming my shoulder with his and spinning me 180 degrees. I nearly fell on my ass again.

He must have been in a hurry to join what I call the zombie parades. Those attract hordes and go all the time. I try keeping away from them but it's not always possible.

Change of plans

For a minute or so I stood where I was, rubbing my painful shoulder. I only thought it, but didn't say aloud or even form the word on my lips: OUCH.

When I turned and bent to retrieve my sunhat, I saw it was flat, downsized from a flying saucer to more the shape of a pancake.

The man holding his device must not have looked before stepping on my sunhat and walking off.

He may not have seen the sunhat, even with its light color, in the dark of night. Or he may have seen my sunhat and purposely stepped on it.

What's done was done, but I decided to at least try undoing some of what had been done.

I held my pancake-shaped sunhat in one hand. With the other hand I made a fist, punched inside, punching out the crown.

The crown ballooned with each of my punches. Then I blew across the restored sunhat to blow off grit and dust.

Standing in the middle of the sidewalk, I placed the sunhat back on my head. I circled the brim of it this way and that. Wearable, I decided.

Still holding the sunhat in place, down around my scalp, I heard shouting in the distance. The shouts came from the pack of runners and made me jump straight up.

For whatever reason, on this night the distant shouting gave me the shivers, as if the weather was freezing, which it wasn't, not yet. Maybe my nerves were frayed from my head-on collision.

Anyway, whatever the reason, hearing those shouts turned me off from the nightly runs with the pack.

Somehow I knew the time had come to run solo and be silent and see where that took me. It was time to transition from group-think to thinking on my own.

Of course I knew my running, solo or not, would sooner or later lead me to where Kit was working.

A crush

In those days, nights mostly, just picturing Kit at her work gave my running purpose. It made each of my runs less aimless and more focused. I had a thing for this woman, you know, a crush.

What was there about Kit that brought the crush on?

For one, she had an exceptional job that she seemed to thrive working at. Two, I liked picturing her at that job and also her being there for me to see, as the need arose.

What I needed, actually more what I really wanted, was for her to blow on me, all over – sustained, soft blowing.

I wanted that blowing to help stay refreshed, for her to blow off any dust that my nightly running missed.

Well, that's not entirely honest. There were other ways of dusting off, like wiping and washing myself, which of course I did, but I wanted to have Kit do some of the blowing and dusting. I've even tried to imagine her doing this for me, and, when I did, focus my imagination that way, well, the feeling was indescribable. Someday, perhaps...

So I'd become attached to Kit, yet I doubted the attachment went both ways, at least not very deep on her part. For my part the relationship was a work in progress. More of a rough draft.

X factor

When it got dark out was when I ran to find Kit. She was easy to find, even with the outside darkness.

Nighttime was the time when Kit worked, when I knew where to find her. So I always knew the when and the where because I knew the times and where she worked.

Anyway, night was also the time when I ran. As I've said, that was to keep from falling asleep, to delay the onset of sleep for as long as possible. Stay awake, alive, run, don't get X'd out – our theory, our credo.

Between running and waking activities, like coffee gatherings, I only permitted myself catnaps. That's because no one can run or be active every second of the day. Get 40 winks here and there, yes, every character took the risk. Had to.

So nights I wound up, at some point, running in the direction of Kit's work. Even when I was running with the pack, I would skip out of the long running line for a detour to see Kit, then, after seeing her, return and rejoin our pack.

Another plus from running solo now meant having more time, if I decided, to hang out with Kit.

There was too much dust in the air, inside and outside, to remain inactive for long and sleep the nights away. And there were also the cobwebs.

Dust and cobwebs settled on things — and characters — that didn't move enough or were shunned.

Like me, the other characters ran at night to avoid overnight sleeping, running to stay awake and lessen the odds of being X'd-out.

But unlike me, now a dropout, the other characters would keep running together, as a pack, more than a dozen strong of them.

I vowed to never again get stuck running with a pack of characters. Looking back, that time was a disaster waiting to happen.

Running in a pack was like getting caught in the chaos of a marathon race. Racing action was unpredictable, potential repercussions were terrifying.

I could have been tripped, knocked down, knocked out, even trampled or maimed by other runners.

Such repercussions might have ended future character roles for me. No more reincarnations. I won't say aloud but only think it: I might've been X'd out, which equals assassinated.

Kit Kat

By the way, some historical perspective on names given to the woman I had a crush on: Kit was a diminutive for Katarina, which to me was an elegant first name for a girl. Katarina – that was Kit's formal first name.

In a book of names I browsed at the old library, I saw the name Katarina derives from Katharine and means pure. In Italian, it is spelled Caterina, which was also the first name of Leonardo da Vinci's mother.

Growing up as a little girl, before she grew into being Kit, Katarina was called another nickname by her friends and family – Kitty.

Katarina told me that over time she must have outgrown the Kitty nickname. She couldn't give an exact date and figured Kitty faded gradually from usage.

By the time she grew to be a young woman, everyone who knew her was just calling her Kit, for short.

So Kit became her new adult nickname. For fun her parents sometimes wrote or called her Kat, also for short, as in the animal cat but spelled with a first-letter upper K instead of a lower-case letter c.

But Katarina preferred Kit to Kat, and she rolled her eyes and stuck out her tongue when a teasing girlfriend combined both nicknames into one – KitKat – after the popular candy bar.

 KitKat's not my nickname, so I'm asking, no, requesting, that you never call me that – it's insulting and juvenile, Kit said. She also asked that her parents, even in jest, stop referring to her as Kat – both in speech and on paper.

The changing, playful names and nicknames finally came to an end. Kit took its rightful place atop the pecking order. Kit's naming had reincarnated, one nickname replacing another, the earlier ones X'd out.

Runners of the pack

My fellow characters who still ran in a pack also try giving their runs more of an edge, to make them less aimless and more focused.

That must be why they – we – all shout up and down the line at each other. When I ran with the pack, was a part of groupthink mentality, I shouted too. For as long as there was air in my lungs.

Our shouting was meant to strike fear. We pretended the person running behind each of us was a threat. This forged a menacing chain of being chased and chasing.

Except for the last one running as the caboose, or the one running as the front engine, there was someone ahead to chase and shout at while at the same time being chased and shouted at by someone from behind.

So the running game amounted to the thrill and menace of a chase. Pretend chasing motivated us to run faster and farther – an all-night running marathon – all to keep awake, focused, keep from sleeping and being X'd out.

Night after night, under streetlamps, running block after block throughout the city, we were spotlighted thus – stick figures with legs and arms pumping, chasing and shouting insanely after each other.

Back then I was no different. As pack runners, the energy we devoted to these noisy, insane chases left us thin, some even skinny.

As nightly marathon runners, our bodies burned off calories by the hundreds, also any excess fat.

Echolocation

This also might come off as absurd, but I have this thing I call my bat sonar. It pings inside me the nearer my running takes me to the old library warehouse. At least I pretended it did. Maybe my bat sonar was nothing more than the sound and feel of my racing pulse.

That was where Kit worked, as curator, at the old library, at least on evenings when it was her shift to work.

Her posting was Upper Floor, Literature Section, but usually between Sci Fi/fantasy and Mystery. Kit's Colony, that's what I nicknamed these genre sub-sections.

Bats locate desirable objects by emitting and hearing reflected sound waves, their sonar a form of echolocation. When emitted sound waves strike a targeted object, they echo back to the bats' ears and guide them where to zero in.

The echolocating I heard and felt – my racing pulse? – pinged faster the nearer I got to the old library. I knew the way by heart but the pinging reminded me I was zeroing in.

Once I reached the old library's entrance, the echolocating pinged nonstop. Now it was more of a dial-tone buzzing.

That buzz gave me a high. I took the crumbling front stairs in two leaps. Then I barged through the revolving door and whooshed in, remembering to take off my sunhat.

Her Night off

Sadly, as expected, the first one I met inside was Ms. Silver. I often meet her first when entering the old library.

Ms. Silver looked up from behind her lofty half-circular desk. She's the library manager. The high desk surrounds her like a fortification.

Ms. Silver's gray hair was coiled in a bun. She wore half-lens readers attached by beaded chain round her ears and neck and wore a colorless sweater like a short cape over her shoulders with a bluish/gray button fastened at the throat.

I rarely had much to say to Ms. Silver. Likewise she to me.

This time she may have shouted to me but, still high from the buzz, I bolted the stairs for the upper floor. That's where I expected to find Kit working.

Kit's favorite task was pulling around a leaning cart of books to be restocked on shelves. The cart leaned because of missing caster wheel.

Ms. Silver claimed there were inadequate library funds to replace the missing wheel. What kind of budgeting was that?

Kit had to be careful not to let the cart lean too far so a row of books spilled to the floor. I can vouch for the care she took so spills never happened.

However, Kit was anything but robotic about restocking. In fact, with her curious mind, she got distracted by the various book titles.

If a title caught her eye, she would open the cover of that book, lean ever so slightly against the leaning cart and, losing herself, begin to read away.

Her reading was like being put under a spell – it could go on and on for page after page after page after...That's what it looked like to me, watching her...

...When next she looked up, Kit would have had the same book open for a half hour, even as long as an hour or longer. Under these reading spells, time for Kit flew by until that dimension of physics ceased to exist.

The old library itself was usually overlooked and forlorn, as it was on this night. Rarely were there patrons who needed Kit's help, so it was rare for there to be many books for her to restock.

Her boss, Ms. Silver, remained on the first floor, behind the fortification. Her knees throbbed in pain and needed replacing, especially the left one, causing Ms. Silver to limp on her left side.

With the elevator broken, Ms. Silver was unwilling or unable to go limping up the stairs to the second floor and oversee Kit's working progress – or lack of.

Ms. Silver again claimed there were no library funds to replace the broken elevator, which would cost far more than the wheel-short, leaning book cart.

Aside from restocking, Kit took her time wiping with a cloth and blowing on the books scattered across the shelves of each aisle.

Most books were seldom read and so, day after day, accumulated dust, even cobwebs, while sitting on the shelves. Kit's wiping and blowing was, on the face of it, their time to shine.

When she was done cleaning these books, even the older ones looked freshly printed.

I got a jealous pang when I watched Kit handle those books. She handled them like sacred texts. I could see this by the way she held and blew on them.

Each of her blows peeled off dust bunnies that caught the light before sparkling down to the floor.

Now, as I took the stairs three at a time to the upper floor, the earlier words of Ms. Silver shouting at me bonked my head and echoed inside: SHE'S NOT HERE… HERE…HERE…HERE!

Duh, obviously. That's why I couldn't find Kit working anywhere upstairs.

There was nothing to see on the upper floor but partly to empty bookshelves and dim overhead lighting. Not a patron in sight. No Kit in sight, either.

Above me, stems from an ivy vine dangled down between ceiling tiles. I reached up to swat at the leaves grazing my hair.

Just another parade

OK, so Kit had the night off from work. I suppose I could survive one night without her. From time to time these absences happened. She deserved her free time. All of us deserved some work time off.

My problem was keeping tabs of Kit's on/off schedule. I tended to think she would always be on, for my benefit, working every single night and never off, but that was selfish thinking.

When I couldn't hang around Kit at the old library, my nights of running seemed aimless and unfocused.

Kit had never told me where she lived. I was too shy to ever ask her. I wish I had asked. If I had, when she had a night off, like tonight, I could run over to wherever that was and knock on her door.

Instead, I stumbled on the warped, dusty floor while stepping over to one of the old library's tall, stately windows.

Starting at my waist, the window rose high above me. I looked out from the low end, leaning my head against the glass and looking down. On the sidewalk below, another parade of zombies shuffled by.

Anyway that's what I called them – zombie parades – my nickname. These went on each day but more often at night when most people had time off from work and chose to use the off time to parade around.

People shuffled like zombies, going mindlessly all over the city in these parades, all over except ever coming in to patronize the old library.

Everyone shuffling by in the parade below me was lit up. That's because each zombie reflected a glow from bending near to his or her glowing mobile device. Their faces looked like a river of full moons reflecting the sun.

At least the zombies of this parade all went as one in the same direction. Nobody to shuffle, run or bonk into – no fear of another head-on collision.

Invasive species

Mindful of stumbling again, I carefully placed the soles of my shoes down, heels first, step by step, on the crumbling stairs of the old library's entrance. While doing so I breathed in the chilly, late-summer night air.

As I breathed out, I patted my cheeks and watched puffs of breath come from my mouth. The puffy breaths mixed with motes of dust that skimmed off my cheeks from the patting.

Dust, it never stopped accumulating – on my hair, face, hands and clothing – just as it did on neglected books over rows upon rows of the old library shelves.

I sure needed a decent blowing, a dusting off. Running by itself didn't always do the trick.

The glowing zombies from the parade had shuffled on, passing from sight. I had the all-clear to resume my solo run without fearing another collision.

Behind me, as I turned, loomed the stark profile of the old library's lower and upper stories. From top to bottom, its masonry walls were cloaked in wild ivy.

Over time the clinging vines, stiff as wires, had chiseled through the crevices and cavities of the stonework. And over still more time, the vines had penetrated and spread into the library – through its walls and ceilings.

A breeze kicked up. The ivy leaves swished and fluttered like pages of a book being turned. The swishing and fluttering soothed me as I ran in place for a minute, then resumed my run.

Like a migraine

I looked both ways for motor traffic. Always do. As a night-time runner, you can never be too alert. I even looked each way twice before crossing the street. Then I took off running on the opposite sidewalk, this time away from downtown.

The night air was bracing. It should keep me alert and wakeful. Soon, on both sides of the street, I was running by rows of houses centered on typical city lots.

Then, briefly, I had to stop. I thought it was to catch my breath but it was something else. When I looked up at the stars, I saw there were none to see and I felt my head pounding.

Was my sunhat on too tight? I felt for it up there, circled the brim this way and that, but no, the sunhat felt just right up there, where it was, on my head.

Was this the after-effects of the head-on collision with the other man, the one who called me asshole and left, device in hand, first ramming my shoulder and then walking over the crown of my sunhat?

I put my hands on my hips, breathed and hoped the pounding in my skull might stop soon. I missed seeing the stars. I waited five minutes or so and kept hoping, but the pounding didn't stop and the stars did not come out.

Rather than wait and hope any longer, I said fuck it and started running again. On the street two pickup trucks passed me and each other, going opposite ways.

One driver flicked high beams. I blinked. Responding to the high beams, the other driver turned on headlights that were off but the truck either had a bad muffler or misfiring engine. For half a minute the roaring motor obscured my pounding headache.

On the next block, from inside a passing house, a child's voice whined: NO, NO, I won't do it...You can't make me! A woman's voice bellowed: Shut your sniveling face and get those PJs on for bed...or else!

I quickened my pace. By the next block my headache had roared back like a motor. It was unbearable. I either needed a new muffler or a tune-up.

To be precise, the headache was not the pounding kind. It felt and sounded more like a clacking keyboard but with a migraine's intensity.

The clacking was nothing like the gentle pinging I felt as I zeroed in on Kit. I was afraid the pressure in my skull would force me to lie down somewhere, even on the ground, and shut my eyes.

I didn't want to lie there like that, exposed and helpless. But I was not anywhere near my basement flat.

To ease the clacking pressure, I took off the sunhat and resumed running, my stick-like legs and arms pumping as I held the sunhat in first one hand, then the other.

From windows I passed, I saw lights inside being turned off and curtains, shades and blinds being drawn closed. Good night, moon, I thought, wherever the hell you are up there.

Clack, clack...CLACK, CLACK...CLACK!

I reached up to rub my head with the hand not holding a sunhat but kept running. If possible, and it was, the clacking was louder.

Could the clacking possibly be coming from somewhere else, from outside my skull, from somewhere outside and not far away? I had to sort out the possibilities.

Bungalow

At last I couldn't stand it anymore, stand that clacking. Somehow the clacks had to stop. Had to be stopped! Make them...stop! Me, someone...stop them for me...please, someone, somehow, help!

I was begging for help from anyone or anything because, on my own, I couldn't make the clacking stop. So I had to stop running, bend and rest my hands on my knees, one hand still holding the sunhat.

In front of me, no, actually, to my side, I became aware of a small white house, a bungalow, with a slice of front yard. The bungalow's casement porch windows were cranked open to let in air through screens.

I stayed bent, doubled over, hands on knees, waiting, gasping and looking down at the cracks in the sidewalk, then to the side, at the white bungalow. It had a low-pitched roof over a partial second story.

CLACK, CLAck, CLack...Clack...clack. Was the clacking easing up? Or was that wishful thinking?

The bungalow wasn't far from the sidewalk. Still doubled over and looking to the side, I was gasping and blinking fast from the residual pain.

One shallow concrete step up from the sidewalk was a narrow brick pathway. The path curled like a vine right up to porch stairs and storm door.

Between my rapid blinking – or maybe because of it – the white bungalow had this funky, wavering facade. As if it too were breathing, with me, my breaths, and not 100% solid.

Once, after a long, slow blink, the bungalow at my side went away. In a blink – gone! When I closed and quickly reopened my eyes, a second blink, there – back. Something not all there was going on. I had to look away.

The pain persisted. I felt close to keeling over and passing out when the clacking eased up so much it seemed gone. And there, yes, I could feel that it had gone away, entirely.

Even so I stayed bent double for a while, catching my breath, feeling, listening and waiting to see if the clacking came back – either in my skull or from wherever, from somewhere else.

But there was nothing else to wait for. The pressure and pain from the clacking didn't come back.

After standing tall I walked, no hesitation, up the one concrete step. Next I followed the curling brick path to the bungalow's stairway.

On the top stair stood a wooden carving, the bark deeply grooved and eroded – the figure of some wizard? But no, the figure was shrunken and more the size of, say, a gnome.

The gnome's head rested crookedly on its shoulders, contorted by a gash across its wooden neck – blow from an ax?

Under the gash was a knotted maroon necktie. Under the tie's knot was a nailed-on metal sign, like a license plate, with words painted to look like dripping blood: LOST GET.

As my breathing settled, I wondered if the two words, reversed, should be taken as a warning. For anyone? A certain someone? The solid facade of the white bungalow no longer wavered or blinked out.

Before reaching the top stair, a thing passed before me from inside the porch. I saw its shape through the casement windows, the shadow of a passing something – short, squat silhouette.

The shorty shadow passed into nothingness as I crossed the threshold and entered the porch of the white bungalow.

Breaking and entry

Why, oh why? Too bad I couldn't answer my own questions.

Why didn't I bother to ring the doorbell or at least knock first on the rusted screen door? Instead I pulled at its loose handle and the door rasped open.

Beyond was a dented steel door, already ajar. Why again didn't I first knock? Instead, the steel door gave way to my slight push so – why not? – I entered.

What I was doing would strike any sane witness – had there been one – as insane. Breaking and entry? For what? Are you shitting me?

Whatever had come over me? I'd never done anything like this before. No shit I hadn't. Then I paused: Had I?

I couldn't be sure because I couldn't recall being told if any of my past characters had ever broken in somewhere – house, store, shop, gallery, factory, fortress, office, bank. Somewhere else?

Just considering this made my inner skull – now free of clacking – feel gummed up with reams of paper.

I had to snap out of this stupor, forget the goings-on in my skull. I pivoted on my heels, looking all around after each pivot. One by one, details of the porch came into focus.

My eyes stayed put on the football-sized head of the Buddha. Ceramic maybe, painted cobalt blue and placed on a corner wall shelf. One of the eyes, left, was either shut or worn away. Was that maybe the Buddha's way of winking?

Buddha's head had a pointy topknot and elongated ears. The more I stared at the gleaming blue Buddha with a possible winking eye, the more drowsy I got.

There was a card table with a floor lamp emitting a cone of light on sheets of typing paper on that table. One stack of sheets was blank; the other stack was typed on.

Also on the card table next to the two stacks of paper sat an upright manual typewriter – looking like a grizzled veteran after years of typing combat.

Near the typewriter, smoke spiraled up from the floor out of a bulging object with a round base. Looking closer I saw it was a hookah.

The hookah's serpentine tube was a gleaming blue like the football-sized Buddha, with rings of smoke rising to the white drop ceiling. I breathed in the acrid smoke and stifled a cough.

So, not a moment before, someone was here, smoking something. And typing something.

A rolled-up page was still in the combative typewriter. I looked down at its red-and-black ribbon. Above the ribbon a cluster of typewriter's keys had jammed mid-air.

Below the ribbon and jammed keys was a half-finished sentence. The sheet of paper in the typewriter had lines and lines of other sentences.

The upper page was dirt black from the lines of typed sentences. By contrast, the lower page was snowy blank.

Someone had been here typing at the keyboard. Someone had stopped and beat it, and a passing, shadowy someone had exited the porch as I entered.

I hunched over the typewriter, coughing as I blinked fast and inhaled hookah smoke. My legs and knees were rubbery. The typewriter image wavered like the bungalow had with each of my blinks.

I wanted to read what the typed sentences on the page in the typewriter said.

Blink, blink...the wavering typewriter cast off its image, shuffling parts like cards and soon reassembling as a whole, a solid, bearing the image of a pagoda. Was that the winking Buddha's influence, or from the rings of smoke? Was the smoky substance in the hookah marijuana, maybe hashish?

My eyesight blurred. I rubbed my eyes and blinked to clear my vision.

I was able to make out that words, many of them, and even whole sentences on the upper page were X'd out by the typewriter's capital X key.

What was the writing content that was X'd out? I wanted to read what there was to read but it was, on the whole, unreadable.

My watery eyes dripped like a leaky faucet. My blinking was frantic. Everything was wavering out of focus. The typewriter/pagoda wavered until, like the bungalow, it blinked out of sight. Then my head got top heavy and dipped forward, my chin plopping against my chest.

This time, no avoiding it, I was passing...out...

Cups of joe, tall tale

And then now, here we were, sitting elbow to elbow and across from each other at our tables.

Two oblong tables were lined up end to end. That made for one long table, room for us all to take a seat and talk to each other.

At this extended table my comrades chuckled. More than that, they guffawed, even slapping their thighs – all at my expense. I had just narrated, or tried to, about my late-night outing that led me to the white bungalow.

My sunhat rested between my thighs. I had taken it off. I didn't slap my thighs so my sunhat didn't get squished. Anyway, I wasn't going to slap and laugh at my own narrative, was I?

My fellow characters acted as if seated for entertainment at a comedy club – not the Dune Buggy Cafe. They dared to call my late-night outing my tall tale. I guess I could hardly blame them.

I'd given up running with them at night, yet here I sat with them, at our cafe, chugging black coffee after black coffee while expecting them to accept and interpret my enigmatic outing.

We were a pack of stick-like characters, our coffee consumption washing down slices of pie with whipped cream, appetizers of chicken wings, onion rings, stuffed mushrooms, and snacks of grilled-cheese, egg, tuna and BLT sandwiches.

Even after stuffing down food like this every morning and into the afternoon, we burned off those calories running each night. As proof, baggy clothes hung from our bodies.

My fellow characters laughed, not from spite but at what I was trying to narrate for them. At what happened to me outside and inside the white bungalow, at how I ended up where I did, which was right back home – back in my basement flat.

Of course I couldn't explain why my headache became clacking, both in and out of my skull; explain what I saw on that porch, starting with that shadowy thing passing by the windows; explain the nerve of my breaking into the white bungalow; explain the winking Buddha; explain the hookah smoking away till it made me woozy; explain the rickety typewriter wavering into a pagoda beside two stacks of paper; explain the typed sentences across a rolled-up page; explain the various words and lines that were X'd out.

Hey, it's OK, easy does it, friend. Don't get upset with us. Start over and tell that story of yours again, from the beginning, how it began and how it ended where you woke to find yourself all the way back home and in bed next morning.

The sensible request came from a yawning woman named Blue. As usual, Blue was not fully awake when I had narrated my not-so tall tale.

Blue was of middle age but a bit younger than I. She yawned and fell asleep at the drop of a sunhat.

Blue had a dainty mole in the middle of her forehead. I fantasized it was a bindi. In my fantasy when Blue laughed, or frowned, some strong emotion, the bindi crinkled like the blinking of a spiritual third eye. That was as far as that fantasy got.

I recalled when Blue's character was named Sandy — or, for short, nicknamed Sand. There was a story behind the character that came from the plot of a romance novel. Her role was that of a paid snuggler.

I'd never heard of the profession, but the novel explained the snugglers were licensed and offered platonic therapy to forlorn men and women who hired these pros for hugging and holding comfort. Being a romance story, Sand and one of her clients fell in love after months of snuggling platonically.

As with any of us, Sand's new name and character Blue simply appeared one day— out of the blue — so to speak. That's how it goes for us. The name was written out for her new character and came with a new story role.

In this novel by the same author but not a romance, the character Blue volunteered for a sleep experiment conducted by a government space agency. She would lie in cryostasis, for months, basically sleeping on a bed that tipped, rotated and floated.

Scientists were testing the effects of artificial gravity on the human body before launching deep-space voyages.

After months of experimenting, her character awoke so disoriented and listless that she was nicknamed Blue, and that stuck. There was much more to the plot, but that's the story behind her nickname.

After the space agency role, Blue's character developed narcolepsy. None of us knew if that was part of the plot or the way Blue was on her own now — waiting, as we all are, to be rewritten and renamed for another story.

What I'm about to explain next may seem as batty as my bungalow outing, but so be it. I've referred to it in passing but here's the gist: Our character names and biographies are subjected to the whims of endless makeovers.

To us, these are baffling and manipulative, but we have no say in the matter and never get used to them.

After a character's latest makeover, conflict can and does boil over. The made-over character with a new name often accuses the rest of us of lies and slander. Coffee time together turns contentious.

The reason: Once made over, none of us recall a single thing about what we were, our old selves and names, and what's changed about our own character. Our slates are wiped clean.

Yet everyone else can recall what their fellow characters were before — their names and the roles they played in fictional stories. But those made over, remade, if you will, cannot recall what they have done before, what they were in the past, any past.

How do you go on living with a revolving history on your back? Trying to peel away layers from the past only leads to dead ends. And delirium.

Me, a stoner?

My coffee mug was drained. I stared at the bottom brown rings, wanting to retell my story but on the verge of giving up.

The others squirmed in their chairs on both sides of our tables, drinking from their mugs. They waited politely but there were smirks.

Look, I'm at the point where I don't give a rat's ass if you guys don't or won't believe me, I said, not bothering to raise my voice this time or start over from the beginning.

As I said, after passing out on the bungalow porch, I woke to find myself in my flat, at sunup, on my bed that was still made up from the day before. I was lying at an angle on top of the sheet and covers and on the edge of my pillow. I had a kink in my neck, probably from the crooked way I'd slept. The curtains were open, the way I'd also left them, and the sun slanting in felt warm and must have wakened me. I've no idea how I roused and got myself out of the bungalow or was able to navigate all that way back home. I can say this about being in that bungalow – it absolutely gave me the chills.

As I finished, I looked across at Blue for sympathy. Her hands were folded on the table. As if praying for me. Blue yawned and nodded. I followed the crinkly motion of her (bindi) mole and felt my tension drop a tick.

There was murmuring at our tables, then Muldoon cleared his throat. That meant everyone pipe down.

Because of his past character (a role he couldn't recall but was told about), Muldoon projected a tough-guy persona. He never let his guard down. The clamor at our tables ebbed after his throat clearing.

In a past story, Muldoon was a special-ops combat hero serving overseas. His character's name was Copper. More recently, as the story character named Muldoon, he wore a civilian uniform and had a mundane role driving a cargo van equipped to transport special-needs clients to machine assembly jobs.

Muldoon ignored that storyline. He found it beneath his past macho glory but relished reminders of his role as combat hero – a role he had no memory of.

Muldoon patted his balding head before holding forth: Forget the bungalow malarkey! Seriously, people, take that garbage out to the can. Here's the real script: You – he pointed at me – inhaled vapors of a narcotic substance and went under its influence. After that, well, who knows but based on the intel, I'd say you were toking on that substance in your very own home, never left the premises, then you passed out in a delirious state on your own bed. You woke up in that hole in the wall of yours because, man, you were there all along! Never stepped foot outside. You dreamed or hallucinated the entire white-bungalow incident. There now, end of story...OK, next!

Muldoon twirled the fingers of his right hand above his head and whistled through the fingers of his left hand for the next table topic. He sure knew how to project the image of an authority figure.

Everyone nodded with Muldoon, calling me a bohemian dreamer, a stoner, then calling for me to rejoin running with the pack, that it was the safest way to pass the night and keep awake, that we survived running together, strength in numbers, etcetera.

At that moment our server, Paige, delivered a round tray of delicious pecan pie slices and set down another steaming pot of freshly brewed coffee.

Oh, how we chugged that pungent coffee, always black, never cream or sugar. The undiluted, caffeinated beverage was our daytime jolt. Differences aside, we existed together through our stories – tall tales, even – all beyond our control.

Our humming, lusty server

This seems like the time for an interlude to describe all things Paige. She had a lean, supple build outlined by a fitted server's attire. Below her dress hem that rose and fell, one glimpsed a tattooed vine climbing the outer right thigh.

Paige hummed while balancing trays and gliding between tables and booths and reaching over counters. Her athletic, graceful movements were those of a gymnast mixed with a ballerina's. Better yet, she never kept cafe customers waiting.

Paige's head had once been shaved. That struck us as exotic, but then she grew out her top portion of hair into a shaggy Mohawk and colored it with silver and blue streaks. More exotica, we agreed.

As Paige glided by tables, booths and counters, her dress hem lifted, revealing more of the climbing tattoo vine. The hem never lifted high enough to reveal where the vine ended. Or if it did.

The tattoo, the streaky Mohawk hair and the ballet-body movements gave me an urge to call Paige by another name. I don't know which one, maybe a nickname like Luna or Lola. Or Lulu. I never did, though.

Depending on how many of us were at the Dune Buggy Cafe, we took up either two oblong tables moved end to end as one table, or, if available, the extended booth against the far wall.

Paige, lusty as ever in her lavender-colored dress and white apron, approached our tables, shaking her head. As always, a paperback book bulged from her apron pocket.

Holding up notepad and pen, Paige stopped humming and grinned before saying, Well, besides another pot of our blackest coffee, what else looks good on today's menu for my motley cast of characters?

Her description of us was so spot on. We acknowledged this by bobbing our heads. Even macho Muldoon bobbed his. It was like we were in class. Then we recited our orders to Paige, knowing we wouldn't have long to wait.

Not business as usual

Later, hours later, Merlin was still recruiting players for one more card game – of course it had to be Crazy Eights.

In his last character role in a short story about feuding crime mobs, Merlin (his last name) was a slick card dealer mentioned only a handful of times over three pages before being summarily executed by crooks. He was only mentioned a handful of times over three pages before being summarily executed by crooks in a short story about feuding crime mobs.

A few of the crooks, just killing time and waiting for orders, kept losing bets to Merlin in rounds of Seven Card Stud. Finally one spat on the pile of cards and pulled out a Glock 19 from his waistband holster. He stood, knocked his stool back and called Merlin a card-sharking asshole before plugging him in the head. Merlin had no chance to defend his integrity or plead for his life.

With us, Merlin never discussed this brief, fatal role. He said it seemed out of character from what he'd been told of his earlier story roles.

Even so, goodness, could the man shuffle and deal cards – like a wizard. We never played poker with him– that was off limits – but stuck to more wholesome card games: Hearts, Old Maid, Go Fish, Snap, Kings in the Corner, Canasta, and, of course, Crazy Eights.

I had played many hands already and lost, though I never accused Merlin of cheating. I simply excused myself, said my goodbyes and walked out of the cafe and onto Main Street.

I felt snubbed because not one believed my bungalow story despite my insisting there were no hallucinatory drugs in my flat.

Before leaving the cafe, I had looked around to say bye to Paige. She was busy by the swinging doors leading to the kitchen, wiping off the condiment counter and refilling ketchup, mustard and various spice bottles.

Though I hadn't heard another chair scraping from our tables, I sensed Blue was on my heels.

I decided to leave the cafe and investigate what the enigmatic white bungalow I'd broken into might be about and how it involved me. I didn't know if I could even find it.

When I used my bungalow investigation as an excuse for leaving early, Muldoon accused me of acting out of character. He called me a gumshoe-wanna-be.

I rather liked the gumshoe role, even a pretend one. My instincts told me to begin investigating for more clues and links to the white bungalow.

It was mid-afternoon. I stood under the cafe's dripping metal awning. Outside it had rained while we had been sitting inside at our tables playing Crazy Eights, snacking and drinking coffee.

In front of me, a fat motorcyclist in sweatpants nearly plowed into a parking meter. At the last second he glanced up from the glowing device in his pudgy hand and with the other hand on the handlebar veered back to a traffic lane. Horns honked.

After that close call I stayed far from the curb. As I walked off in the direction of my flat, fingers tickled my jacket collar.

I guessed Blue, turned and was right. We stood facing each other like cutouts from a still-life picture.

Blue reached up to cover her yawn and nodded, her forehead's third eye crinkling. When she uncovered her mouth her smile radiated. I couldn't help but mimic her by smiling back. I doubt if mine matched her radiance.

Of course you can't remember anything from your past — none of us can — but that's why I believe in the importance of what you're doing with the bungalow-investigation, Blue said, brushing a strand of hair from her eyes. I sincerely hope that what you find out brings closure — for whatever destiny awaits you. Meanwhile, I wish you bon voyage!

Before I could respond, Blue leaned in and gave me a peck on the lips. Then she pulled away, paused, and did it a second time, more of a real kiss, before turning and trotting off in the opposite way, waving at me without looking back.

As I watched, I wanted to call out and remind Blue that I recalled her past roles, all of them, vividly, especially the character of the Sand woman — she whose snuggling therapy comforted lonely clients before one turned into a love affair.

Instead, I kept that to myself, turned and headed toward my flat.

Better to mind my own business, I decided, even if I hadn't a clue what the business of mine really was.

Her polka dots

Back in my basement flat, I remembered to sprinkle grass and oat hay inside the hutch for the pet rabbit. A white tail wiggled as the bunny hopped over to sniff at the evening's entree.

I fell back in the loveseat facing the upper front window and stretched my feet out on the floor. I needed a footstool. The window's vertical bars reminded me of a prison cell. I slipped a pillow behind my head. It felt lumpy, either the pillow or my head.

I looked up through the bars at passing cars, buses, trucks, scooters, bicyclists, even a golf cart along with several pedestrians, including children and dogs, on the sidewalk. No one looked down to see me looking up at them.

How isolating it felt to look up from here, below ground, as people passed above me at ground level.

Before long two women in matching large-lens sunglasses and leather sandals strapped above their ankles walked by. They could have been twins.

The one in shorts tipped her head to sip from the striped straw of a fast-food soda cup. Her puckered lips shone red by the late-afternoon sun.

The other one, holding a container of fries, wore a pleated sundress that billowed whenever the wind blew. As she walked past me, spilling a fry, I looked up her legs and saw a pattern of blue and silver polka-dots on white panties.

Those blue and silver dots folded and unfolded as if blinking at me with each of her steps. The woman never thought to look below her to see me looking up.

A truck horn blared twice as a semi-rig chugged along in the same direction as the walking twins. The polka-dotted twin raised a hand with fries to wave at the truck driver. The other twin raised her soda cup to salute.

I felt more alone, even jilted, once the truck and two women were out of sight.

Stars not aligned

My loneliness reminded me that, unlike Blue and the other characters, I was going through an unnameable stretch. My character, that is.

That was why no one called me by name anymore. Not even Blue.

The reason was simple: I no longer had a name, one that stuck. At least not sticking now and actually not for the longest time. The longer time passes without a reincarnation, the more a character's most recent name fades from usage, even by fellow characters.

I don't know why this is. I can't fathom the logic. It could be there is nothing logical to fathom.

When I mused on my namelessness, as I was doing, it scared me to death – figuratively, at this point.

My fellow characters tell me to stay patient, that I had been named, unnamed and renamed countless times, that the trend was on my side.

Once or twice, to be funny, a character had called me Bub. That generic name didn't stick, which was fine by me. It seemed like a charity case to even call me Bub, and that I didn't want. Plus I didn't like being called Bub. It made me feel like a bum.

Trying to cheer me, Blue still recalled that at one time, long ago, I had the name of Robby. Or, for short, the nickname Rob.

How about that? Blue asked. I said the name Robby, or the nick-name Rob, was OK, but of course I had no memory of being named either.

Still, I would have felt cheered if Blue had started calling me Rob or Robby again. But she didn't. Given enough time, all our names blow away and get lost in the void, like our dreams.

My namelessness was linked to my being between roles as a story character – for longer than I cared to imagine.

I was reminded of several past roles: One of me toiling as a monastery gardener; a second of me pining away as a bookkeeper in a far-flung edifice dubbed The Vault; a third as an apprentice learn-ing the ropes with a crew of robots at some sort of rehab clinic.

Gardening? Bookkeeping? Robotics? I shook my head. Greek to me, and the plot details, as revealed by my fellow characters, only grew fuzzier with time.

In my gardening role, I was posted at a cliffside desert abbey. I assisted the top monk, Gobi, who wore a hooded cloak and was addressed by our legion of monks as Most Venerable Lama.

The abbey was inaccessible to all but the most devoted spiritual seekers. Our duty was to preserve sacred texts inscribed on bound, camelskin pages.

Not all monks were honorable. Certain sacred texts vanished, poached for commercial value and sold to curiosity seekers returning to the outside world. The story had this element of intrigue. My role as humble gardener was incidental.

The abbey had only sparse green space to garden. I had other menial tasks, such as walking Most Venerable Lama's dog, a pug named Wu, through labyrinthine corridors. The dog was so named because instead of a woof his bark came out as woo, woo, woo.

I had no inkling of that or any past life, character role, personal relationship, etcetera. I just waited and waited for what would be written next for me – that is, for my reincarnation.

Characters at the Dune Buggy Cafe, especially after my bungalow outing, looked on with mock sympathy. Yet I could see from their looks how they sensed my ill fate. We were all waiting and hoping for new roles, but my wait to reincarnate had gone on longest.

So here I was, unnamed, not gainfully employed in any story, holed up in this underground studio flat with a barred living room window. The stars were not aligning for me. In fact, they were blinking out.

The depressing metaphor made me look away from the prison window and step over to the kitchenette to microwave a frozen pizza. The pizza choice for my meal emptied the freezer. On a side shelf of the empty fridge was a jar of spicy dill pickles. My side dish.

I simply had to step outside again and delve into the bungalow business. And step on it soon.

Then what? Well, even for a gumshoe, but especially for a rookie, please, one question at a time.

Catnap

Instead of stepping out, what I did, after eating my pizza/pickles meal and letting it digest, was let my eyelids close. Lying the length of the loveseat, curled up to fit, I gave in to a short nap, call it a catnap.

This was unavoidable. Now and then, here and there, a little cat-napping.

Belly filled, sleep crested over me like a down comforter. Bite by bite, I had consumed the pizza, eight sliced wedges, vegetarian, thin crust, black olive, green pepper and mushroom toppings.

I was famished and ate that entire pizza, last edible food in my fridge, and then, after eating it all, got sleepy. I dreamed in my sleep. The dream was short, because it was a catnap.

The two walking women from my waking reality, possibly twins, returned for a dreamy encore.

Both walked backward in my short dream, back from the way they'd come. Wherever that way was.

In my dream their sandals were replaced by high cowgirl boots. Those click-clacked on the sidewalk. The clicking and clacking am-plified the nearer the two got to my sub-window. On their heads were cowgirl hats.

The woman with her soda finished it and flicked the straw down in my direction. The straw sailed between window bars and bounced off the glass before landing in the well filled with pebbles, sand, weeds and litter.

The one flicking the straw didn't look down to where the straw was flicked. She still didn't see me looking up at her

In my catnap dream the wind had died down so the other wom-an's pleated sundress didn't billow up.

Still, from where I lay looking, from below in my loveseat, I knew what she had on underneath. I knew about the blinking blue and silver polka dots.

The walking dream women with their cowgirl hats passed back-ward, cowgirl boots click-clacking, across my line of vision, reversing back to wherever they had come. That was all, and with that I woke from the catnap. I sat up, patting the pillow on my lap.

Like a page torn from a book and fed through a shredder, the dreamy snippet was soon X'd out from memory.

Incinerate, bury?

After the catnap and dream, I woke feeling refreshed. Energized.

This time I got down to business, climbing up the stairway of my basement flat. Outside at ground level, feeling the surge of energy, I swung my arms like a wind-up toy soldier and walked the length of Main Street before cutting over toward the old library.

The refreshing nap also left me feeling grateful: I had not been X'd out while asleep.

Getting X'd out is a fact of life, our lives – a character goes out like a light, goes to sleep that is, same as my lightbulb burning out, only never wakes, never lights up again.

Character assassination. Same thing. That's right, the forbidden words. End of story, end of everything. Period.

On Main Street people gawked. Or seemed to. They stereotyped characters like us, like me, assuming we belonged to some voodoo cult. I'm sure the sight of skinny me in a floppy sunhat on a cloudy day reinforced the occult stereotype.

In reality there were few if any gawkers. People rarely gave us, gave me, a second glance. We were eclipsed by the glows from their mobile devices.

I decided this evening to walk, not run. I didn't want to rush running off those veggie pizza calories.

Soon I would need groceries. That is, if I wanted to eat and not waste away. Even for story characters, eating was essential for keeping alive.

I wondered if I still had funds in my bank account. To buy food to keep eating, to keep alive.

A dump-truck driver honked at me. He was so short behind the wheel that I couldn't see most of his face. I leaped back to the curb as his truck belched smoke and fumes while grinding by.

As it passed, I did a double take at the driver's haul — a cargo bed overflowing with junked books.

Another driver facing me in a minivan and ready to turn also honked. She waved out her window for me to get a move on as I tottered at the curb.

The woman's other hand held the steering wheel. And her device, which she looked at. The wheel glowed faintly from the device she looked at while waving me on. Since it was only dusk, the device's glow was faint.

Thanks, lady! Thanks for seeing me — as well as your device — and for paying barely enough attention to give me a break to cross a busy intersection.

Meanwhile the short, barely seen dump-truck driver had reached the next intersection. Were those really books being hauled for disposal? Or was I seeing things?

My mind pictured Kit browsing her sub-section of the upper old library and handling books like sacred texts — blowing away dust so they sparkled for patron readers. Contrast that with what I'd just seen in the departing dump truck — unless I was seeing things.

Books as physical objects — how rare that had become. Seldom were there enough readers to keep books circulating. But had it come to this — their remains hauled and dumped to burn in an incinerator or buried in a landfill?

The minivan's driver, still waiting to turn while staring at her device, honked again — without looking up. Made glum by that dumping load of cargo, I stayed frozen at the curb a moment longer.

Make way

But then, next minute, I managed to shake myself off and defrost before stepping down from the curb and continuing my travels.

I had to sidestep another parade of zombies before getting to the old library. And, once I got there, I was in for more disappointment. Again, I couldn't believe what I saw.

This had nothing to do with seeing the dump-truck's cargo of junked books. This library sighting was more personal.

Last night Kit had been off. I found that out too late. Tonight she was back on, but I could see that I would not have her to myself.

The village drunken idiot, so called, had already wormed his way up to the library's second floor. I found him hovering over Kit and her leaning cart of books.

I was so bummed by the sight of this because just getting to the library had been a hassle, like zigzagging over an obstacle course.

I had to jump off the sidewalk and walk for blocks in the street to avoid the passing parade zombies. Then I had to zig and zag to the curb and back to avoid the passing motor traffic.

The sidewalk had been taken over by a two-way parade. Zombies on the right, going one way, south; on the left, going the other, north. That left no way for me to walk on that sidewalk.

Naturally the zombies, going both ways, had glowing devices nearly shoved up their noses. Almost all shuffled their feet, but one wiggled along on roller skates, going north, while another, going south, wobbled forward on a unicycle. Somehow these two, eyes on their devices, advanced without looking where they went or disrupting the two-way foot traffic.

By itself a feat like that could qualify as a form of voodoo. Not one zombie going either way, north or south, ever looked over to see that I was forced to vacate the sidewalk and dodge street traffic.

Eventually, like tearing a sheet of paper in half, the two-way parade separated as each half shuffled off in opposite directions.

That's the how it goes with these parades. No spectators, permits, everyone marching with one hive or another of glowing zombies.

Booze and books

I had raced up the old library entrance – three stairs at a time, two leaps – mindful of the crumbling concrete. I batted away wiry vines under the arch before charging through the revolving front door that whooshed as it spun me inside.

Ms. Silver was staring down at the bare surface of her fortified desk through half glasses while unbuttoning and buttoning the cape at her throat.

When she looked up I was halfway up the stairs – four at a time! – to the second floor. This time she didn't call out to me. A good sign, I hoped.

But at the top of the stairway the potential good sign turned bad. Kroner was deployed between the Sci-Fi/Fantasy and Mystery aisles. As usual, Kit was in the same fictional sub-section, scanning titles on book spines spread across the leaning cart.

Kit ignored him but Kroner imitated her by pretending to scan titles near to those she scanned. Every so often, Kit touched a spine with a slender finger, as if tempted to pluck the book out. Right after this Kroner touched a nearby spine with his stubby finger.

Backs to me, they were nearly shoulder to shoulder. I cringed. With his drinking, I could only imagine how Kroner's breath must reek.

To be honest, Kroner was once a decent guy. He dabbled in poetry, mostly limericks, scribbling out verses on cheap notepads, on receipts, napkins, paper shopping bags, even on public toilet walls.

As far as I know, Kroner was never published – unless you count the walls of public toilets. I don't know if his submitted limericks were rejected or if he never submitted them. He seemed indifferent to publicizing his work.

Then Kroner's life took a nosedive. His wife or live-in girlfriend ditched him. Instead of poetry, he drank now. Instead of a notepad in his hand, now there would be a silver flask of whiskey. Or bourbon. Or tequila. Or vodka.

Nowadays Kroner spent more time boozing in pubs than browsing the old library. He was mainly here to cozy up and flirt with Kit.

This time, I couldn't contain myself. I stepped forward and said to Kit, Excuse me, ma'am, but is this person bothering you?

Kit slowly turned from her cart of book titles and let her eyes rake over me. She scrutinized me, up and down, as if it was I who was the village drunk/idiot.

Peaceful feeling

To save face, I forced out the most unnatural smile. It stretched my lips taut across my cheeks. As if I just had plastic surgery. Then I held out my arms on both sides, palms up and shrugged. I know, both gestures, dumb.

Kit held a chosen book in her hands, face up and half open. I thought she wanted to go under one of those reading spells of countless pages and get borne away beyond the dimension of time.

But then, after I had blinked, what's this I saw? The pages of the book Kit held were swishing back and forth – as if on their own.

That was the cleverest magic I'd ever seen – or recall seeing. Kit didn't even bother to glance down to see what those swishing pages, on their own, were up to.

I wondered if she was going to wipe and blow on the book or read it, or do all three. Either way, what a fortunate, enchanting book.

A natural sunrise of a smile spread across Kit's face. She spoke to me: Of course, I do remember you. You come here often and like to watch me. Maybe, even, to watch over me. Didn't you mention once that your name was...wait, let me think...oh yes, Robby?

I nodded, saying, I may have mentioned the name, but it must have been long ago. And for short, I had a nickname to go with it: Rob.

Well, whatever your name is, long or short, then or now, thank you for asking, but I'm trained and capable of handling any patron – this one included.

Kit tilted her head at Kroner before turning back to the leaning cart. I saw Kroner's shoulders from behind. They shook as if was laughing silently. I'm positive that's what he was doing.

What a jerk he'd become. This was nothing but a joke for him, a win over me as we vied for Kit's affections. But then, unexpectedly, Kit put the book on the cart, turned back and came up to me.

She patted my bony shoulders, raising clouds of dust. Trying not to sneeze, Kit raised a hand to shield her nose and mouth.

Without my asking, she did a swift dust off of my clothing with her other hand. She dusted away my latest dusty layers.

For my pants, Kit knelt and dusted both legs, using both hands. It was like being frisked by a cop only not at all threatening.

Kit finished off the cleaning by blowing on me. This was what I had been waiting and hoping for. I didn't forget to remove my sunhat.

The air from Kit's lips emerged as if from a toy fan, caressing my bare head (fluttering the hairs), face, neck, lips, ears and throat.

Each blow was delicate and soothing. The dust blew off me in sprinkles. My skin tingled.

For the moment, like the books she had blown on, I felt dust free and newly published.

Kit rose from her knees and stood. She dabbed at my clean cheeks and looked me in the eyes. Our faces were inches apart.

The kinky stalk of a vine poking down from a ceiling panel hung above our heads. I imagined it as our mistletoe.

I know you like to come here to keep watch on me, Kit murmured. And I don't mind the attention, it's flattering. But don't get upset about Kroner. Deep down he's a sweetie pie. Sure, he's had some bad breaks. We all have our problems, our troubled pasts. Life's short. All we can do is carry on and handle whatever turns up next. You understand that much, don't you?

Behind her Kroner, now facing us, rubbed his stubble as if sanding his chin. He was also looking straight up at the vine and grinning.

The outline of a silver flask showed from the waistband of Kroner's frayed corduroy pants. Only the neck and cap peeked out above his belt.

Second encounter

Kit and I said our goodbyes, actually goodnights, but never did kiss under the mistletoe vine on the old library's upper floor in the Sci-Fi/Fantasy/Mystery sub-sections of Fiction.

Back outside, at the entrance, the drooping vines under the arch seemed even lower and to have thickened. I shoved at them but their folds swung back, whacking me in the face. Hastily I stumbled down the crumbly stairs.

Stumbling onto the sidewalk, I stared back at the vine-cloaked building. A row of cooing mourning doves was outlined along the roof's parapet.

How inscrutable back in there, up there, being with Kit. First she made me feel like the village idiot; then she smiled like sunshine at me, had her book pages swish back and forth on their own; and then she dusted and blew all over on me – my wish fulfilled.

All that attention, the sleight of hand, the physical contact – none of those had ever happened between us. Was all this some new phase in our work-in-progress relationship?

Before I could analyze the evidence, I was forced to leap out of the path of still another parade. This one put me back out on the street.

The bent faces of parade zombies were infused by lights from each of their devices. It was night proper now, so the devices emitted a brilliant glow and the faces before the screens seemed lit up by floodlights.

My leaping to the street distracted one zombie from his device. That might have been a first.

Turned out the distracted zombie was the guy I'd collided with, head on, and bounced off of the other night. He recognized me and jumped from the sidewalk to the street, yelling that my bouncing him had damaged his device after it fell.

This time he didn't call me asshole but did give me the finger. Then he flicked at my sunhat with the same middle finger. It was a feeble try to knock off my hat, which he had stepped on and flattened last time, whether purposely or not.

I dodged so his middle finger missed flicking off my sunhat. He himself wore a baseball hat, backwards, probably so the bill wouldn't block seeing his screen.

Without another insult or flick at my sunhat, he jumped back to the sidewalk, rejoining the parade ranks, bending to the glow of his device and returning to a trance.

He had replaced his old, damaged device. The new one would have more updated, hypnotic features. From behind as I watched, his parade shuffling looked like a waddling duck.

No one else in the parade was distracted by our run-in. Parade zombies stop for no one, no interruptions, at least hardly ever.

After the parade passed, a silhouette pedaling a bicycle whizzed past me on the street. I recognized the rider's silhouette and shouted at him in the dark: Hey, you! Can't you see it's me here? Pump those brakes.

Merlin's confession

The pedaling silhouette braked and made a wide arc before circling back to where I stood waiting. The bike tires whizzed since the road was still moist from the earlier rain.

We stood facing each other, just the two of us, on a lit curb by a marked crosswalk. The old library was a half-block behind, slightly north I believe. The downtown was one block to the side of us, I believe that was west.

Merlin straddled a single-speed blue bicycle with wide seat, tires and rims – quite retro. We stood breathing in the late-summer night air but not yet speaking.

There was also something retro about our meeting, maybe even deja vu, with the two of us isolated at this crosswalk, haloed by the street lamp.

It had me feeling hollow, as if we were the last surviving characters, stranded at the rim of a black hole. I waited for Merlin's breathing to settle.

Biking can't be as hard as running, can it? I asked, breaking the silence.

Merlin waited another moment to catch his breath, then said, I've got a few years on you, old friend, quite a few. Besides, you may not have noticed, but I no longer run, not for a very long time. That bone-jarring activity was wearing out my joints – hips, knees, ankles – also my arches.

My mouth fell open. What was he talking about? Not just another character who gave up running in a pack, like me, but also not running solo? No more running, period? Had I failed to notice his absence when I still ran with the pack? Were we too strung out in lengthy running lines in the dark night for me to take attendance?

I kept staring at Merlin. He fiddled with his handlebars, twirling them and the front wheel round and round as if practicing a form of sorcery.

Besides bicycling, he went on, I now swim at the Y. I try doing so daily. Swimming laps is like traversing gravity-free space. When I'm done with a swimming workout, my head has cleared, my muscles feel toned and my body joints have no aches or pains.

Merlin pulled out and smoothed his tangled beard. He seemed amused by the shock of his words.

While I no longer ran with the pack, it shocked me to hear that Merlin didn't run at all – either with other characters or solo like I still did.

A car came up from behind, the driver signaling a turn west toward the downtown. Merlin lifted his bike from the street to the sidewalk next to where I stood.

He patted my shoulders. Thanks to Kit's dusting, barely any dust puffed up.

Merlin whispered in my ear: News flash, old friend. That faith in endless running so we don't get X'd out is pure quackery. More bluntly, it's a crock of shit.

For emphasis, Merlin waved his arms in the air like some cosmic conductor. I stepped backward, two steps, shaking my head at him: NO!

Listen up. I don't know who, how, or when the rumor began that you can save your ass by endless running, but it's a big fat lie, Merlin said, still near my ear but raising his voice. Our lives and personalities as characters, despite what we do, yes, they're reincarnated time after time. But then, despite what we do, or don't do, a time comes along and ding dong, your number's up, characters are, as you know, assassinated. Dare to say that word! It's liberating.

And, here's a juicy tidbit to blow your mind: Runners get X'd out in the very act of running. You bet they do. We choose to ignore this, preferring blinders and reassuring cliches. For us, oh yes, running shows that we're active, not passive, characters who take control of our destinies. Well let me tell you old friend – that's nothing but feel-good therapy. We are never, I repeat, never in control.

After he was done speaking, I was speechless. Finally all I could come up with was: Then why do you...go on biking...and swimming?

Merlin pushed off from the curb with the retro blue bicycle, switched on a headlight and called back: That should be obvious. It's healthy, keeps the heart ticking, and, even better, it feels exhilarating. Try it and get some more shuteye. A good night's sleep is far better for your health than running yourself ragged, even the way you do it – as a soloist.

Merlin was out of range before I, old friend, shouted that he should be wearing a bike helmet – for his health.

One big clap

For the next week I actually did it, giving it a try. I followed Merlin's advice, not about bicycling and swimming, but about running and sleeping.

Fellow characters regarded Merlin as a misfit but also a sage. So why not try his advice? I gave up late-night, long-distance running. Instead I stayed put, stayed in.

Instead of going out to run from here to way over there, going around and around before finally coming back, I slept in, in my flat, sleeping all night long. Unless I woke during the night because of a nightmare, or to take a leak.

This lifestyle change was liberating. It seemed normal – staying put, not chasing around, and especially sleeping the night through. A long, good night's sleep – part of a normal lifestyle, one I'd been lacking.

For a while I even gave up regular runs to go watch Kit at her job. I couldn't be sure where our relationship stood. Was it even standing, or on hold?

Of course I did miss Kit's blowing and dusting of me, but that happened only the one time. Now I took more responsibility for my hygiene, especially daily showering as well as regular laundering of my clothes. This seemed quite normal and more responsible of me.

Staying in overnight also made me a devoted caregiver for the bunny. Before there were times when, keyed up to run, I forgot to change the soiled bedding in her hutch or replenish the food and water trays. No more.

Running, however, was recreational. So I still ran, but only when I felt like it, and now for shorter distances and not for any set time or overnight.

With overnight sleeping, my dreams lengthened, no just longer catnap snippets. Sadly, I could only recall fragments from these long, nightly dreams.

I did recall one perverse dream that, while fragmented, woke me like a nightmare from a sound sleep before dawn.

In the dream, I'd accepted an invite to join a seance. During the first session I felt myself growing sheer and gauzy until gravity released its grip and I floated up like webbing, merging in the airspace with the brainwaves of someone – more like some kind of entity. I sensed it was the someone who lurked in the white bungalow which I'd broken into.

The bungalow entity and I were soon telepathically entwined. Our brainwaves formed overlapping funnel clouds that churned up dust, sand and large debris. Ours was not an equal partnership; I was by far the lesser.

The stormy merger and its eruption had me gasping and then, poof, the dream sequence zapped out – like my lightbulb. I found myself twisting a pillow while feeling the clacking of a migraine. I flinched in pain and waited, hoping to capture more dreamy details, anything more, even a shred.

But within moments of waking, I could recall fewer and fewer details, and what I still recalled was shredding. The headache, thankfully, was also short and soon shredded itself to oblivion.

Yet the bad dream's essence draped over me, like webbing. Something seismic had occurred in the uncut version, something eluding my conscious grasp.

Right after the headache and dream ended, I shot up in bed, sweeping the covers to the floor, freeing my body. I watched my hands come together in a big clap – as if slamming shut the front and back covers of a dream book.

Off The Record

During coffee I found myself having less to share with the other characters. And I was caring less about them.

What a shame because we all shared the ultimate fate – assassination. Even that suddenly mattered less to me.

I no longer ran with them in a pack since Merlin enlightened me that mindless, endless running night after night was a crock of shit. So, while my drifting apart was a shame, it was undeniable and probably inevitable – another fate.

Also, over time, there were fewer characters gathering each day at the Dune Buggy Cafe. Had the subtracted characters been reincarnated to fill new story roles? Or were their numbers up, literally – meaning, character assassinations?

Those who remained never referred to these subtractions – reincarnations? assassinations? – or speculated about their fates. Denial in the form of silence was the unspoken code.

With fewer characters sitting for coffee and snacks, there was no need to bring two tables together, to seat us at one long, combined table. Now we sat at a regular-sized table or in a smaller booth. For the six or seven of us still remaining.

Either at a regular table or smaller booth, I still took off my sunhat and kept it on my lap until leaving. It seemed the way for my character to act at the Dune Buggy Cafe. I was attached to and protective of the old sunhat.

One of those recently subtracted was the character Blue. I won't deny how much I missed her presence.

Yet no one referred to Blue's absence or that her name before Blue was Sandy – nicknamed Sand, the Sandwoman – a trained snuggler of forsaken clients.

Blue's subtraction – reincarnation? assassination? – was not deemed a topic to discuss. Why play favorites by singling out her character when other characters, one by one, had gone missing, too?

If we had dared discuss the subtraction topic, characters now subtracted from our midst, we'd have despaired.

So we bypassed despair, tried anyway. Instead, with our silence, we settled for plain denial. We never discussed those no longer able to be present with us for coffee.

As if character subtractions were officially stamped: Off The Record.

From Amelia Earhart to Pocahontas

So what did the rest of us, the few remaining, discuss while at the Dune Buggy Cafe? Predictably, what we had done in past story roles as characters. Call them career highlights.

As always, as seasoned characters, we got caught in feedback loops of reliving the past.

We relived past stories of what fellow characters had done. While we couldn't remember our own stories, we could be reminded of them by what others repeated. The repetitions, over time, became copies that passed for our very own memories. And our dreams.

Take one remaining character, Thorn. We regaled him with his doomed role in a satirical suspense novel about a disputed inheritance. The plot begins when he and other characters, hardened villains, dress up as blood-thirsty zombies who pursue terrified family members – who were themselves squabbling and even fighting over shares of an inherited fortune – down a winding stairway that dead ends in an underground vault.

The victims are pursued inside, locked in, key disposed of. But during the mayhem, Thorn and his comrades are also betrayed by the mastermind who locks them all in the vault with the trapped family members and departs. One by one, day after day, the underground captives turn on each other and are decimated by torture and grisly deaths.

Then there was Lydie. We sometimes kidded that her name rhymed with Kitty and even gave her the childish nickname of Lydie the Kitty. Lydie's character took center stage in a science-fiction tale. Her innocent role began as a nondescript custodian at a top-secret military research base.

Late in a work shift, Lydie became drowsy and misread the sign to a laboratory door for that of a lavatory. She entered the lab and found what appeared to be a broken-down toilet.

Straddling the lid, Lydie got to work fixing the flush lever as it flapped uselessly. Before long she had the toilet flushing again, but doing so caused the room to revolve like a whirlpool. The lightning-fast revolutions sickened her till she passed out.

Lydie had activated not a lavatory toilet but an experimental laboratory apparatus. The lever flushed her down the chute of a spacetime portal.

As a time-traveling novice but also a born fixer, Lydie couldn't resist tinkering with history, such as distracting pilot Amelia Earhart from taking off on her fatal flight in July 1937, or, flushing further back in time to rescue the kidnapped/held-for ransom Pocahontas from Jamestown colonists in 1613.

But each of Lydie's well-meaning fixes only worsened humanity's destiny. Ever-more desperate to keep fixing what was broken, Lydie kept flushing herself backward – and forward – in time until the apparatus she straddled ran out of power. By then, Lydie was stranded as sole inhabitant on an unrecognizable and uninhabitable – for humans – planet.

Another remaining character was Dusty, a character written for a series of 1870s-era Westerns. It was hard not to laugh or giggle at the mere sight of Dusty and not go through pretend motions of dusting him off.

What a name – Dusty! Oh, how we all could relate to that name.

But our Dusty took pride narrating the adventures (and misadventures) of fellow characters. He would tip back the brim of his 10-gallon Stetson and loosen his bolo tie before tapping a spoon on a bowl or cup and stand at our table or booth to get our attention and begin his narrative.

Having heard it so often, Lydie was bored by the narrative of her character's time-travel plight. She poked Dusty with a screwdriver from her tool belt and told him to sit down and wait for when he could regale our group about her comeback exploits – her reincarnated character! – in the highly anticipated sequel.

How we kept at it, reliving the moldy oldies, going over the narratives virtually word for word, pausing for breaks marked by banter and jest.

The first time or two around, such storytelling was a riot. Later it got boring, then more boring, and finally stifling. Even with the black-coffee consumption, nothing held our attention. We were bored to death and putting ourselves to sleep.

Buffering

How startling to see Muldoon – for all his projected virility – wracked by sniffles. Add a runny nose and sneezing, and he seemed almost dainty. Others tried distancing themselves, but crammed in our smaller booth made that awkward to do. Was Muldoon next on the subtraction list?

Undeterred, Merlin shuffled and reshuffled his card deck but couldn't tempt recruits for another round of Crazy Eights.

Like rotating thunderstorm clouds, my thoughts darkened vertically. I kept picturing the white bungalow I'd broken into: Who was lurking there, unseen, in its depths? And why?

I could barely recall the bad-dream fragment that woke me but what I recalled had to do with merging brainwaves – mine and whomever or whatever had taken up residence there.

The more bitter black coffee we consumed, the louder Dusty and his deadly dull narrative got. Dusty was sweating so from his theatrics that he undid the silver clasp of his bolo tie and let the blue cords dangle.

At last Paige swooped into the rescue, gliding to our booth, humming away but shushing us.

She swept back a swath of her Mohawk mane and knelt on one knee by our booth: Hey, dudes. Gotta chill. Let's start chowing down instead of all the monkey jabber. Customers have complained, the cook is getting pissed. Now, what else can I bring to put meat on your sorry bones?

We guffawed at her description of us – monkey jabber, sorry bones! How true, that was us. Paige had us pegged exactly right. We elbowed one another, slapped our thighs. I was careful not to slap and flatten my sunhat.

An elderly couple sat hunched at a nearby table. Their flabby bottoms oozed out the sides of their chairs. Both peered down at glowing tablet screens.

Reacting to our raucous booth, the oldsters swiveled their chairs so their broad backsides faced us. All the while they kept eyes riveted to the tablets while blowing on chicken-noodle soup and dipping spoons into the broth.

I watched them grimace and shake their heads, muttering about us while exchanging salt and pepper shakers to sprinkle into the steaming bowls.

Suddenly the old man lunged against the table, cussed and rapped on his tablet. He put a hand to his chest and whined: Ma, my heart. Do something. Save me, woman. Make it quit doing all that, what do you call it, that buffering? My heart keeps skipping when this thingy buffers like that.

I tipped back my coffee mug for the dregs before asking Lydie the Kitty to slide out so I could go. Lydie held a brownish hanky over her mouth and nose because of Muldoon's sneezing.

While saying adios and slipping out of our booth, I heard the old lady berate her partner: No, Daddy, no! You listen to me, and if you can't, they'll be no chocolate lava cake for dessert. Quit dribbling chicken soup on your thingamabob and it'll quit buffering. Simple as that. Got it, Simple Simon? Now dry off your screen with that napkin and here, nibble on a Saltine, but don't you dare spill crumbs.

Pickpocket

On a night soon after, as I ascended from the basement flat, the inside of my head lit up. Just a flash of light, like lightning, but it also felt hot. A second or two later the flash narrowed to a laser beam burning words before my eyes: THE JIG'S UP.

I shook my head. Up what? Was I becoming a head case? If so, it hardly seemed worthwhile to analyze this internal message, but if I did, I interpreted this one to mean that this was my character's last chance to get to the old library for one more visit with Kit.

In no hurry for this final visit, I just walked there casually after first remembering to feed bunny and put on my sunhat.

Earlier that day, at our cafe, character attendance was down again – dramatically down, down to only Merlin and me.

Subtracting characters had resulted in a major reduction that equaled just two of us left. Even so, both of us stuck to the code of denial and spoke not a word about the lack of elephants in the room.

Merlin and I sat side by side at a ledge lined with tall round stools. We were in front of the cafe's smudged, plate-glass window. Between smudges we stared out as pedestrians and motor traffic zipped back and forth.

Of all absences, the one that still hit me hardest was Blue's. I didn't admit to Merlin how much her presence – and now absence – meant. Had her character been assassinated? Or reincarnated to another venue, only to return here later as a new character with a new name and story while totally ignorant of Blue's background?

I doubted the latter. What we were witnessing, those who remained, the two of us, was a character assassination binge. We were on the brink of extinction.

As the morning hours passed, my mug of coffee cooled before turning cold. I stared at a fly buzzing in erratic loops on the windowpane. It barely registered how Merlin towered over me on our side-by-side stools.

Paige served a row of customers at the counter. After she finished taking more orders, she patted her apron pocket, patted it a second and third time before yelling, What the hell! Not again. Gone. Where did my book go this time? Did it fall out somewhere?

The short-order fry cook reaching for Paige's order slips kept his empty hand stretched out, wiggling fingers at her to give.

Paige yelled once more: My book, the second one gone missing today. Has anyone seen either of them? They're from a family collection. Please look.

Customers dutifully bent down from their cups, plates and bowls to survey their areas of linoleum floor. At floor level were crumbs, balled-up napkins, wrinkled receipts, driver's license, bottle caps, a twisted spoon, fork, some shiny coins, and dust bunnies to be vacuumed. Two customers grabbed and argued over the driver's license.

Paige shook her Mohawk, huffed and handed the slips across the counter to the cook who snatched them.

Ignoring the fuss, Merlin wiped his bearded mouth with a napkin before riffling a deck of cards. Then he rubbed his palms, winked at me and began squirming.

I glanced under our ledge to his stool. The towering Merlin was sitting on top of two, thick, paperback books.

It's OK, he put a finger to his lips. I'm just smoothing out the creases. Paige's books get all dog-eared, stuffed any old way in her apron pocket. Before we go I'll lay them neatly on the ledge. They'll be in better condition than before. It's just something I feel like doing every so often. Sue me, I'm a pickpocket – but for a good cause.

True to his word, Merlin later piled the smoothed-out books on the window ledge. Ready to depart, we left generous tips with our receipts for Paige on the top book cover.

Before laying out the books and leaving tips, Merlin blew away a fine layer of dust and three upside-down dead flies from the ledge's surface. A spider crawled out of a crevice to scramble down the wall after the fallen flies on the floor. A centipede was waiting.

While he couldn't remember anything of his past, I wondered if Merlin ever had dreams or flashbacks from his long-ago time as the character Gobi, the desert abbey's Most Venerable Lama? I clearly remembered his name and story role there, but of course not mine; he remembered mine, my role there, but not his.

Solitaire

So that evening, on my way to the old library warehouse, a squat tan dog with a flat snout lumbered out before me. I figured this bulldog must be chasing what looked like a gray cat, but it was actually a squirrel, gray though.

A walnut bulged from the squirrel's mouth. The bulldog had a silver-and-blue studded collar, so no stray.

The squirrel proved elusive for the bulldog. It scaled a maple tree before scampering across a power line and leaping to the slanted roof of a house. The squirrel perched upright on the edge of the gutter, held the walnut in both paws and bit.

From far off in the neighborhood, a voice rang out: Chhhhhh-heeeeeeeeeeeeeeeeeeee...

The bulldog glanced toward the voice, then up to the tree, power line and the roof's gutter as shards of walnut shell fell like hailstones from the squirrel's paws. One shard bounced off the bulldog's curly tail.

The dog woofed and whirled to see what the falling object was, chased its tail then sniffed a garden weed before lifting a leg to squirt a yellow stream at a birdbath pedestal before trotting off toward the still-ringing human voice.

The dog-squirrel skit amused me but I felt the onset of another headache – with a hint of clacking.

I wondered what Merlin was up to. Was he swimming laps at the Y or out pedaling his retro bicycle or by now back home relaxing with a deck of cards? Tomorrow, back at The Dune Buggy Cafe, if I wasn't there, would he improvise with a game of Solitaire while wondering if we would ever meet up again?

If not there, my mind messaged, who knows, maybe somewhere else – another venue, another plot with other character roles and names. Or had we already played out all our roles and names from days gone by?

Another head-case message, I thought, as I trudged up the entrance stairs of the old library. This time, stalling, I took each crumbly stair one at a time. And slowly.

I thrust aside the ivy's clinging vines that hung like massive folds of a stage curtain. I whooshed in a half circle and then coasted inside behind a gust of blowing air from the revolving door.

Shearing

First thing, on the first floor, I saw that Ms. Silver was not at her post, not behind her fortification. Beyond the vacated desk, rows of book aisles everywhere were, as usual, devoid of patrons.

I took the stairs to the upper floor. Again, stalling, I slowly took the stairs one, by one, by one. The soles and heels of my shoes clopped down heavily on each stair. Each heavy, slow step echoed.

I doffed my sunhat. When I scratched my lightly clacking head, hardly a speck of dust spilled off. I'd sure been keeping myself clean and fresh.

Looking around for Kit, I peered up and down empty aisles. There she was – in an ankle-length plaid skirt, white pleated blouse, hair pinned up like a schoolmarm. She looked old-fashioned but alluring, though I would never be so bold to tell her that. Her allure, that is.

Kit was at the far end of a vacant aisle, on tiptoes and balancing on top of a stepladder between lofty shelves. She clipped away with garden shears to prune a thick stalk of vine dangling low between displaced ceiling tiles.

After stepping down the rungs to pick up the trimmings, Kit noticed me. She waved the hand with the shears and said she found them in a storage closet filled with her book-repair materials – trimmers, scissors, squeegees, rulers, magnifiers, weights, binding cloth, press boards, wax paper, glues and adhesives.

A curator's job here means dealing with contingencies, she sighed, mopping her brow, folding the stepladder and leaning it against a wall. I wished I had come earlier to lend Kit a gardening hand. From what fellow characters told me, my experience qualified me for the work.

Is that Kroner character around here tonight? I asked, glancing suspiciously behind each shoulder.

No, not this evening, he isn't, Kit said. And I'm afraid poor Ms. Silver has gone home ill. So, it looks like you have me to yourself.

Cast of characters

Did I misspeak about Kroner? By referring to him just now as a character? He was never part of our cast of characters at the Dune Buggy Cafe, sitting for coffee and snacks, let alone running for his life with us at night.

And what about my Kit, the old library's curator? Was she a story character or did she inhabit the town as one of its flesh-and-blood citizens?

I suspected my worldview was too small-minded to realize all the answers. There had to be more story characters scattered across the big world – many, many more – than the local ones I associated with.

And then there was Ms. Silver? Hers, such a familiar name somehow. I frowned just imagining the woman and her name but couldn't decide how each fit into the bigger picture.

Not everything in the world, or in a story, can be rationally analyzed and explained. I fell back on that for my conclusion.

Anyway, I couldn't be sidetracked by unknowns that are likely none of my business, whatever that business is.

Hot air balloon

Kit and I took our seats on a padded bench by a group of upholstered chairs. These overlooked the stairwell between floors. It was like sitting on an island from an archipelago. For a full minute, we just sat quietly, looking down.

Last time Kit commented at how dusty I'd gotten myself. She couldn't do that this time. Would she be surprised, disappointed?

Maybe my self-cleaning wasn't wise. I looked forward to Kit dusting and blowing on me, even though it only happened once, but now she could see I needed neither.

But knowing how much I liked it last time and with Ms. Silver off now for sick time, Kit humored me and went through the motions. That meant she first patted me up and down, all very proper, before brushing my pants and shirt, even my shoes, and then dabbing at my face and blowing over it like a rotating fan.

Only a few specks of dust blew off, but Kit continued the ritual of fanning her hands to clear the air between us of pretend dust. Her pretense soon had us doubled over and giggling.

Above, the lighting from a ceiling panel had blinked out. Inadequate funds? I saw other vines poking down – more potential mistletoe until they were trimmed with the shears.

Kit's hair had loosened, gotten wispy from the vine trimming and maybe from the dusting and blowing of me. Her sweaty upper lip gleamed. I could barely feel or hear any clacking from my headache.

I worked up my courage and asked for a farewell kiss. We were sitting, hip to hip, on the island bench.

Our lips came together under what I imagined was a mistletoe of multiple vines. Not a long kiss, not a French kiss, but a kiss lasting longer than the one I'd had with Blue.

When our kissing was done and without being told, I stood, propelled with the buoyancy of a hot-air balloon.

A clock on the wall between windows read five to nine – closing time. Because of the overgrown vines on the outer stone walls, only ragged black holes were visible through the windows.

I donned my hat. The keyboard clacking in my skull resumed.

Kit stayed sitting on the bench. She gave an itty-bitty wave and, with the same waving hand, blew a kiss.

Her kiss off sent my hot-air balloon adrift. When I had floated halfway down the stairs and looked back at Kit – still on the bench – I saw her tears.

That hum

Balloon-like and propelled by a current, I whooshed through the revolving door and then flailed through the stage-curtain vines.

Outdoors, teary-eyed myself, I looked up before tiptoeing down the first of the crumbling stairs. The late-night sky was a starry dome.

It was very chilly, nearly freezing. I nearly sneezed. Instead I breathed in, then out, again in, deeper, before finally seeing a faint patch of breath.

I also saw the dense cloak of vine leaves on the old library's stone wall. Were there hints of autumn color, reds and golds, showing on those leaves?

Hard to tell in the dark and, anyway, I was color blind. An unusual case, I was told – I could only see black, white, and, of course, shades of silver and blue.

I heard what sounded like laundry flapping in the wind. Sound of wings. I looked up and saw flying shapes, small black ones, bat shaped. They flew up and over the roof, the bats, then beyond and out of sight.

My attention was redirected by yet another oncoming parade. I tiptoed down to the last crumbly library stair, maybe for the last time. On that stair, before the sidewalk, I held on to a railing post.

This parade was so vast, almost like the dome of stars, that it spilled from the sidewalk to the street and across to the opposite sidewalk.

At intersections near and far, tactically positioned officers blew whistles. Their batons pointed this way and that to direct motorized traffic.

A hypnotic, ice-blue glow from countless hand-held devices formed a solid, wide bar of light passing before my eyes.

In front of me, Kroner, unmoving, leaned against a parking meter in the midst of the icy blue bar. Parade zombies shuffled by him, both on the sidewalk and on the street. Was this parade why he was not upstairs in the old library trying to cozy up to Kit? If so, my lucky break.

Eyes on the parade, Kroner suddenly stepped from the parking meter and shouldered his way among the shufflers. In his free hand, Kroner held a silver flask partly hidden under a long shirtsleeve. Officers were too busy with traffic to notice the village idiot taking a nip and hiding a flask up his sleeve.

I saw Kroner had somehow acquired his own device, the latest version. He was mesmerized. The paper-thin device adhered to his forearm like a tattoo. The sleeve of that arm was rolled up to his biceps.

After merging, Kroner dropped the flask, either purposely or absentmindedly. The flask, a mere silver smudge, was lost among shuffling legs and feet.

As if nearsighted, Kroner held his forearm with the tattooed device an inch or so from his eyes.

I became aware – maybe due to my clacking head – of how the oversized parade of zombies emitted a collective hum, like those of chanting monks or, I don't know, the mechanical droning of robots.

Whatever the sound, the humming lulled me into a stupor. But as the parade's icy blue bar rounded a corner and went out of sight, my headache blew up: Clack, clack, clack...CLACK-CLACK-CLACK... CLACKETY-CLACK!

The clacking came like hoof beats against the interior keyboard that had to be my skull. The gumshoe in me messaged that time was now an hourglass, overturned and fleeting, that I had to run for my life again – and not just run, but sprint.

One problem: The dire message came with no directions, none on exactly where my sprinting should go.

Hot, cold

I had only an inexact notion of what direction to go to find the white bungalow. That meant there might be signs along the way to detect or miss, clues to read or misread. Yet success or failure might also hinge on a plain old hunch.

I sprinted solo through the grid-like blocks of residential neighborhoods. I felt the racing spirit fire up in me, that thrill and danger, like old times. Outlines of houses on my periphery blurred. I tripped once on a cracked sidewalk but caught myself before falling.

It must have gotten very late. I met no one on the sidewalks – walkers, bicyclists, tricyclists, skateboarders. None of those, just random passing cars, their headlights and taillights appearing and disappearing. I had to look down so as not be blinded by the high-beam headlights.

One car with a hitch pulled a boat the size of a yacht. It seemed the wrong time of day to haul cargo of that size. Yet with minimal traffic and no pedestrians, maybe it was the right time of night for pulling such a boat.

No dogs, cats, squirrels, or chipmunks but a raccoon to my right sat huddled on a trash can by a garage door. The coon patted around to find a grip on the rim of the lid to lift.

It warmed me to know I'd fed bunny before leaving but, seeing that bulldog earlier, I wished for my own dog. I missed not having a running/walking companion.

I picked up my feet while sprinting so I wouldn't trip during interludes between streetlamps and hurt myself, delaying or stopping my progress.

The keyboard clacking was unabated. I passed a certain house and heard the child shriek: I won't! I hate you, I hate you! And the woman shrieks back: Little ogre, that light better be off when I get to your room – Or else!

The familiar household strife meant I was closing in, getting warmer. Sure enough, the clacking in my skull got louder, more painful.

As I accelerated my sunhat sailed off. I reached back for it, as I ran, missed but didn't bother to stop, turn back and retrieve it on the ground. No stopping me now.

As I sprinted to the next block the clacking subsided...no, no, no. Must be getting colder, losing the trail of signs and clues.

I retraced my steps and sprinted in another direction. The clacking pounded more painfully...Oh yes, yes, yes, getting warmer again.

I followed a series of highs and lows from my clacking skull – first warm, then cool, warmer, colder – monitoring each clue to know what sprinting direction to go to next.

It was hit-and-miss, less satisfying than echolocation, but, at last, the clacking clues did lead me to the block where the white bungalow stood.

At first I wasn't entirely sure if the bungalow was real or not. Again, its image wavered in and out as if in sync with my heavy breathing. As my breathing lightened, the bungalow rematerialized. As a solid.

Breaking and entry, II

As expected, this residential block set off memories. Recent ones. It wasn't that long ago that I was last here.

It was here where I found myself before. And here where I somehow got away and made my way back to my basement flat and my bed.

Unless, as know-it-all Muldoon claimed, I had only hallucinated my way to here and back.

Across the road from the bungalow stood a big house. Gutted. Windows boarded with plywood. Tarp covering part of the roof. Front sidewalk in pieces. Dumpster overflowing with construction debris, taking up two curbside parking spots. It didn't look like home renovation had gone on for ages.

One thing I'd missed from my first and last visit – the bungalow's road, the very block, was a deadend. With potholes, stones, shattered glass, more construction debris, weeds, litter and sand, the word deadend surely defined this block.

A high concrete wall separated the end of the deadend road from something – not a noisy freeway – but something undeveloped and primeval. Neglected vegetation slithered over the wall from unseen depths on the other side.

As before, I was so close to the bungalow – so hot – that the clacking in my skull nearly knocked me cold.

But as I stepped up to the curved brick path, the clacking let up, then ceased — as before. What a relief to regain my breath, to end that dreadful clacking. Still, the inside of my skull felt cratered.

On the top porch stair, I saw the wood carving was disturbed. I looked closer and saw that not only the LOST GET metal sign was gone but so was the gnome's crooked head. I peered down the cavity where the head had been. The body's interior was all air, hollow.

After peering, I shrugged and looked up. My breath was no longer visible in the freezing night air. I huffed and puffed. Really hard. Nope, nothing, not even faint. Was I still alive?

Nothing passed before the porch windows as I reached for the storm-door handle. As before, the steel door was ajar. It swung open with my fingertip touch.

I hardly thought of consequences for breaking into this bunga-low — for a second time. Legal consequences, that is. Normally I wouldn't presume to be above the law but, at this point, well, did it matter?

I vaguely recalled what happened the last time I was on this porch...After I came upon the cobalt-blue Buddha with the left eye shut, as if winking; the archaic typewriter with pages blackened by type, some words and sentences X'd out, other pages blank; the hookah's spiraling smoke...

This time the porch had been cleaned out — emptied. I turned and looked all around. My steps here and there on the hard floor echoed the emptiness.

Opposite the front windows, on the beadboard wall facing the street, hung a clock. The ticking told me it was going.

I listened to the clock: Tick, tick...tock. Tock, tock...tick. Irregu-lar but, still, ticking and tocking away.

The clock's pendulum swung back and forth, but the black hands of the white face showed the time as nearing 5 o'clock, maybe nine minutes to.

Nine to five? Early morning or late afternoon? That couldn't be the right time...could it? It was still dark outside.

Wasn't it five to nine, at night, when I left the old library, just before closing? How much time had elapsed during my search for the white bungalow?

On the same wall as the clock, a small circuit breaker box with the cover open an inch. Circuits inside screeched like electrical-charged cicadas.

Then I saw a thing, something short and squat, appear and disappear over in the living room. It skimmed like a shadow through a wall in that room.

After the short thing's disappearance came swishing sounds — some sort of fabric, clothing, sheets of paper?

Beyond the porch

I had to lower my head and neck, as if for a noose fitting, to pass under a triangular-like entrance to the living room.

The apex of this near-triangle, instead of reaching a point on top, formed a line about a foot across. As I passed under I stooped so as not to ding my noggin.

Never had I been in a living room, any room, with such a low ceiling. I wished I was shorter, maybe the size of that carved gnome at the front door – at least the original carving, before it lost its head.

The living room ceiling was barely higher than the triangular entrance. Its cramped interior was not made for a normal-sized human, which, as a character, I modeled myself after.

Unable to stand up, I stood hunched. It was like navigating a crawl space. The inside of my head still felt cratered and as hollowed out as the porch – or the body of the headless gnome.

I thought it might be easier, instead of bending and walking on my feet, to walk on my knees. Without carpeting, I knew that knee walking would cripple me.

The living room, if it was one, had no light switch. The blinds of the only window were drawn shut. In a corner were outlines of an upright vacuum cleaner, straw broom, dustpan, mop and pail.

Where had that short, shadowy shape skimmed off to?

Walking on knees, I hobbled around, tracing my fingertips over surfaces of each blank wall. As if reading braille. There was no hanging artwork. Maybe I could feel for a clue to where that shadow had gone.

It took hardly a minute of hobbling on the bare floor for my kneecaps to rebel. There was only glimmering light from the closed blinds, enough to make out a series of notches on one wall. I hobbled closer, resumed my braille tracing.

I traced the notches up and down. These formed an upright rectangle. Two parallel lines, maybe three feet apart, extended up and down from the floor, where the trim was cut away. These were linked by a crossover line just above eye level as I knelt.

The rectangular outline seemed rather like a sort of door in the wall. Would it open to a second exit, a conduit, out of this crawl space of a room?

Problem was, I could neither see nor feel anything resembling a doorknob.

As any clue-seeking gumshoe would do, I acted on a hunch. I reached to one side of the possible door, halfway up, and dug in with my nails – and there, yes, I dug out a chip of folded metal.

Dug until I got a finger hold, held on to it, a ring handle, and pulled the ring to peel back the door – the cover? – from the wall. Dust spilled from the opening as it widened.

The part of the door opposite the ring was hinged. The door's cover was made of cloth stretched over some kind of pasteboard.

But what was the cover for? Still on rebelling knees, I leaned in to peruse.

Inside the hinged, peeled-open door were sheets of paper. They were arranged like pages in a book. Hundreds of bound, white pages.

The pages matched the size of the door. I used both hands to flip through. Before I knew it, on their own, the pages were swishing back and forth.

The breathing air from the pages swished over my face with a lover's intimacy. Soon the draft, more of an updraft, was so strong it lifted me off my knees. OK, wherever it led, I was bound to follow this trail of clues.

Were these pages blank or lined with printed words? I can't say. If that was another clue, sorry but this gumshoe missed it.

Too much else distracted me. I was now off my knees and feet, elevated and exiting the low living room, not on my stomach or back, but sideways, being pulled or pushed in, not sure which, but levitating through an interior passage.

The door-size book pages kept breathing at various speeds before settling at an even tempo. I sniffed a pleasing, woody fragrance before scenes from past lives – desert abbey gardener, reclusive keeper of books, and more – swished before my eyes.

The breathing pages caressed my brow, eyebrows, nose, lips and chin. I was flowing on an airy carpet, on my side, out of the crawl space and toward somewhere else.

I wasn't fearful. No, in fact, the transport was putting me in a catnap mood.

My eyes opened and shut before shutting for good. I heard, or imagined I did, a familiar, feminine voice cooing: Sweet dreams, Bub. Sweeter the better...

Homecoming

I woke. I may have only half woken. I felt groggy and drowsy. Maybe I was not fully awake.

Maybe I was partly asleep or maybe between realms of sleeping and waking there was no difference anymore.

Before me, an ancient stump of a man sat on a silvery throw rug, sitting in the lotus position, erect but sideways – if such a sitting angle were possible.

On his one side was a hookah, looking the same as the one from the porch, and a floor lamp.

A young woman knelt on a knee on his other side, on the same rug, arm over his shoulder.

From my view everything, objects and these two, was skewed sideways by 90 degrees. These were impossible angles.

The stumpy ancient man and the young woman seemed posed for a portrait. Both barefooted. Now and then the toes of the woman's one foot wiggled; the toes of the man's feet did not.

She wore Navy blue – tank top and boxer shorts. Her exposed limbs and midriff were sleek and supple. Because her boxers revealed more skin than a server's uniform, I could see more, but not all, of the climbing vine tattoo.

The vine climbed the woman's thigh horizontally and vertically. If that made sense, which I knew it didn't, but I realized my view was skewed from lying sideways, the side of my head against the hard floor.

My sideways position passed on a perspective of seeing things that way – slanted and sideways.

So the vine-tattooed woman had to be Paige, our server from the Dune Buggy Cafe. She kept an arm over the stumpy man's broad shoulder. His short, chubby legs were tucked in like a pretzel's.

Eyes shut, he inhaled through coils of the flexible pale blue tube attached to the hookah.

Top-grade hashish – relieves pains, melancholy, he exhaled, without batting an eye or taking lips from the tube.

When he did open them a sliver, eyes and lips, it was to expel a plume of hash exhaust.

The stumpy man's scalp had only threads of white hair. Threads of a white goatee dangled like baby vines from his chin.

Across the scalp, exposed under the threads, was a birthmark shaped as a spiraling galaxy. With my color-blindness, the galaxy's spirals reflected, faintly, silver and blue hues.

The stumpy man wore loose, off-white pants. Also a wraparound tunic cinched by a cloth belt. Lotus positioned and still, he seemed not only stumpy but ageless.

Pardon my marooning you like this, old pal, he croaked. The stage curtains are closing for me. Actually, for you, too. My needle, our needle, is pointing to empty. I can no longer tap out creative ideas, not a one. The writing is blocked but, at least, I have my beloved granddaughter by my side. She will lend aid and comfort for this, my obituary.

He turned and nodded up at Paige, as if her turn to eulogize.

Paige held a large leatherbound book in her free hand. She took the other hand from her grandfather's shoulder and pulled on a ring to open the book's worn covers and riffle its dog-eared pages, blowing on them.

Powdery dust sprayed out. As the spray entered the lamp's prism of light, it sparkled before falling darkly to the floor.

Paige looked directly at me, cooing again: Fear not, Bub. This is it, where you came from and, by rights, where you'll return. Hey, we should be throwing you a homecoming party…

Ass

…After passing out, or sleeping – after coming to, or waking – again, one or the other! – I found myself still lying on the floor. But now on my back, instead of lying on my side.

How was that switch done? I didn't recall switching positions from my side to my back. Had I been switched, or did I switch myself, unconsciously, after passing out or going to sleep?

Lying on my back gave me a feel for how rigid and uneven the floor planks were. Over time, probably a long time, the planks had warped.

A nail from a warped plank jutted into the back of my head. I tried to raise my head, just an inch, for relief, but I couldn't get it to rise even a fraction of that inch.

The place where I had transported to was some kind of mezzanine. More of an attic or a loft. How had I gotten up to a loft when I seemed to have passed sideways through a door in the wall, the book-cover door, from the crawl space room below?

Did being here mean I was still in the white bungalow? Was there space for a loft this size in the bungalow? Or had I been transported across the road, to that bigger, abandoned house.

I listened for cicada screeching from the porch's circuit breakers. I listened but heard no screeches, heard no noise except for water gurgling – as if from a running bathroom toilet.

Above me the ceiling's beams angled down to the floor – maybe on both ends. One end was impossible to see without rolling my eyeballs to the back of my head. I tried but couldn't get them that far back.

The wall before me was lined with shelves holding up rows of books and stacks of crinkly brown manuscripts. Sections of the overloaded shelving tilted precariously.

Up and down the middle of the loft were more shelves. These formed aisles and aisles that held more books and manuscripts.

The loft's dimensions wavered, the waves appearing endless. Must've been a mirage from my prone position on the floor. My eyes strained to correct the distortion.

The hookah and floor lamp had been moved. Both were crammed against a wall shelf by the battered typewriter and a set of shiny chrome weights. Did Paige stay buff by weightlifting?

Before I looked away, a humpbacked rodent scuttled across the planks, slipping behind the typewriter.

I shifted my eyes to look over at Paige, still kneeling, then at the lotus-sitting, ageless man. He was cradling the cobalt-blue Buddha in his lap. Paige cradled a burly Maine Coon whose bushy tail flailed her hips.

While on my back, I was still lying to the side of them, sideways, looking out from the corners of my eyes, especially the eye closest to them. I'd rather have looked at them straight on, both eyes equal, sitting up.

Paige released the hairy cat, calling out, Feast! The cat launched in an arc toward the hookah, typewriter, lamp and weights. Where the mouse had been.

Then Paige spoke again: With this ever-growing inventory, Grandfather was eventually nicknamed the KOB – Keeper of Books. Well, look around at a bookworm's collection. As the KOB, grandpa preserved every book acquired during his prolific, man-of-letters life. Doesn't the nickname fit?

I didn't answer the rhetorical question. I saw the leatherbound book Paige had earlier opened. It was by her wiggling toes – down at my eye level, which was still sideways on the planks.

Now the book's covers were closed. I wanted to reach for it, lift and feel its heft, but I couldn't budge, not even twitch.

The ageless stump man either wheezed or hacked before croaking more words. His ruddy complexion and glinting eyes were those of a Himalayan Sherpa.

Beloved Paige inherits this, he rasped, waving a stubby hand like a club. She will carry on with her own writing – as I have for so long. What she writes and creates will distinguish hers from my body of work – all the stories and characters that comprise my legacy.

The man's wrinkle-free, beaming face suddenly crinkled into the spidery lines of a wadded-up ball of paper.

With my next blink, he and I were eyeball to eyeball – only he was leaning over my face, upside down to me, elbows on the planks, propped up.

Smoky breath blew down with these rasping words: Know this, old pal – Paige is no different from you. I repeat, Paige is another story character of mine, only she so adores the granddaughter role I created on a whim, along with the aspiring writer's role, that I cannot bear to spoil it by saying otherwise – that she's a figment, like you, a made-up story character.

After the revelation, I had to blink. What I saw next was the man, back in the lotus, cradling the Buddha head whose right, not left, eye was squeezed shut.

Had the Buddha given me a new wink? Had the stump man moved? What he revealed about Paige – did I hallucinate that? My delirium?

No need to resist, he went on in a confessional tone. Resisting the end is futile. You were often my alter ego, my first created character – also my last. I'm attached to my stories and characters, especially yours. Your obscure roles were subtle but endearing. You were my observer's eyes. That's why I waited this long, until the end of my life, to X you out. Together, you and me, we X it, ha, ha.

Assassination, bah, vile concept. You can't feel a thing, can you? Even those sore knees, right? Can't move even a fraction of that inch, not a twitch, can you? Old pal, there are only so-called endings. If there are still readers to be found, a big if, then story characters live on through countless electrical impulses that network human brains. Webs of neurons, like highways. Characters travel them, going on with their own lives, their own dreams and visions, yes, even their own delusions and deliriums. This traveling goes on, and on, characters overlapping, blending, recasting. Yours, too. Do you see?

With my next blink, I saw Paige propped on her elbows, also above me and upside down, up to my eyeballs and snorting: Seriously, Bub, get this. Pay no attention to the old fart and his hocus-pocus behind the curtains. He's delirious! I haven't the heart to clue him in, but hey, he's just a figment of mine, one of those sparks traveling my neural highway. He was plucked from this fantastical story I've been trying like hell to finish.

Look, it's Grandpa – that's my nickname for him! In my story he's a shriveled old dump-truck driver. He hauls scrap books. To a recycling plant. Book pulp there gets remade into shipping cartons, bags, napkins, confetti, and tissue for tears and snot blowing. Gramps smuggles out story characters, like you, before the books are pulped. Saving lost souls. I've only done a rough draft – got stuck, the old writer's block – but the poor Gramps character does get snagged in gears of the plant's machinery. You try saving him, get snagged yourself and you're both shredded, pulverized. To dust! Sorry for the gory end. Oh well, stuff that plot in your pipe. Light it, inhale the assassination fumes.

Paige dropped her head, wiggling her Mohawk hair over my nose. I sneezed, saw stars. I'd never witnessed this side of Paige – upside down, maniacal. She cackled so hard she drooled, got the hiccups.

When I blinked again, neither of them – characters? writers? a blend? none of the above? – were visible. Either straight on, sideways or upside down. I blinked again and again, trying to restore them, but they had, what, been X'd out, assassinated, reincarnated? Traveled on to the next highway?

My entire life, all my lives, had been fictional, so what truth was out there for me to hold fast to? For dear life.

I kept my eyes closed. When I opened them again, I was standing in the middle of parched landscape. It was near dusk and cloudless. My stringy shadow, in the setting sun, wavered toward the skyline.

Rows of stalks, shoots, tendrils, leaves and vines had withered to stubble and lay flat across the baked earth. From one side of the land, maybe from all sides, the wind blew, stirring up funnels of sand, grit and dust.

The crisscrossing currents met in the middle, where I stood, blinding me.

I held out my hands to shield myself, at least my eyes, but I couldn't see a thing with all that dust, always that eternal dust. Then my legs buckled. I lost my footing, somersaulting through a trapdoor, eventually landing on my ass.

This time falling didn't hurt, but I was alone. I sat there for a minute. Something kept swishing against my face. At just the right tempo. I nodded, waiting for my eyes to reopen, and I breathed.

THE END

ABOUT THE AUTHOR

Philip Pfuehler grew up in Oconomomoc, Wis., and is a University of Wisconsin-Eau Claire journalism graduate who spent most of his newspaper career as editor for the River Falls Journal. He also edited suburban papers in the Twin Cities of Minnesota and has published prose poems in several literary magazines. Pfuehler and his wife, Kim, a social worker, are retired and live in Sturgeon Bay. They have two adult children, Maria and Julia, and two granddaughters.